'Intr

'In this compel
created a fictional setting which is at once magical and believable'
Times Literary Supplement

'The storytelling is masterly. Just as you notice a loose end, the
author deftly ties it . . . Loss is stacked upon loss, and yet this novel
leaves you oddly uplifted; for all the suffering the characters
endure, their courage never deserts them, nor, in the end, do their
hopes betray them.' *Independent on Sunday*

'Martin Davies pulls out all the stops . . . in this heady, breathless
mix of history, mystery and romance' *Daily Mirror*

'A remarkable novel which deserves to be shortlisted in 2009 for a
serious prize. Davies' prose is poetic and erudite, his plotting
superb, the narrative gripping' *Historical Novels Review*

'A romance in the traditional sense. It conjures the brutality and
beauty of the lands it crosses, and speaks of love, honour, greed
and power. In its final unfolding it comes down to the importance
of words: their power and their limits . . . and how much can be
said without them, and how far they can be trusted. A few
philosophical questions are raised along the way, but mostly it is a
story, to be enjoyed in and of itself.' *Bookbag*

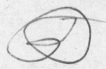

About the author

Martin Davies grew up in North West England. All his writing is done in cafés, on buses or on tube trains, and an aversion to laptops means that he always works in longhand. He has travelled widely, including in the Middle East and India, and substantial parts of *The Unicorn Road* were written while travelling through Sicily.

Also by Martin Davies

The Conjuror's Bird

the Unicorn Road

MARTIN DAVIES

HODDER

First published in Great Britain in 2008 by Hodder & Stoughton
An Hachette UK company

This paperback edition published in 2009 by Hodder & Stoughton

1

A CIP catalogue record for this title is available from the British Library.

ISBN 978 0 340 89636 5 (B)
ISBN 978 0 340 92011 4 (A)

Typeset in Sabon by Hewer Text UK Ltd, Edinburgh
Printed and bound in the UK by CPI Mackays, Chatham ME5 8TD

Hodder & Stoughton policy is to use papers that are natural, renewable
and recyclable products and made from wood grown in sustainable forests.
The logging and manufacturing processes are expected to conform
to the environmental regulations of the country of origin.

Hodder & Stoughton Ltd
338 Euston Road
London NW1 3BH

www.hodder.co.uk

Journeying is hard,
Journeying is hard.
There are many turnings . . .
I will mount a long wind some day and break the heavy waves
And set my cloudy sail straight and bridge the deep, deep sea.

Li Bai
'The Hard Road'
Translated by W Bynner

ζ

To lose a small boy in a world so wide is an easy thing.

I have learned that now, just as I have learned the names of places unimagined by me then, names that strike my ear like strange verses. *Socotra, Kinzai, Samarkand. Malabar, Nicobar, Pem.*

I had not thought this Earth of ours so large, nor Christendom so small. I had thought the lands beyond our maps no wider than the beading edge that runs around Christ's table. Had I known the truth, that the wild plains and forests of the heathen reach so far and so unforgivingly, I should not have let him go.

I should not have let him go.

To find him now I must trust to God and to the good offices of the traders, Jew and Arab, who come to this place with their tales of foreign lands. They are good men, fathers themselves. I see the truth in their eyes as they pledge to ask for news. Sometimes they tell me I am not alone in asking. They say there are others, men they neither like nor trust, who ask the same. They tell me this to warn me, but I will not be warned. I keep no secrets. I simply want my son.

Perhaps one day these good men will find him for me. There hangs around his neck a tablet on a chain. It was my father's. And on that narrow chain there hangs my hope: that my merchant friends might know him and one day bring him home.

He will be full-grown now, my slender son. I need to know what kind of man he is become. A better man, I think, than those who led him hence all those years ago. And yet I envy them, that mismatched band, for the time they have had with him – for there are days when I'd surrender all the time still left to me for one brief word with one who watched him grow.

Soon I will leave this place for home, and journey back to the children that remain to me. They too are dear but, being grown, they have no need of me to watch for them. And so on this high tower I stand and face the east, and pray that if he sleeps he sleeps in peace; that if he lives, one day he will come home.

ζ

Damascus

The sun had done its work on him. In only two months of travel, it had burned and coarsened his skin and bleached his hair so fair that to avoid attention he concealed it beneath a Saracen cloth according to the custom of the land. In front of him, a tall Kibruni merchant was waving his hands and speaking in a strange, guttural tongue, the immaculate whiteness of his robes far more persuasive than the lump of skin and shadow he described.

The mermaid must have been dead many days. Even where he stood, a step behind his master, the boy could sense the odour rising from its skin. A stale smell, pungent, like dried dung and rotting seaweed, stronger even than the smell of sweat that the boy and his companions carried with them into the cool, fragrant darkness of the souk. In the shadows of the merchant's inner room, it was hard to make out the creature's form. The boy's eyes, still narrowed by the glare outside, could distinguish only a clumsy, lumpen torso tapering to an indistinct tail.

A mermaid? The boy could not be sure. Certainly the markets of Damascus were not short of wonders, clustered as they were beneath walls as old as the desert. A holy city, the scholar had told him, and in the spice-scented alleyways where the light barely penetrated, the boy saw Syrian monks and Saracen holy men brush shoulders with men and women of every sort, from sallow Copts to black-faced Ethiopians in bright desert robes. It seemed there was nothing that could not be purchased there. The market stalls were piled high with magic charms, from dried scorpions to living snakes, and there were other wonders too: ice from the mountains, and fine-grained pottery as smooth to the touch as a child's skin. And now a small crowd had gathered behind them as the merchant described yet another marvel, another wonder for sale.

The boy could see his master was listening intently: Antioch, the scholar, grey and gaunt, his face strained. When the merchant finally fell silent, the old man turned to his interpreter, who stood a little apart.

'What says he, Venn?' he asked, and as the man moved forward the boy felt reassured. Of all their small company, the interpreter alone seemed unruffled by the ways of that arid land, so far from home that it seemed neither strange nor unlikely to be smelling the remains of a mermaid.

'He says that a mermaid is a rare creature. They are found in the southern seas in the shape of women and they call out to the sailors that pass. But when touched they turn instantly into sea creatures. He says that only if struck dead before they change will they retain their female shape. This one was killed when half changed. Had it been slain a moment sooner, he says, it would be different, but now only the outline of a woman's face remains.'

The interpreter stopped speaking and stepped back and the boy peered again at the mermaid. His eyes were better adjusted now and he could see for himself the sorry specimen that lay before them, its skin grey and its jaws slack, human only in its fleshy lips and the dark lashes that fringed its eyes.

'What think you, Count?' the scholar asked.

This question was addressed to the person beside him, a dark-haired man with the eyes of a raven.

'I think it is no true mermaid,' the man growled. 'A freak thrown up by the sea, then a tale spun around it. The infidel lacks nothing in enterprise.'

'A freak, yes.' Antioch nodded, turning the thought over in his mind. 'And yet I think we should acquire it nonetheless.' He straightened, relieved by his own decisiveness. 'And tonight we shall agree a plan. We must decide whether to continue east or else turn south to the warm waters whence these wonders spring.'

The pause that followed this remark was long and uncomfortable. The boy looked from the weary face of the scholar to the cold eyes of his companion and shivered.

It had begun with a summons, a messenger flapping crow-like through the corn. Sicily in September and the morning promised heat. Visitors to Antioch's villa were rare, and the boy watched carefully as the rider crossed the plain below, growing with each minute that passed until, rising through the lemon groves, he disappeared beneath the gatehouse walls. Then came the ringing of the bell and the commotion, and Antioch, flustered, calling for his best cloak regardless of the season. And then the day-long journey through the gathering heat of the Sicilian plain, wheat yellow for harvest, sky blue, summer defiant. Only on the long climb upwards to the citadel of San Julian did the sun weaken its grip on them, slipping slowly behind their backs and into a quicksilver sea.

Then came the palace gates, a courtyard, the rough hands of ostlers and finally a stone-flagged room at dusk where the king of a stolen kingdom stood waiting. The shadows were long when the two men met. What light there was fell on their faces, one strong and commanding, the other thin, bookish, nervous. Watching them from the shadow was a third man, a man whose eyes were carrion black, a man who neither smiled nor spoke but waited and missed nothing. And before them on the table lay a book: huge, heavy, firmly shut. The more the large man talked and made no mention of it, the stronger its presence grew. In the corner furthest from the fire the boy held an ermine cloak and listened.

Much of what he heard meant little to him. The king spoke, of war, of great armies, of an empire reeling and a Pope triumphant. As he spoke, the boy could sense the growing perplexity of his master, who listened and nodded fitfully: Antioch the scholar, a man of sixty, stooped and uncertain. Like the boy, he knew nothing of such subjects and was struggling to understand why he had been summoned into the presence of this warrior king.

'Charles of Anjou is marching under the Pope's banner. An army of 30,000 men is at the door of Italy . . .'

As the large man continued to speak, the boy's eyes wandered around the chamber. On the hills above the Sicilian plain the autumn mists come down quickly, and the heat of the day was long gone. The boy held back a shiver. It was a high-arched room, cold despite the fire, and smelling of the damp autumn evening outside. By some act of neglect the torches were not yet lit, but by the firelight the boy could make out the patterns on the banners that shrouded the walls; the imperial arms, the insignia of Charlemagne, the gold crosses on purple. Above them all hung the tattered banner of Frederick, the last emperor. And although the boy knew little enough, he understood that this

7

lord, Manfred, was that emperor's son, said to be the only man in Europe still brave enough and strong enough to defy the power of the Pope. The boy's eyes returned to him constantly, taking in his vast solidity, his red hair. A handsome face disintegrating into creases. Hugely strong despite his bulk, he seemed immense, powerful, remarkable, a man who could order death with a wave of his hand.

And then the boy saw something else. The Lord Manfred was facing away from him, intent on Antioch. As he spoke, he stood chest forward with his hands behind his back. It was a pose of great confidence, of great authority. But it was the movement of his fingers that the boy had noticed. As the large man's voice continued firm, the fingers of his right hand were working vigorously, turning something over and over in his palm, stroking it, kneading it, twisting it around before beginning again in a restless, urgent cycle.

From where he stood, the boy could make out the object being so caressed.

This heir of Charlemagne, defender of the Cross, descendant of emperors, Christ's soldier on earth, was clutching – like a frightened squire – the severed foot of a hare.

That sight changed something, although it was not until later that the boy truly understood. But there entered into him at that moment his first doubt about the man before him, his first doubt about the ruthless certainties of kings and crowns and order. Startled, he looked across the room and realised that the man with the raven's gaze stood watching him. His was expressionless, but something in his eyes told the boy that his surprise had been observed and noted. To this man, evidently, the perpetual nervousness of those fingers was not a revelation.

At the table, the Lord Manfred was still speaking, his manner calm, as though the hands behind him were somehow independent of his body.

'His Holiness rebuffs me, Antioch. My envoys return unheard.' In speaking to the scholar he used rough court Latin, fortified with the dialect of the Sicilian plains.

'Your father, sire . . .' the old man replied, then tailed off, confused.

'My father is dead,' the other said softly. 'My father is dead and I am his true heir – his son by blood and his heir in spirit. I have held Sicily in his name when his other sons could scarcely raise an army. I am the only man in Europe strong enough to rule it. And yet his Holiness will not recognise me. And until he does I am a renegade, a usurper. There can be no peace until he gives the world a sign I am accepted. I need to be crowned, Antioch. I need to be crowned in Rome.'

The seriousness in his voice gave his words a greater emphasis. It was the speech of a man accustomed to command. Aware of it, the old man's confusion grew.

'I'm sure if his Holiness was offered a settlement . . . Perhaps some sort of tribute . . . ?'

'Ah, yes.' Manfred moved around the table then and guided the old man to the fire. 'His Holiness's liking for gifts is famous. But what gift would win such a man as he? A man who simply takes by force anything he might desire?'

'Perhaps a sum of gold . . . ?' the scholar began, then stopped on seeing the other's expression.

'Enough gold to buy a pope?' Manfred laughed bitterly. 'There is no sum large enough for that. Besides, any man possessed of such a sum would soon be parted from it by other means. A quarrel would be found, or a heresy discovered. Denunciation, disgrace . . . Or simpler still, a troop of well-armed men one day, waiting at the roadside into the forest. The Pope has his methods. No, I will not attempt to buy my life, nor barter for my own birthright. Besides, I have a better plan than that.' The King's voice grew softer then, and the boy could feel he was drawing near the true purpose of the visit. 'You have heard tell, perhaps, of the Great Menagerie in Rome?'

The old man blinked, surprised at this unexpected shift to a subject he understood.

'Indeed, sire. His Holiness's own collection. It is said to be a great marvel, unrivalled anywhere in east or west.'

'It must surely then contain a great many beasts. Is that not so, Antioch?'

'So people say. If the stories be true it holds nearly every creature known to man. Lions, panthers, deer, great oxen, even birds that speak the tongues of men . . .'

Manfred nodded. He seemed calmer now, and when he spoke next his voice was almost soothing. But still the boy could see his fingers turning, faster now even than before.

'Come, I have something to show you,' he said.

Only then did he guide the scholar to the table where the great book awaited them. 'Please, open it. It is yours, my gift to you.'

The old man blinked again and approached the book with caution. Before touching it he wiped his hands three times against his cloak, and when he reached out towards the great volume those hands trembled slightly.

The boy heard a little gasp escape his master when the book fell open. And he saw a change in his face, as if the book itself were lighting it.

For a few seconds the old man stood still, and then, with a sudden start, all semblance of caution left him. His fingers began to turn the heavy pages and with each one his touch grew wilder, more urgent, until his eyes scarcely scanned a page before he turned again. Bright images tumbled into view before him, sumptuous in gold and scarlet, twisting and turning on the page as one leaf followed another.

'Lion, tiger, panther, pard,' the old man breathed.

'Each one magnificent. Such work! Such skilful touch . . .'

He turned the heavy pages both forward and back, not knowing where to rest his gaze, until the frenzy passed and he looked up, his eyes bewildered.

'It is exquisite,' he said. 'The finest bestiary I have ever seen.' His eyes moved down again. 'Each creature brought out in gold, each one depicted with such perfect delicacy. See the eyes of the wolf, the snarl of the tiger! Is it Breton? No, English . . . It matters little. It is the work of a master. Is this the gift you intend for his Holiness?'

'A book?' The other's scorn was barely concealed. 'No, Antioch, this book is just the beginning. Look here . . .'

The hare's foot was pushed beneath his belt as he reached down and moved deftly to a particular page.

'Tell me, Antioch, does his Holiness own any beast such as this one?'

The picture at which he pointed showed a white beast with the heavy body of a horse, a great curved horn extending from its forehead.

'The unicorn? Why, no, I would have heard of it . . .'

'And this?'

'The bonnacon? I think not . . .'

'And this? And this?'

Then it was the Lord Manfred's turn to move from

page to page, his strong fingers practised at finding the leaves he sought.

'The leocrota? The satyr? The basilisk?' The old man stammered. 'No, no. None of these. No ydris, no dragon, no jaculus. These are all rare creatures, rare.'

'So rare that few have ever seen them,' the King agreed. 'So rare indeed that none are found in any lands we know.'

'No, sire. These are creatures of the desert or the mountains, or of the great rivers. They live in lands we scarcely know. But the Greek masters knew of them and taught us of their forms and habits. And indeed there are men alive today who claim to have seen such creatures in their travels.'

'So they say. Now these would be gifts for a pope, would they not, Antioch? Gifts his Holiness would value more than gold?'

'Indeed, sire! These would be gifts beyond value. With creatures such as these in his menagerie then truly it would be a wonder for all ages.'

The Lord Manfred smiled in satisfaction. His hand behind his back reached for the hare's foot and the boy watched him stroke it softly.

'And tell me, Antioch, how would a man go about obtaining such creatures as these?'

The old man blinked and furrowed his forehead. 'Why, with the greatest difficulty, sire. The ancient scholars have left us clues about where to seek them, but they are vague and incomplete. To arrive at definite locations would involve much reading, much searching . . .'

'And a stout heart too, my friend.' Manfred turned then to the man with the strange eyes and gestured at him lazily. 'The Count Decius here has a battalion of men in readiness for the search. But who should lead them? Decius here can marshal them, of course, but he is a soldier and this is a mission of peace. A bishop, perhaps? But the infidels have no reason to love our church. Besides, I know of neither bishop nor soldier who is scholar enough to follow the clues of which you speak . . .'

The stout man's fingers began to move faster as they rolled the fragment of fur against their tips. And as the boy began to understand what was happening, he found his chest tightening, a chill of excitement growing from the base of his spine.

'I want you to find them for me, Antioch. All these beasts that men here have never seen. This book and others I have gathered are yours to guide you. Count Decius will be your deputy. You are to travel east, to the court of the Great Khan himself, if you must. But you *will* find them, Antioch. You shall be the man who completes the bestiary.'

And with those words his finger fell idly onto the open book. Beneath it, picked out by chance, the twisted figure of the basilisk looked back at him with angry eyes.

ζ

There is little here for me when the night falls. By day I meet the ships and ask for word. The captains and the traders know me now and make me welcome, tell me where they've sailed and any news they've heard. But by night the port is still. Its life drains to the narrow streets below the fortress, to the inns and wine shops where talk is thick and travellers tell of wonders. Sometimes I go amongst them and watch the weather-worn faces. They have become for me a new and unexpected family, these strangers in this place so far from home. My son perhaps has known such men as these, perhaps in some far tavern he sits and tells his story.

Some nights the talk here turns to Antioch's lost mission. It is an oft-told tale now and mysteries help the evenings pass swiftly. But no one knows for sure what tale to tell, and the passing years have given story-makers licence to imagine. With time the tales have grown fanciful, embroidered with rumours of a curse, or of an ill-omened treasure that Antioch carried with him. Some say it was the lost gold of Albion, others a treasure meant for Aragon by the Saracen emperor, a ransom for the captured city of Cordoba. And there are those who say that Antioch's party took the Devil's money, paid to the crew by Satan for the keeping of their souls . . .

I shake my head when I hear such whispers. These are the tales that grow when truth is absent, taller with every day that passes. The truth is different: an expedition of hardened soldiers, provisioned well and in good order, sent by a Christian king, vanished without trace or explanation in the lands beyond the east. It is a mystery fit for any fireside – fit for my own, had I not still the memory of one child's face before me.

It was three nights ago, on such a night as this, with stars so bright they seemed to write words in the sky, that I received the Catalan's visit. I had seen him before, in crowds around the harbour, had thought him then perhaps a rich man's agent, one sent to oversee the handling of goods or set a mark on purchases. He was a man of forty years, lean, sour-faced. His eyes moved quicker than his lips. He seldom smiled.

His page must have been awaiting my return for his knock came quickly. He was small and dark, in a livery I did not recognise. I have no servant to answer for me, so I attended to his knock myself. My lodgings are simple – two rooms high up in the town which I rent from an Andalusian merchant. By day they have a view of the mountains. By night I can hear the sea.

'Sir,' the boy began, 'my master, Raymond of Nava, begs an audience. He asks to be allowed to wait on you this very evening, for he departs for Narbonne at dawn.'

It was a late hour for such a visit and I told him so, and yet I bade him bring his master to me, for the nights are long when one sleeps so little and even an old man sometimes covets company.

The visitor who followed within the half-hour was a little shabbier than I'd thought him from my observations in the market. He dismissed his servant at the door, leaving the two of us alone. When he spoke, his voice was quiet, but there was a harsh edge to it that told of a man who did not deal in kindness.

He told me he was an agent for the Count of Mirande and that business sometimes brought him to the Moorish ports. The count, he told me, had long heard tell of Antioch's missing expedition, and now would like to know the truth behind the tales.

His eyes had taken in my simple room — a bed, a table, chairs, a drinking jug — and now came back to mine. 'They say you are the man to ask, that you have looked beyond the tavern gossip.'

I shrugged. 'I know no more than anyone could learn by asking. I know they sailed eastward, bound for unknown lands. I know I still await them. That is all.'

His eyes brushed quickly over me, then away. 'I've heard the expedition was lost at sea, or overwhelmed by brigands. Surely after so many years you must believe the same?'

I considered him carefully. Through the open window a breeze from the sea stirred the hot night air. Below, in the town, I could hear men laughing as they left the inns and wandered to their lodgings.

'A lost ship leaves traces,' I told him. 'An empty line in an owner's ledger, a fortune lost. And a skirmish leaves wounds, or widows to remember it. Survivors talk and tell their tales. Brigands boast of their deeds. Sometimes the goods they've plundered are recognised at market. And yet I have heard nothing.'

The Catalan had remained standing and now he turned to the open window, as if listening to the sounds from the town.

'You talk to many people in this port.' There was, perhaps, suspicion in his tone. 'Jews, Arabs, Greeks. You talk a great deal for one who knows so little.'

'I talk to everyone I meet. I ask each man the same: whether he has seen my son.'

'Ah, yes. Your son. When did you last have word of him?'

A deep breath to dull the pain. 'There has been no word of him since Antioch left Italy.'

The Catalan wiped his palm across his jaw and slid his gaze away.

'That's strange, is it not? For a son to so neglect his father?'

'A boy that age has other things to think of. He believes his parents live forever. I would not have had him neglect his duties for thinking of his home.'

My visitor ran his palm across his face again. 'There were others with your son who perhaps have sent you word? Some messages to give you hope that they are safe?'

I looked at him. 'I have received no word.' And then, perhaps foolishly: 'The count's curiosity is very considerable, is it not? If he wishes to know more, let him come like I do and listen to the news from foreign ports.'

He looked hard at me then, and I saw I had surprised him. 'Be careful, merchant. You stay for a while in a Moorish city but step back into a Christian land and you will answer to Christian powers once more.'

I returned his gaze steadily. 'So you come to threaten me?'

He smiled then, a dry, juiceless smile. 'No, I did not come to threaten. You are right that the count's interest in this matter is more than careless curiosity. I am here to offer his support.'

He waited for me to respond but I stayed silent. A successful merchant quickly learns when to say nothing.

'Tell me, merchant, did you ever meet the Count Decius who sailed with your son?'

'I did not.'

'What do you know of him?'

'I know he was a soldier of Manfred, that he fought against the Pope.'

'Not always.' The Catalan paused in his pacing. 'He made his name as a young man fighting for the Pope's allies. He fought with the papal armies at the Siege of Montségur.'

I shrugged. It meant nothing to me. The next question followed quickly.

'Have you heard of a man known as Pau?'

I looked up, curious. 'He was one of Decius's men, was he not?'

'You knew him?'

'No. He was mentioned in Antioch's letter from Sicily, the last he sent me.'

The Catalan shook his head, his face disapproving.

'You knew very little of the men to whom you gave your son.'

'I entrusted my son to Antioch the scholar. I did so at the recommendation of Richard of Lincoln himself.'

As I had expected, the mention of that churchman had its effect. When my visitor spoke again his tone was more respectful.

'Sir, the count understands your sorrow for your son. He would wish to compensate you for your suffering. If you receive any word of your son's fate, he would like to hear of it. In return he will be generous. You understand?'

Again our eyes met.

'Why?' I asked. 'Of what interest can it be to him?'

He paused, paced for two, three strides, then stopped. Finally he seated himself in the chair opposite my own.

'If you ever find out more about Count Decius it is unlikely to be to his credit. His reputation for brutality lives on to this day. He is a turncoat, too. A man who changed sides, a man who has fought alongside the Saracens against Christian armies. And worse than any of that, a man who cheated my master out of a large sum of money.' He smiled that same, dry smile and rose to his feet. 'Where money is involved, men have long memories. While there is any chance that Decius might be found there will be people in these parts willing to pay for information. My master is a more generous man than most.' He looked at me again; that hard, cold look. 'If you hear anything, merchant, anything at all, then send for me.'

With that he took his leave but, with the door open and the night breeze fresh in front of him, he paused on my threshold. This time, when he spoke, his voice had changed. It was softer than before, and with a note of genuine puzzlement in it.

'Tell me, merchant,' he said. 'In all these years you say you've had no word. Nothing to give you hope. You ask me to believe that. But why else would you remain here, waiting?'

I felt sorry for him then. Sorry, because for all the cleverness in that sharp face of his, there was something absent, something lost. Somewhere in his forty years he had forgotten how it feels to love.

'I wait here,' I told him, 'because this is all I can do.'

Late at night, when the backstreets fall silent, I repair to my room and to the charts I keep there. There are some who say that beyond the Arabian Sea the world ends. By this they mean the last safe coasts are left behind you and the ports beyond do not know the rule of law. This is Christian talk and I too believed it once. But those I live with here tell a different tale: of desert coasts and then the fruitful Indies, ample harbours built of stone where goods are bought and sold, and strangers welcomed.

Beyond that coast, they say, another sea begins, a sea at once a mystery and a challenge. They say the islands here can float, and that their forests steam by day so each seems caught by fire. These lands are less well charted and so I ask each man I meet to sketch for me the outline of his voyages there, what course he set, what capes and bays he noted. Much of what I hear is second-hand, the reported word of cousins, brothers, friends. Yet even so, these rough plans have grown into something larger. An old man here, a chart-maker, has made for me three maps from all these sketches. At night I study these, wondering at a world so wide, at names that tell·of half-imagined coasts, and cities deep in jungles: *Sumatra, Bintan, Lambri; Andaman, Comorin, Kaif.*

I do not believe the tales of cursed gold. I do not believe that Antioch set sail with a great treasure. I spoke once to a prisoner in Venice, a man who had held office in Genoa. He could recall the time of Antioch's departure from that city, of the money spent and the high prices, and the old man's fear for his dwindling coffers. He recalled no talk or sign of treasure, only a handful of tough Sicilian soldiers and an old man fretting over the cost of flour.

I asked that man if he recalled a fair-haired page.

'There *was* a boy,' he told me. 'Yes, a boy who helped me once. My prayers for him.' And then he paused in sadness. 'Know, though, that those were dangerous times. The states boiling with hatred. Violence festering in every hollow of the land. And the cruelty . . . such cruelty . . . Sometimes it seems we live as beasts . . .' He spoke the words as if the blame lay on his shoulders.

No one knows for sure the route that Antioch took from Genoa. I hear them say he sailed south to a floating land and there found streets of gold; or that he travelled east and found the golden unicorn of Tartary whose magic horn made fortunes for them all. Some say the old man died and all his men went on to conquer unknown lands; others that they sailed beyond the sunrise, from whence in time they will return.

The truth is plainer. I know they sailed from Genoa a force of forty-odd. Sidon was their destination and that was reached, for traders there recall them. And I know from Sidon they went east, to Damascus, then south until the port of Basrah was achieved. There a ship was leased, and sailors hired. And from that place Antioch's men set sail. After that there's only rumour. From there the trail is lost.

ζ

A Lost World

She was born into a world of mists. Every spring, when the heat of the day and the cool of the night first came together in the water meadows, their mingling gave rise to silver fogs that cloaked the river at dawn and dusk, and dimmed the lanterns of her father's house. It was a season of mystery and stillness. But on the night of her birth, the skies had cleared, and for that reason they called her *bright moon* and said that one day the stars would show her the way to happiness.

Few strangers ever travelled as far as the water meadows of Zaiton. Even as a child it was safe for her to walk there, for the foreign traders who thronged the docks were allowed no further than the city limits, and the local merchants who built great houses on the land beyond the walls had interest only in the breathless clamour of the markets. And so the water meadows lay in peace, and every summer of her childhood she walked there undisturbed until the year the stranger came.

She was fifteen then. That was the year of the troubles in the north, when her uncle's house was burnt and the stone dragons of Angzhou were seized by the Great Khan's armies, the year when the closed boundaries of her world began to fray. She had learned nothing then of the treachery of words. Later she knew much more. Yet even later, when she had learned so much, she struggled for words to tell how vivid it had seemed to her, that summer when she saw him first.

She remembered the colours most. It had been a hard, yellow season – the grass scorched, the earth baked ochre, the sun huge and red and unrelenting; tempers were short and arguments flared as quickly as the fires that burned on the borders. Sickness plagued the country, and lawlessness came with it. Foreign merchants stayed away amid the rumours of invasion, and tales of bandits spread from town to town more quickly than the fever. Her father ruled the meadows unsafe and tried to make her stay within his walls.

Into this discord, astride a cream-brown horse, rode Song Rui – bold, urgent, brilliant; a favourite of the Emperor; already a field commander; and, beneath all the renown already attached to him, a young man of twenty-five.

She first saw him in the water meadows, early in the morning when the light was still milky with dawn. She heard his horse before anything else, the steady caution of hooves feeling their way down the dusty river-bank. They were both fugitives that morning, she from the heat of her father's house and its stifling sleeplessness, he from the responsibilities of his command and from the tedium of a five-day route march. She was courting disgrace on the river-bank, with her bare toes dangling in the water; he had left his men under the command of a captain and was scouting ahead for his own amusement. He rode with a light heart, enjoying the serene hour before the heat would narrow the day. She watched him coax his mount through the undergrowth of the opposite bank to the water's edge, then dismount and drink.

To Ming Yueh he seemed like a creature from the tales of her childhood, the impossible stories of heroes and princes who, through their brilliance and their beauty, were unfettered by the rules of common men. He wore the uniform of an officer but he wore it lightly, open to the waist and hanging loose, as if to let the cool air closer before the rising sun dispersed it. His hair was long, far longer than was respectable in the salons of Zaiton, where the scrupulous propriety of merchant society enforced the strictest codes. And there was something in his travel-stained state and the ease with which he wore it that spoke to her of a world much wider than her own, where rules meant less than the people who lived under them. Even much later she could recall the blue of his jacket that morning, the brown streaks of dust in his hair – and the sense of wonder that opened in her at first sight of him.

Song Rui was in a good temper. He had left his men in good order, making excellent progress on the way to Zaiton. They were few in number, but good soldiers under a captain he trusted. He planned to arrive in Zaiton ahead of them and from a different direction, as that way, he'd learned, he often heard and witnessed scenes not always shown to a senior soldier of the Emperor.

From the north, the river was hidden by willow trees and by a high escarpment, and only as he edged down the slope towards its bank did he become aware of the broad stretch of water meadows, still green, beyond it. The sight was a pleasing one after so many miles of brown, drought-crippled fields. And the river still ran strongly, still almost filled its banks; deep enough to swim, he thought, when the day grew hotter.

It was only as he drank from its waters that he noticed her. She was so still amid the reeds that he had to look twice to be certain. Then he rose and re-mounted and nudged his horse forward towards the opposite bank, his military instincts piqued at being observed without observing. As he grew closer, he saw her better: slim legs covered to the ankle, bare feet, dark eyes that followed him and did not flinch from his gaze.

'Girl,' he called out, taking her for a peasant because her feet were bare and her skin darker than a lady's. 'Will this path lead me to Zaiton?'

She watched him, intrigued and awkward in his presence, trying hard to decide if she risked disgrace by being discovered in such a place in such a way. Her household, she knew, was not like those of other merchants. Her mother had died within a week of Ming Yueh's birth. Her death, they said, had cut into her father's soul. For months after it he had not left his house, had scarcely spoken. Then he had returned to his business with savage energy, talking little except for business talk, keeping no company except for business company. His daughter he hardly saw, leaving her to the women of his household: the old women, her nurses, the sympathy of servants. He seemed content simply to watch from his room from time to time as she went about her day. And yet, she knew, a scandal would appal him. She knew this instinctively, without understanding why, or what it said about his feelings for her. And so she watched Song Rui's approach with a mixture of curiosity and concern.

When he called out to her, it crossed her mind to run, or perhaps simply to remain silent. But he was coming closer – and she found that she wished to know more.

'There is no path,' she answered him, still four-fifths hidden in the reeds. 'But if you can find your way across the water meadows you'll reach a road that you can follow.'

On hearing her voice, he realised she was no peasant. She spoke clearly and rather beautifully, with none of the village slang he'd expected from such a girl in such a place. On reaching the far bank he hastened to dismount, tugging closed his jacket in embarrassment.

'Is it hard to find a way across?' he asked her, turning to scan the high grasses that lay in front of him. When he turned back her bare feet no longer touched the water but had been discreetly withdrawn and were hidden in the reeds. 'It doesn't look too difficult,' he concluded.

She laughed then, and he heard for the first time the mischief in her voice.

'Many think so. We drag them from the ditches later, when they lose their way and stumble.'

'Is there someone who can show me?'

She stood up before replying and he saw her properly for the first time: taller than was ideal in a woman, long hair tied behind her, straight and slim like the reeds.

'The men are in Zaiton with the militia,' she told him. 'I could show you, but people would say . . .' She flushed and tailed off. 'I don't care what they say, but my father would.'

He laughed. 'And do these people think it proper for a lady of good family to go bare-legged in the fields? The customs of Zaiton must truly be exceptional.'

Seeing her blush again, he took pity on her, taking his leave with a short salute. 'If I survive my journey, I shall return this way,' he called, 'to show the water-spirit of this place that her warnings were unnecessary.'

He did not look back as he rode away. Yet he too was reminded a little of the tales of his childhood, where princesses hid themselves in rags and only the brave and the pure of heart were able to discover them.

Two days later, at the same hour, he returned and found her waiting. It was an unlikely meeting, the first of a series that defied every rule and every convention. Whenever Song Rui could put his duties to one side, he would ride out of the city to the place he had first seen her. He never failed to thrill at the freedom he felt on passing out of the city walls, nor at the scent of the countryside that awaited him. And the water meadows of Zaiton, green when the whole land seemed brown, pleased him greatly. It was a luxury to ride through them of a morning, and with every yard he covered he found his heart grew lighter. He would pass a mill and two low dwellings, then a forge where an incurious blacksmith ignored his passing, and only a mile or two further on he would find the place he was seeking. Even in that volatile summer there was still peace there, still trees and shadows, and on the river margin the grass grew as high as his horse's shoulder. It released a fragrance that roused in him memories of

lost childhood mornings. And there, on the very edge
of the water, his water-spirit would be waiting.

First he would swim and let the slow green waters
press against his body. And then, as the sun dried him,
they would talk. He would tell her of the things he
knew which she did not, and she would listen to his
words and marvel. She heard in them the sounds of a
world quite different from her own: a world without
the smothering, respectable restraints of Zaiton. She
heard in his words the cries of the great city and the
hubbub of its streets. His words drew pictures and her
imagination coloured them, until Song Rui half believed the embellishments she added and, smiling,
helped her draw more.

Soon his courtship of Ming Yueh was being con-
ducted with the urgency of a military action. He had
met no one in Zaiton so enchanting, he told himself.
Her simplicity delighted him and the stubborn determination he detected beneath it made him smile. So
what if she was a merchant's daughter? Surely she was
as graceful and delicate as any man could wish for.
And if her father was a merchant, what of it? Had not
his own mother's grandfather been a simple infantry
officer? A little education in the ways of the court
would make good all her faults, and her father's
fortune would dispel any scent of the marketplace.
Yes, he decided, when the time was propitious he
would send for her and continue her education. It

was a pleasant prospect with which to enliven a tedious season.

And so that fierce summer burned itself upon Ming Yueh's memory. They met in dappled green darkness, cloaked by shadows from the glaring world beyond. They met often, sometimes every day for a week or more. She knew herself in love before she had framed the words to name it: it came to her as a joyful, stabbing certainty in the very centre of her being, a pain and a passion that she had never known before and would never forget. And she vowed she would one day share the wonders he described to her, for they were surely part of him and he of them, the two of them one whole which beckoned her.

For Song Rui, this rapture in the water meadows helped him bear a mission that had quickly ceased to entertain. The merchants had met his demands for extra money promptly – their fear of the Great Khan's armies had ensured it – and with their gold he had strengthened the militia. But before any chance of action had arisen, the crisis of midsummer had passed. The desperate heat lasted longer, but soon the rivers were seen to fill again, revived by rains in the distant west. And it seemed these faster waters washed away the foundations of unrest, for the lands around Zaiton grew calm and in the north the raids of the Great Khan's armies paused, then halted. Orders came for Song Rui's return to court.

As the summer passed the young pair had grown more confident, yet he had never dared to touch her. Perhaps the green river had washed away his city instincts, for he found himself both pleased and proud of his restraint. Even so, the excitement in her eyes drew him close to her and he let his fingers rest on the warm earth of the river-bank so close to hers that both could feel a current of feeling pass between them. And when at the end of the summer he came to say farewell, there on the banks of the river, he spoke to her passionately and earnestly, full of a raw desire that flared up and surprised him. He told her that he'd send for her when the time was right, when the Emperor was prepared. And he told her that no other woman had affected him as she did, that no happiness could be his without her.

He left her repeating those words, her mantra against the days to come.

Twelve months after Song Rui's departure, a message under the imperial seal arrived in Zaiton, and was delivered to her father in the house by the water meadows. His daughter, it informed him, was summoned to the Imperial Court. This was an order that allowed no hesitation and no questions, one that was stark in its directness. Soldiers were being sent to escort her. She should set out as soon as the preliminaries for such a journey were complete. She was to bring with her a dowry – an enormous sum in coin was specified – and all the jewellery, silks and adornments that would be expected. In return the Emperor would smile upon her. One did not attempt to put a price on such a smile.

And so a convoy to escort her was assembled, the date for her departure set. And she waited, seized by a restlessness that her father neither recognised nor understood. He had watched her for so many years, watched her grow, wondered at her flowering. But he had always kept himself apart, unused to children, at a loss how to speak to someone at once so precious and so vital to him. There would be time later to speak, he always told himself. But now there was no time left to him, and in trying to reach out to her he realised she had changed. Somewhere out in the meadows, unnoticed by him, his child had disappeared. This creature in front of him now was new to him, a determined, strangely poised young woman, who hid from him her fears and hopes. And when he tried to talk to her, he found she had outgrown the language of the schoolroom. Her restlessness was her own. He could take no part of it.

Side by side, silently, they sat and waited for her life to begin. That was the summer when a strange party of travellers from a distant land arrived by water in Zaiton. Amid the confusion of its welcome came the order to depart.

Genoa

Before the sea, before the desert, before the strange steaming islands, there was Genoa. Heaving, over-confident Genoa, city of spies. To the boy who tra-velled with Antioch, a place unlike any other: a city grown grand on trade, its arteries plumped with wealth, people choking its streets to a standstill. Every-one hurrying, and the worship of God all but lost beneath the rituals of commerce.

And yet the provisioning of Antioch's expedition was slow and difficult. Goods were expensive and permits were refused or delayed while the wait on the docks grew longer. For the boy, they were lonely times. With so much to do, Antioch had little time for a page he considered no more than a child; so the boy found himself ignored while those around were overwhelmed with work.

It was Decius who had insisted that the party was equipped in Genoa, where the provisioning of such expeditions was more common, rather than in any port of Sicily. His decision meant that Manfred's battalion of men must be reduced to a force of no more than forty, for all agreed that any larger force, even marching under Antioch's household banner, would not be allowed to enter the uneasy, feuding states through which they must pass. So Decius had selected forty men, hard-faced veterans under a young captain named Pau, and had dressed them in Antioch's colours. Together they had ridden north cautiously and without incident.

On arrival, Antioch insisted on a mixed and muddled cargo. His books must go with them, but so must his Arab instruments of navigation and a gold casket containing a finger of St John. He insisted on a multitude of gifts for the great kings they would encounter: cloth of gold, swords, lances, barrels of Cyprus wine, holy texts, Spanish leather, vessels in silver and in copper, ivory chess pieces, fine oil, carved knives, even a toothless ape that was bought, apparently at random, from a sailor on the quayside.

The only help they received was from the harbour-master, a man who negotiated for them a ship and sailors. He seemed to take a liking to Antioch and it was he, on the very eve of their departure, who asked a question none had considered: who in their party would speak the foreign tongues of the lands they were to visit? For although in Syria they may get by with that form of market Latin that served for trade around the Roman Sea, they would, he told them, one day come to lands of strange and complex tongues, some scarcely ever heard by Christian ears. In these lands, who would ask directions or bargain for supplies?

'There is a man in Genoa now,' he told them, 'a man by the name of Venn. He travels with many expeditions. Merchants who wish to trade in distant lands employ him for his special way with other tongues. He has a gift unlike any other and they say no language can defeat him. They say he can learn the speech of a new land by simply walking in the markets and listening to the talk.'

Antioch nodded eagerly and agreed that such a special gift would be invaluable, and so it was agreed that the boy should be sent the next day to summon the man before them.

Before the boy set out, the harbour-master took him aside and pressed something into his palm.

'Take this to the man you seek, boy. Tell him it is sent with my compliments.'

Only when he was alone in the street outside did the boy pause to study the object. It was a Saracen coin of a sort he had never seen before, with Moorish writing on one side and on the other a constellation of five stars. One – the second smallest – had been deliberately scored through with the shape of a Latin cross; and another, the one in the middle, had by the same hand been scratched around with a hasty circle.

The boy considered it a while and then for safe-keeping hid it tight in the hem of his trousers, next to the locket his father had given him.

The old quarter of the town, where he was sent to look for the interpreter, gave the boy his first idea of the lands he was to visit. There, in the narrow, squalid streets, foreign traders and itinerants were allowed to find cheap lodgings, and in the crowds were many Moors and Berbers laughing and talking in their own tongue. The sound both worried and excited him. It told of a world unknown to him, where even the streets made different sounds.

He found Venn's door at the top of a narrow staircase that led from a courtyard where caged birds were sold. As he ascended, the cries of the traders faded but somehow the cries of the birds remained clear, so that as he climbed the last twelve steps all he could hear from below was the faint calling of songbirds. His first knock received no answer but he had walked for half an hour in the heat of the day and dared not return with his message undelivered. After he'd persisted with his knocking for a full minute he heard a movement behind the door and it opened wide enough to reveal a woman looking down at him. She appeared to wear nothing but a length of cloth which she held tightly to her chest and which trailed downwards in uneven folds. Her legs and feet, he saw, were bare.

'What's your business?' she asked him, using the port-side slang the boy had heard Pau's soldiers use. He prepared to reply in his best, most formal Latin, yet instead he found himself hesitating, taken aback by her bare shoulders, which were dark and smooth and very close to him.

'What?' she asked again, and when he hesitated she looked past him to see if anyone else lurked in the gloom of the stair. Only then did the boy find his voice.

'I bear a summons for the man Venn,' he announced. 'He is required to attend the scholar Antioch, envoy of the Lord Manfred, King of Sicily.'

She showed no sign of listening, her eyes still studying the shadows behind him.

'You are alone?' she asked.

He nodded and, satisfied, she opened the door and stood aside for him.

After the darkness of the staircase, the room he entered seemed fresh and bright. On both sides of it the shutters were pulled back, letting in sunlight and a breeze that had not been apparent in the musty streets below. The room was white-walled and sparsely furnished; in it there was no sign of the man he sought.

Left alone with the woman, the boy felt at a loss. She moved past him, to where a pale blue cloth lay across a pile of cushions. She bent to pick it up and wrapped it loosely round her shoulders before turning back to him.

'In there,' she indicated, nodding at another open door. And then, surprisingly: 'I told him you would come.' But when the boy looked back at her with astonishment, she had turned away and was standing at the window, looking out over the town to the distant hills beyond.

The next room was a bedroom, cooler and darker, with a mass of blankets lying in disorder on the floor. It too was empty, but in one wall a small doorway led to a narrow ledge that overlooked the bird market. There Venn was standing with his back to the boy, leaning over the wooden balustrade as if listening to the sounds rising up from below. He wore a pair of rough breeches of the sort popular with Arab sailors, and his shirt hung open. On hearing the boy approach, Venn turned and began to fasten the garment, but not before the boy had glimpsed a scar on his chest, a great dark crucifix across the centre of his body. Unsure where to look, the boy raised his eyes to the interpreter's face. He was a man of middle years, thirty perhaps, perhaps half a dozen years more – the weathered skin, scored with brown creases, gave little away, and the blue eyes were edged with fine lines. A face that hid more than it revealed, yet was neither unfeeling nor unkind.

'You are one of the Sicilian's men?' he asked. His voice was calm.

'Yes, sir.' The boy had arrived intending to give orders to a common mariner, a man for hire. Instead he found himself standing to attention. He hardly

knew why, unless it was because the man had spoken
to him in the same court Latin that the Lord Manfred
had used in Sicily.

'They say you head east,' Venn went on, 'and have
need of someone to speak for you.'

'Yes, sir. We go as far as we must to find the missing
creatures of the bestiary.'

Venn shrugged. It seemed a gesture aimed not at the
boy but at himself.

'Your mission is your own business. But perhaps it
is time for me to travel again.' He looked back, into the
room, hesitant for a moment, then crouched down on
his haunches so that his face was level with the boy's.
'Your masters know what pay I ask?'

'Yes, sir. A silver piece a day.'

'Tell them that this time they must pay in advance.
Six months. Tell them you are to bring it here and give
it to the woman who greeted you today.'

'Yes, sir, I'll tell them.'

Venn smiled. 'I thank you,' he said. 'Now tell me,
child, what's your name?'

'Benedict, sir,' the boy replied, and smiled too. It
was the first time since leaving Manfred's court that
anyone had thought to ask it.

Only after he had returned with Venn's message did
the boy remember the harbour-master's coin.
Ashamed of his lapse, he said nothing, thinking to
deliver it instead the following day. But the following

day was a busy one, and when eventually the interpreter joined the ship, the boy's desire to win his good
opinion was such that he could not bear to confess his
forgetfulness. And so the coin, and the message it
conveyed, remained in the hem of his trousers, remembered for many days with shame and eventually
forgotten.

They had come to Damascus almost by chance, carried
there by winds of rumour, each twist in their route
decided by the murmur in the local bazaars or by
extravagant tales of strange creatures that were whispered into Antioch's ear. In the lands to the south, they
were told, countless wonderful beasts roamed the
grasslands; and in the islands of the Indies sea dragons
basked openly on sunny shores. There were tigers
there, and orange apes, and also, it was universally
declared, a kind of elephant no bigger than a dog.

All this seemed possible to Antioch, who seemed to
change with every mile travelled. Manfred, in selecting
him, had little understood the old man's passion for
new learning. But that passion burned deep and now
its flame was fanned to extraordinary heat by the
glorious bestiary he carried with him. And yet
Manfred had also been shrewd in his choice, for the
magistrates and the local governors of the Arab lands
were men who placed a value on learning. They
recognised in Antioch a true scholar, and his learning

won a safe passage for his party. They would invite
him to their tables and listen to him speak, then send
messages ahead that the old man posed no danger.

The night the mermaid was acquired, Antioch
called a council. They were camped that night in a
caravanserai near the souk, and it was to their
temporary quarters, hung in brown desert cloth
and lit by strongly smelling torches, that Decius
and Antioch retired that night. The boy was in
attendance, as also was an old Lascar pilot, a person
recommended to them by the city governor for his
knowledge of the lands beyond Hormuz. Venn accompanied him, lest the pilot's understanding of their
Latin proved too meagre. In that hot chamber, so
very different from the echoing room where Manfred
had first addressed them, the future of their journey
was decided.

Antioch proposed to sail south, down the Ethiopian
coast, where great wonders were to be found. There
were travellers in Damascus who claimed they had
seen with their own eyes creatures unknown to other
men: triple-tusked elephants, huge unicorns, deer with
necks like snakes. But Decius would have none of this.
Lord Manfred, he maintained, had stipulated that they
travel east, to the realms of the Great Khan, and in that
remote and barbarous region they were to seek the
beasts they came for. These were their orders, which
they were honour-bound to follow. And had not

Antioch himself once said that it was in the east they would find the famous Asian unicorn?

The thrust was a shrewd one and for a moment the old man looked down at the book that lay beside him. The Asian unicorn! This was something more real to him than the strange creatures of the southern seas. This was a creature he had learned about since childhood, had dreamed of as a boy; a beast made magical by story. Surely such an animal – just one of them – would in itself be enough to satisfy Manfred? With such an animal they could return in honour. For a moment Antioch thought of his home, his quiet room, the spring light angling across his study; and Decius, watching him, felt sure he had carried the day.

It was then the Lascar pilot spoke, hesitantly, awkwardly, uncertain in their tongue. The road to the eastern kingdoms was an arduous one, he told them. The mountains were high and the snows deep; the deserts spread wide across the routes, and the passes were infested with brigands. Meanwhile, in the port of Basrah stood a fine ship, ready to depart, that would carry their lordships in comfort to the place they sought.

'I know a way though the islands of the Lesser Indies that brings you by sea to the port of Zaiton, the greatest port in the world. From Zaiton it is but a few days' ride to the lands of the Great Khan.'

The boy saw from Antioch's face that the city's name was not familiar to him, but there was a certainty in the pilot's tone that commanded respect. By taking ship, the pilot explained, they might achieve all their desires: they might come in safety to the lands of the unicorn and yet still behold the many wonders of the southern seas. And they should travel by ship like men of breeding, not on rutted paths like common muleteers.

For Antioch this solution was ideal. His mind was made up, and nothing would move him. The next day arrangements were begun for their great sea journey. In seven months they would be in Zaiton.

The Women's Script

In the house by the water meadows she watched the preparations carefully with a calm that never faltered. Her father, who had observed her for so long and spoken so little, had tried again to find words with which to approach her. But silence can breed silence, and the language of his own home had somehow become a mystery to him.

Instead he spent lavishly on her trousseau, filling her caravan with the most brilliant of things, determined she would want for nothing. His neighbours marvelled at his spending, little understanding that what they witnessed was an awkward, stumbling outpouring of love.

But Ming Yueh barely noticed. She longed to be away, free from the confines of Zaiton, free of her clucking neighbours and the city's suffocating expectations. And before she could leave she had a letter to write: a letter of farewell, an invitation, a promise, a letter that had been written before, countless times, by women preparing to make a journey. Hers, like all those others, would be posted in the marketplace – on the Women's Wall – for a dozen minutes and no more. Then, before it could be noticed by any but those who watched for it, it would be torn down and destroyed.

She knew those dozen minutes were enough to announce her journey to her sisters in Zaiton so they could send her their messages, their greetings for loved ones along her route.

Her writing was good, she knew, but in the writing of this letter she must excel, for in the few minutes it remained on the wall the whole of it would be memorised, to be passed in whispers from one woman to another. Thankfully she had learned the art well, the traditional forms, the subtle cadences, the use of certain characters to echo others and enhance their meaning. With these the formal style could be rendered into something simple yet full of feeling.

She rehearsed the lines in her head for many weeks before she dared to write them. How to tell so much in so few words? Her name, her birth, the destination of her journey, all the places she would pass through . . . And more than that. She must tell the women of Zaiton of her plans, of her dreams, of her love for Song Rui, and ask them for their prayers on her behalf. And she must show them her strength, for if they thought her a mere girl, why should they trust her with their messages?

That was why, when she took up her pen, it was with a seriousness and a solemnity written in her face that Song Rui would not have recognised.

'*To the Women of Zaiton, Notice of a Journey,*' she began.

Nothing had prepared the boy for his arrival there. Even Venn, who had seen many things, had seen nothing like it. A city that seemed to reach forever, a harbour so densely packed with ships, six deep in places, that from a distance they could not tell where the water ended and the docks began. Closer in, the detail grew clearer, and the boy could see the countless wooden cranes on the harbourside and realised that the slim pontoons which stretched like fingers into the bay were not of firm construction, as he'd thought them, but were in fact long strings of smaller craft all roped together into floating thoroughfares where foreign merchants traded with each other beyond the boundaries of the mainland tariffs.

Through this tangle of ropes and timbers their hired vessel nudged its way in the hands of a local pilot, while Antioch's party lined the deck and wondered at what they saw. The boy stood close to Venn, inhaling all the land smells that assailed him and listening to the sing-song cries of Zaiton's sailors. For the previous month a fear of reefs had made them cautious of the coast, but now the breeze brought the scents of seaweed and pitch and cheap cooking oil and, rising from the slack waters, the familiar stench of human waste. From each ship they passed, sailors called to them, greetings that sounded to the boy more like the songs of birds than the shouts of men.

'Do you understand them, Venn?' he whispered.

The interpreter nodded. 'A little. I was once in a land far west of here where they speak in such a way. Quiet, let me listen.'

And the boy was content to wait. In the course of the journey Venn had become his regular companion. Antioch, in whose household he had lived for so many months, was kindly, but the rigours of the journey had left him little time to worry about a young boy's need for company. Instead, for the sake of his education, the scholar would call the boy to him every evening and talk to him about the great tome they carried with them.

'The leocrota,' he would muse. 'A strange beast. Half deer, half lion. Our book tells us it is a beast of India, but India I fear is a very broad land, with many forests and rivers. We must hope to find some scholar there, or perhaps a nobleman skilled in the hunt, who can guide us to its lair. Otherwise I fear it will prove a very hard beast to track . . .'

The old man would sigh as he pondered the difficulties he faced. But then his face would lighten as another creature came to mind.

'Next in our book is the monoceros or unicorn, a very famous beast. From my studies, boy, I have deduced that unicorns of different types exist and must be sought in different places. In Ethiopia, we know, they are big as bulls and built as stout as oxen. These beasts are valued for their horns but in themselves are oafish, clumsy. The unicorn of Asia is a very different creature, a graceful beast, in shape more like a horse. Many mystical properties are attributed to it. This perhaps is the rarest beast of all.'

Whenever he could, the boy avoided Decius. The general's reputation went before him: a harsh leader, a hard man; no ounce of mercy in his heart or drop of tenderness in his veins. And even worse than Decius's forbidding manner were those aberrant, unnatural eyes – eyes with no colour at their centre, only blackness, as if some elemental humanity had not grown in him as in other men. Decius's soldiers would grimace when they spoke of the discipline he demanded, and they were seasoned troops, hard-faced and hard-bodied. Even through the desert marches their equipment was always gleaming and ready for use. Their captain, Pau, said little to the boy. He stayed close to his men, his expression constantly clouded as if brooding on the challenges ahead.

In avoiding the soldiers and their leader, the boy turned to Venn. There was something comforting in the interpreter's quiet company that made him feel safe. Late in the evenings when Antioch had retired, the boy would find the interpreter on the edge of their encampment, looking out at the darkness. He would approach him quietly and sit in silence next to him until his thoughts distilled themselves into words that he could not help but speak.

'Venn, Count Decius has ordered one of his men to be flogged tomorrow. Will it happen, do you think?'

Often Venn would reply without moving his gaze, still scanning the darkness.

'If the count has ordered it.'

'But it is harsh, is it not? The man's mistake was a small one.'

'Decius's men know what to expect. He is at least consistent.'

'I'm afraid of him, Venn. He has cruel eyes.'

Venn shrugged. 'Cruel? Perhaps. He is known in the Pope's lands as a ruthless man, hard on friend and foe alike. I only know what I have seen.'

'But you have heard of him before?'

'Yes, I've heard of him. Nothing good, although he is said to be loyal to Manfred. Before that he was on the other side, a general in the Pope's crusade against the Cathars.'

'Cathars?' The boy had never heard the word. 'Were they infidels, then?'

Venn turned back to face the stars on the horizon. 'So they say. The Pope decides.'

The boy considered this for a few moments. 'But there is only one true way, Venn, is there not?'

The interpreter picked a stone out of the sand and threw it into the darkness. 'This is an ancient land, Benedict. Prayers have been said here since time began, in different tongues to different gods. But I've found that wherever I travel people always pray for much the same things. And whatever gods they pray to, some get them, some don't. What do you pray for, Benedict?'

The boy looked at the night sky. 'I pray that my father will be proud of me. And that one day I will have the chance to show the world my courage.'

And their conversations would end with Venn smiling while the boy fell silent, soothed by the thought of great deeds in a distant future.

They edged into the port of Zaiton, always finding a way through the reefs of other vessels, the pilot occasionally speaking a word or two to Venn who would nod or venture a reply in that same birdsong language. Decius and Antioch stood together at the prow of the ship, united for once in a common amazement at the scale of the city before them.

'Surely nowhere in Europe can rival this,' Antioch mused, as the size of the city became apparent. It seemed to have flooded outwards from the great buildings at its centre, like the flow of some unstoppable human eruption. Adding to the sense of a seething, smouldering mass, the smoke from ten thousand fires filtered upwards from it into air still clear with the freshness of morning.

Decius contemplated the sight grimly but said nothing. Venn, who was beckoned forward to join him, was unable to read the emotion in his face.

'What now, Venn?' he asked, his voice low.

'They are taking us to that quay over there,' the interpreter replied. 'It is a closed berth, I think – all foreigners must dock there. There we will be expected to declare our cargo.'

'We do not come to trade,' growled Decius. 'We travel to the lands of the Great Khan.'

'Or to whatever other places the rare creatures are said to inhabit,' Antioch added. 'They say these are the lands of the unicorn and the wyvern. We must ask their learned men where these beasts can be found.'

Venn's eyes were scanning the quayside, where a crowd was gathering to meet them.

'They are confused,' he said. 'The officials here are familiar with foreign traders; they have seen people from our lands before. But the pilot says for foreigners to travel beyond the city limits is unheard of. He says special permits are required.'

Decius glanced at him. 'What else?' he asked.

'He says no man may go from here to the lands of the Khan. The Emperor of these lands has decreed it, on pain of death.'

The general met the interpreter's eyes and raised an eyebrow. 'Very well. Then we must persuade the Emperor to change his mind.'

The Women's Wall did not appear on maps. It was not even a single edifice. Rather it was a moving and altering location, any one of a thousand places. It moved with the seasons, with the month, with the day of the week. It followed the markets, altered with the arrival of the caravans. One day it would be in the silk bazaar, the next at the place for household goods, a third by the marketplace for spices and for saffron. There was nothing but tradition to signify when a wall became the women's wall, no marking to distinguish it, no symbol, no announcement. It was simply *known*, a repeating calendar passed on through so many generations, learned so gradually, that women came of age uncertain how they knew it. And yet, at certain times in certain places, those who looked for them might find what they sought: messages in a curious script posted briefly on a market wall.

The walls of the market squares were working walls, grown accustomed over many years to bearing the bills and posters of a thousand earlier markets, walls papered thick with the dry, forgotten carcases of long-dead announcements. Against such a background in a frantic marketplace, a short message would only be noticed by those who looked for it. And a message posted in that particular script did not last long. It was read and memorised by eyes accustomed to the task, and then would disappear – an ancient ritual, grown strong through repetition. Few men came to the corners of the markets where the messages were posted. The better sites, where the rich merchants traded, were always avoided. The darker corners were left to the women.

That particular spring, however, there came to Zaiton a man for whom the old writing on the walls *was* interesting. For all his quick eyes he never saw the fleeting notes upon the women's walls, but once, by chance, he came across a scrap of muddied paper at his feet, one evening in the flower market. On it was a script of slender elegance he did not recognise, different in its sloping and its characters from the writing of Zaiton. This was strange and puzzling, for he collected languages as other men learned prayers, and something so new and different was a rarity for him. But the scrap in his hand was too little for interpretation and he put the fragment out of his mind. If it was part of a language he had not yet encountered, then in time perhaps he would encounter it again.

And in this Venn was right, although it would not be in Zaiton. And even though her message was a bare ten minutes in the public gaze, the replies to Ming Yueh's letter very soon began to reach her.

They were in length and form so very different from each other. Some were but a few lines long, scratched in uncertain characters by hands frail or unskilled. Others flowed like verses, the soft cry of the writers' voices held by them like the echoes of a melody. Each had as its beginning the name of a distant loved one, someone separated from Zaiton by more miles than could ever now be bridged. *To my sister in Ti-chien, a greeting . . . To my niece, the loyal Shan-ti, news of home . . . To my daughter in Pian, if the gods have spared her . . .*

Ming Yueh read them all and learned each one, committing every character to memory before destroying them, that she might write each note again, exactly as before. She had such zeal for her task, and such excitement, that at first she didn't see the pattern. She only saw the trust being placed in her and felt a surge of pride, eager to prove herself to so many others.

But then, as message followed message, she began to see, beneath the greetings and the blessings, beneath the honest words of love, that a common sense of sadness linked each one. It was as if the same sigh of pain breathed through them all, and touched Ming Yueh with an unexpected melancholy.

For these were notes of separation. Women prised apart by marriage or by custom reached out their fingertips to touch their loved ones. Mothers called to daughters taken from them thirty years before and told them of their undiminished love. Women cried out to the sisters who had once been their comforters.

Young girls new to marriage hid their loneliness from mothers who could read of it in every line. For all the clarity of the messages, for all their delicate phrasing, absence weighed on every one of them like a stone sinking through water.

Ming Yueh felt her own heart following them into cold and lonely depths. By way of comfort, she promised herself to carry every message as truly and as safely as if it were her own.

And then she found one note unlike the rest. A note without a greeting. It was not addressed to an absent sister but to Ming Yueh herself. Its prose was terse and urgent.

'Be careful of your dreams,' it told her. 'You wish for freedom, you wish to fly. But the markets are full of caged birds. Take care, for in the Imperial City the lime is set thick upon the branches. And I have watched limed birds struggle. They beat their wings and cry against the traps, betrayed by the weakness that tempted them to rest. They never fly again, though some almost tear off their legs in frustration at their capture. Do not be weak as they were. If all else fails, fly at the sun, for better to die in flames than to live as I do, pinioned by my own regretting.'

Only on reading this note a second time did Ming Yueh realise with a sharp twist of surprise that the characters used to write *limed bird* were, but for a line or two, the way her own name was written.

* * *

Even in a city as cosmopolitan as Zaiton, the arrival of this party of adventurers from barbarian lands caused a great deal of consternation. Pau and his soldiers had been forbidden to land at all, while Antioch and the count, with Venn and the boy beside them, were held on the dockside for many hours.

They might have stayed there much longer, might even have been refused entry to the city altogether, had a late arrival on the scene not taken up their cause. At first the boy thought this curious figure was some sort of local official, for he was dressed in fine robes. But on looking again, he noticed his pale eyes and pallid skin and realised with a shock that from some angles the man's features resembled his own. There was nothing in his bearing to suggest he was a stranger. In fact he strutted onto the dockside like a gaming cock, his chest to the fore, accompanied by two servants, both local men and both in livery. His arrival, the boy noted, was greeted with a stirring of respect. The chief customs officer, who had been talking volubly to his entourage, straightened visibly and hurried to greet the newcomer. To the boy's surprise, after a short discussion, this pale newcomer then turned and spoke to them in excellent Latin.

'Greetings, sir,' he began, addressing Antioch. 'My name is Yang Lun, and I am a merchant of this city. My father, bless his memory, came to Zaiton many years ago from the city of Pisa. A fine city, I believe, though I have never yet visited it. My father chose never to return to it, but decided instead to live out his days in this humble town.' He turned to eye the assembled officials who stood behind him. 'I fear your arrival here is causing some confusion,' he went on.

'From Pisa, you say?' The old man was startled, having not observed the new arrival closely. 'I am astonished. By your dress and your command of the language, I had taken you for a man of Zaiton.'

The merchant laughed at this. 'I have lived here all my life. But by blood I am half Pisan, and at your service. Please, I have suggested that while the officials wait for guidance, you and your companions may come with me to my home and rest there. When we are seated more comfortably, perhaps I can explain some of the difficulties of your position . . .'

The merchant's quarters turned out to be a very grand house indeed, built in the local style, with fine spacious courtyards and curved gables. To reach it, Antioch's party passed on foot through streets bustling with porters, lined with booths, where meat was cooked or bread baked and where the crowds turned to stare at them. They crossed a bridge over a canal and passed down a narrower lane to a small but heavily ornamented gate.

'Look,' said Antioch, as they passed inside. 'Dragons!' He pointed to the doors and the boy saw, laced into the intricate carvings, a pair of sinewy beasts entwined around each other.

Ever since their departure from Genoa, Antioch had kept Venn close to him, and the interpreter had, as a matter of course, been expected to accompany them to the house of the merchant. But at the front door, to the boy's regret, Venn was hurried away by an attendant to the rooms at the back of the house, to be entertained as one of Antioch's servants. The boy, as a page, remained at his master's side.

It was perhaps a significant moment. Yang had wealth, good connections, and knowledge of both the manners and the language of the country, and he very quickly became relied upon for all their dealings in Zaiton. Venn, from being essential to both Antioch and the count, was now no longer to be constantly at their sides. To the boy, this change was a cause for sadness, for he missed Venn's constant company. To Venn, the change was less unwelcome – it was in these days without duties that he was able to lose himself in the cramped intestines of the city, walking and listening, building up his understanding of the place and its languages. If he resented the new-found influence of the man with Pisan blood, he did not show it.

And from that first day in Yang's house, it was clear that Antioch's party would be in need of assistance, for the situation in Zaiton, and in the country as a whole, was far more awkward than they had understood.

'You come here at a difficult time,' the merchant told them, once they had been seated on cushions in an elegant chamber and provided with food and drink. 'This is a divided land. Before the coming of the Tartars, the Emperor's family ruled this entire continent, but the ancestors of the Great Khan seized the northern half of the country and camped their armies on our borders. For many years now the Great Khan has been threatening to advance again, and the lines are drawn from east to west, from the sea to the great deserts. For this reason strangers are treated with suspicion and may not travel beyond the trading centres. All movements must be authorised, permits must be obtained. And you must not say you wish to visit the lands of the Khan – such a request amounts to treason here.'

'But these are grim tidings,' Antioch complained. 'They say the unicorn of Asia is to be found only in the deserts of the west, where the Khan holds sway. That is the destination we have sworn to achieve.'

'I fear the Emperor might view things differently,' the merchant replied. 'He is not a man of scholarly interests. He is interested only in gratifying his senses. It is sometimes said that if he made as much use of his armies as he does his concubines, then we would have nothing to fear from the Great Khan for many generations.'

Decius fixed his dark eyes on the merchant. 'It would seem to me that such a man might be persuaded to change his mind. Is that not so? We are determined to continue our journey into the wild places if we must.'

The merchant looked at him carefully and there was a knowingness in that look which made the boy realise that this new acquaintance did not lack in shrewdness.

'For foreigners such as yourselves . . .' He paused. 'Well, a great deal can be achieved here by putting one's money into the right palms.'

'And I imagine that a man such as yourself might know which palms those were?'

Yang nodded, and it seemed to the boy that the two men had reached some sort of understanding.

'We have gifts on board our ship, don't we, Count?' Antioch broke in. 'We have many goods from Genoa . . .'

Yang's reply seemed to be aimed at Decius. 'To win imperial favour, I fear they will need to be lavish gifts indeed.'

Decius responded with a nod. 'Fear not. We have come prepared.'

Yang opened his mouth to reply but before he could speak, Decius had risen to his feet. 'If you will excuse me, I would like to return to our ship before we dine. It is my duty to see to the needs of my soldiers. But never fear, merchant, I am confident you shall find us sufficiently persuasive to win the Emperor's favour.'

And it was this remark that, when the boy repeated it to Venn, caused the interpreter to raise an eyebrow and purse his lips in thought.

In the house by the water meadows, the arrival of the foreigners in Zaiton was barely noticed. True, Ming Yueh's maid had seen them on the harbourside, great brutish creatures, she said, coarse-featured, with beaks for noses and rough hair that grew on their faces like the fur of apes. She swore the Indians and Arabs she had seen were comely by comparison to these great northern bears. Indeed, a frisson of excited horror ran through Zaiton society at the sight of the barbarian travellers. It was said that one had eyes that saw beyond men's smiles, that when they spoke they barked like wolves, that they were seeking strange and barbarous beasts they wished to worship.

But in Ming Yueh's house, with the exception of the maid, there was little interest in the strange visitors. For Ming Yueh's departure was imminent and cast a shadow that not even the most sensational news could dispel.

Outside the gates of her father's house, the Captain of the Guard also waited for the day of departure. Waited more anxiously than any of them, perhaps, for his mission was not to his liking and he was impatient for it to be over. It was clear to him that guarding a woman was a waste of his time. And it was a fool's errand to go by land. The roads to Lin'an were secure enough, but they were slow. The sensible way to make the journey was by sea. Let the navy look after the Emperor's women so his soldiers could get back to where they were needed. But he was a professional soldier – a veteran at thirty-five – and knew a little bit about the conflict between the Emperor's counsellors and his generals. This sort of mission, he felt sure, was meant to put the army in its place. Sometimes he would spit upon the road at the thought of it.

So it was not the thought of brigands on the road that furrowed the captain's brow. It was the late spring rain that made him anxious, rain that would be turning the roads to mud and swelling the rivers. If he was a day late in Lin'an he would be expected to pay for his failure. He would not be able to smile easily until the last carriage of the merchant's heavy caravan had rolled into the capital. Until then, he was determined to watch the skies and scowl.

He paid little attention to the young woman he was escorting, though he had glimpsed her more than once through the narrow windows of her father's house. She seemed to him little more than a child, small-framed and slight like all the fine ladies. Pah! When he retired from the service he would take a wife with hips, a woman who could heft a sack of rice on each shoulder and who would not need a party of soldiers to escort her down country roads.

And the captain's humour was not improved when he found himself summoned to Zaiton's prefecture to be informed that the merchant's convoy was not to be the only one on the road to Lin'an that month, and the merchant's daughter was not to be his only responsibility.

The boy found he did not much like their new companion. Yang the merchant was glib where Venn was silent, familiar where Venn was reserved. And he seemed at ease with Decius, whom the boy disliked and feared as much as ever. To avoid both men, the boy would persuade Venn to take him out into the bustling streets and show him the city's wonders: the spice markets and the gem markets, the butchers' alleys and the tea houses; and, down streets that smelled of smoke and urine, the great presses that made paper, a substance so light and strong that in Zaiton all parchment was redundant.

It was some three weeks after their arrival in Zaiton when the merchant called them into the main hall of his house.

'You are to leave this city in two days' time,' he told them. 'I am to escort you to Lin'an, the Imperial City, where the Emperor will give you audience.' He allowed himself a little smile of satisfaction. 'I hardly need to tell you it is a rare honour for foreigners such as yourselves. There is a caravan here in Zaiton ready to depart. It is carrying a young woman to the Imperial Court, and there is a military escort ready to accompany it. Unfortunately, a lady of the Emperor's household travels in strict quarantine. No one but the officer in charge of her escort is permitted to speak to the lady, or even to see her face. The impropriety of having two such parties on the road together has exercised the magistrates here. It has been decided that the lady's caravan will go ahead, as planned. We shall follow a day behind. The permit allows just you and your immediate attendants to travel. Your soldiers must remain here until they are called for. A small part of the lady's escort shall be detached to accompany us and to ensure that we adhere to our itinerary.'

'But this is excellent news!' Antioch replied, a look of great relief upon his face. 'Pau shall stay here with his men until we are able to summon them. The rest of us shall be heading north, nearer to the great deserts and the strange beasts that live there. And on the road there will be opportunities to enquire after the creatures that we seek. I have heard tales of serpents in these parts that have on their backs the feathers of birds. And now, with your permission, we must return to our ship and make our preparations.'

When they arrived at the port it was already dusk and Decius ordered his men to assist in the unloading and sorting of their baggage. While they worked he told Pau of the changes to the expedition's plans, orders which the young officer heard in silence and greeted with the familiar, brooding frown the boy had come to recognise. And while the work on the docks continued, Venn gave the boy a nudge and nodded towards a group of local people who had gathered on the quayside to watch.

'Listen. They are counting our soldiers,' he said. 'They think a merchant who travels with such an escort must be carrying unusual riches.'

'But the soldiers are just here to guard us, aren't they, Venn?'

And standing there in the heart of a city both great and greedy, with the evening air salty from the breath of the sea, the interpreter looked down at the boy, and his eyes were serious.

'It is a large number of men to guard one old man and his books, Benedict. Manfred of Sicily would seem to be peculiarly concerned for our safety.'

It wasn't until the moon rose on the first night of her journey that Ming Yueh truly understood the step she'd taken. She had first noticed it low in the sky when the afternoon was still golden: a pale disc in the east, the faint outline of a pebble glimpsed through water. But as the afternoon ebbed, the moon grew in persistence and shadows began to gather, stretching over unfamiliar fields. She had never before watched the moon rise over a landscape she didn't know, and the sight made her shiver, for it showed her the truth: that she had stepped out of her own world forever.

Instead of elation came an unexpected sadness. Ahead of her lay a world of untold wonders: the Emperor's city, the love of Song Rui, a brightly painted chaos for her to shape into a landscape of her own. But that night, as she watched the moon rise, she felt a gossamer mantle of regret settle on her shoulders, a fabric so light that she was scarcely aware of it. She had not parted properly from her father. It seemed clear to her then. There were, she was sure, words she should have spoken, words she had not been able to find. But twelve hours earlier they had not seemed so important to her. It is only with practice that we learn to say goodbye.

Venn watched the same moon rise over the water meadows outside Zaiton. Antioch's caravan, less grand and less luxurious than the one which went ahead of it, was assembled on the edge of the town, ready to depart. It consisted of two wagons, one for supplies and baggage, one for the scholar's comfort, where Antioch would be able to travel and rest in relative ease, cushioned against the worst rigours of the journey. Four soldiers from the forward column had already joined them, led by a grey-haired guide. Both guide and soldiers were already asleep, wrapped in blankets on the edge of the camp. This close to the city, it seemed, no watch was set.

The boy slept too, warm under one of the awnings that had been stretched like tents from the side of the wagons. Venn had left him there and had slipped away to a clump of trees by the edge of the meadow from where he could view the entire camp and the night sky above it. He often found it difficult to sleep at the start of a journey. As a younger man he'd thought it was excitement that affected him, but later, when he knew himself better, he had come to wonder if perhaps it was a low, soft whisper of regret that stopped him sleeping, like the sound of a crowd heard from a great distance. He had learned to sit quietly and let the silence of the moon soothe him until it passed.

The only other figure still moving in the camp was that of Decius, cloaked in shadow, going about his nightly round. Venn watched him as he tested the fastenings of the baggage wagon one by one. Ever since Genoa he had done the same, checking and double-checking the baggage and supplies, never sleeping until he was content with his inspection. And perhaps not even then. More than once, returning late from his wanderings, Venn had passed the place where the commander rested and had seen those black eyes watching him. *He sleeps a soldier's sleep*, Venn thought, *always wary, always watching*. Or perhaps it was something else that kept those eyes from closing. Venn wondered what ghosts rose up at night to keep the general from his dreams. Of one thing he was certain, there was no peace in the heart of the man whose eyes met his in those dead hours of the night.

His inspection complete, Decius returned to his sleeping place beneath one of the awnings and Venn was once again alone to watch the moon. He had seen it, in his time, from many angles and in many guises – blistered and red over the desert or green above an ice-strewn sea – purple, once, before a storm in Lombardy on the night when lightning struck three churches. Always, whatever its mood, it awoke in him the same emotion: a helpless, overwhelming sense of wordless-ness, as if in the face of such simple, naked beauty, every language he had ever learned was rendered useless. And while he sat and watched, the silence of the moon would seem to strip away the layers of words that weighed upon him, leaving him clean and empty.

But that night he was not to be alone. A movement in the camp caught the corner of his eye and tugged at his gaze. At first he couldn't see its source. All seemed still and unchanged. But gradually, as his eyes grew more focused, he realised that Decius had once again emerged from his tent and was standing motionless in the shadow beside it. Venn was perhaps a hundred yards away from him and his eyes struggled for detail. So still was the commander that the interpreter began to think perhaps he'd been deceived, that there was no one in the shadow. And then, very slowly, Decius raised his arm as if in signal. Sweeping his eye across the open meadow, Venn saw two figures approaching. They came from his right and passed close to him. One was tall and Venn was able to see his pale skin and features: Yang, the half-blood Pisan. The other was much shorter, a local man most likely, but dressed in ragged clothes and balancing a small pack upon his back. The two moved steadily towards Decius until the three figures were wrapped in the same shadow and then they were gone, hidden beneath Decius's awning.

Intrigued, Venn thought of moving closer, to see if he might hear what was being said. But stealth did not come naturally to him and, besides, the silence of the meadow was as delicate as frost: the softest footfall must be heard. Instead he drew further into the shadow and measured the wait with his own breaths. Some ten minutes later the merchant and the shorter man emerged. Yang returned the way he had come, passing close to Venn. The other struck out across the meadow in the opposite direction, his pack upon his shoulder, his quick strides taking him northwards, in the direction which the next day the caravan would follow.

The Journey Begins

Of all his journeys by sea and by land, the slow ride to
Lin'an was one of the boy's happiest. It was a great joy
to be on horseback again after so many months at sea,
and the chestnut mare he was given delighted him. She
was a fine animal, light-footed and responsive, and
clearly the mount of an adult, superior in every way to
the slow and patient cobs of his youth. And for the
first time since leaving Genoa they were travelling
through a lush, green land. It was true that the nights
were cold and the mornings swathed with mist, but the
days were growing warmer and there was an intoxicating scent of spring in the air. In such a place and on
such a mount, surely the ambitions he had whispered
to Venn were in his grasp? Yes, in this new land he
would prove his courage and make his father
proud . . .

They quickly left the flat plains outside Zaiton and
from there the way twisted through a gently rolling
landscape of forests and hills, where pigs foraged and
villages were announced by the outraged gabble of
hens. On the higher passes the air was fresh with pine

and wild sage. Descending again, they found meadows deep in flowers, and orchards only just relinquishing their blossom.

Best of all, once they had left behind the last vestiges of the city, the boy found he was given the freedom to roam the length of the column at will, spurring hastily to Antioch's side when the scholar summoned him, dropping behind to ride with Venn when the old man rested. For most of the time he rode with the interpreter at the end of the column, separated from Decius and Yang the merchant by the whole length of the caravan. Those two rode up with the Captain of the Guard and it was Yang who translated for Antioch and the count whenever necessary. That left Venn and the boy at leisure and the small band of accompanying soldiers seemed content to let them fall behind the column, confident that in such empty places they could cause no trouble. So they took their time, stopping to study the roadside shrines, sometimes swimming in the streams that ran down from the mountains. Afterwards, to warm themselves, they'd gallop hard and rejoin the column at a break-neck pace.

For many of their hours on the road, they travelled in companionable silence, for the boy had understood the contradiction in Venn's nature. For all his skill with words in different languages, he seldom initiated a conversation unless some event arose to provoke it.

But when he did find his companion inclined to talk, the boy would ask him about the land they travelled in, and Venn would tell him what he'd gleaned from his previous travels and from his wanderings in Zaiton. He told him that the people of that land valued courtesy and cleanliness above arms and fighting. He said that it was the custom to seek advancement through learning rather than physical strength, and that the Emperor valued his secretaries and his learned courtiers more than the opinions of his fighting men. He explained how printed paper could be used as money, how wine was made from rice, not grapes; how it seemed that the Emperor was both feared and scorned by the common people of the country, for his cruelty and for his countless pampered concubines.

Of himself, Venn said little. Once the boy ventured to ask about the woman in Genoa but the interpreter only shrugged and fell silent. Then the boy was embarrassed, and did not ask again.

But that was a rare grave moment on a journey of great happiness. Indeed it seemed to the boy that the spring freshness lifted every member of the party, for Antioch's brow appeared less furrowed than for many months. Whenever the caravan halted he returned to his books, a vision of unicorns dancing in front of him. Truly, he concluded, this was the most majestic and magical of beasts. It was said its fierceness might only be tamed by an innocent maid. It was said the hairs of its mane were a cure for fever or sleeplessness, or might bring a loved one home. The ancient lore was so full of stories that only a fraction could be true. The thought of examining such a beast himself made him thrill with pleasure.

Only Decius seemed as grim and unforgiving as before. Once, when the boy rode too close to the baggage wagon, Venn called him back.

'Take care,' he warned. 'You'd better keep your distance.'

'From the supply wagon? Why?' The boy was puzzled. 'The supplies are for us all, are they not?'

Venn nodded. 'That's true. But even so, stay clear of them. The general takes an interest in them, and he is a dangerous man to mix with.'

The boy turned to look again at the supply wagon. 'But why should he care so much? Yang says we have ample for our journey.'

The interpreter shrugged. 'Who knows? He carries his secrets deep. But he keeps a close watch on our supplies. There are two boxes of his, plain ones that look unimportant. Yet ever since he joined us they have never been touched except in his presence. Decius travels light, like a soldier, and whatever he keeps in those two small cases he hasn't needed yet. They haven't been opened since we quit Genoa, for the ropes around them were sealed then and the seals are still intact. And now that his soldiers are not around him, his care of them is greater still.'

The boy looked up at him, studying his face. 'What does it mean, Venn? What are they for?'

'I don't know. Maybe nothing. Just keep clear, that's all.'

That day they were travelling through upland meadows, the air tranquil with the murmur of insects. Very slowly the party was climbing into the mountains that had for many days stood ahead of them.

'There's another thing, Benedict,' Venn went on. 'Have you ever wondered why the great and feared Count Decius has come so far and put himself to so much trouble just to escort an old scholar on his travels?'

'Because Manfred ordered it,' the boy replied simply. 'Surely he had no choice but to obey?' But the question lingered in his mind, and he began to wonder whether perhaps, after all, it wasn't a little surprising that Manfred could spare from his court such a fearsome and famous warrior.

After that, the two rode in silence for a little, each of them thoughtful. But Venn's warning did not go unheeded, for in the days that followed he often saw the boy watching Decius, watching too the progress of the small wooden boxes.

For Ming Yueh, after so many months of waiting, the slow journey to Lin'an came as a surprise. For so many months she had been desperate to escape Zaiton. The great city of Lin'an seemed to her to be a hope of freedom – a city older and more beautiful than hers, where the air was pure from the mountains, a city with the most beautiful lake in the world lying like a mirror at its feet. It was a city ancient in legend, where there would be no place for the petty concerns of the Zaiton merchants, where people would understand that life was about higher things – about joy and passion and daring. A city of poets and artists, of gardens and great buildings. A city of lovers.

The thought of being again in Song Rui's arms stirred her with longing. Often the days of waiting at her father's house had grown so intolerable she'd wanted to beat her fists against the matting floors and to cry out in frustration. But women in Zaiton did not display such feelings. They had learned that emotions were to be treated like fabrics at the dyers' – to be compressed with weight upon weight until the weave became pliant and took the dye. After that the natural colour was lost forever and would never show again.

Silence and endurance were the feminine virtues of Zaiton, and the women there had perfected them as arts. Only in the messages they wrote to each other could they venture to find release.

But Ming Yueh had not grown up in the company of women. She had been taught the script by her nurses and by the old widows with cracked, leathery faces engaged by her father to teach her womanly virtues. They had been kind, and she had loved to learn the script they taught her, but only with Song Rui had she ever felt the freedom to confide. And when he left Zaiton it had been harder than he would ever know for her to sit and wait for his call. He had released a torrent of longing. It was beyond her power to stop its flow.

So desperate was she to reach Lin'an that she'd expected the slow progress of the wagons to throw her into a fever of impatience. But instead, to her own surprise, the gentle rhythms of the days contrived to dissipate her fretfulness, and the daily pageant of new sights soothed her. Shu-chen, the elderly maid who travelled with her, wondered at the transformation and decided there must be something in the pine-scented air that made all of them turn a little peculiar. Surely a young girl should be bored to tears, with nothing to do and no gossip, and every day the same? And yet Shu-chen too found herself oddly content to sway with the wagons and count the pigs in the fields and watch her young charge grow happier as the days passed.

And it was certainly true that Ming Yueh's days had no great variety. She would wake to birdsong and to the sunlight already bright on the silk that enclosed her carriage. Outside, Shu-chen would be already on the move and the camp was beginning to stir. She would lie listening, studying the shadows of leaves on the awning above her until suddenly the activity outside would grow more urgent and the camp would ring with the laughter of the guards as the cooks scolded them. Then orders were shouted, followed by the chimes of bridles, and she knew she must be dressed in minutes because the Captain of the Guard was most punctual with his visits.

He came every morning, to pay his respects and to give the day's itinerary. Relieved of his anxieties about the weather and the state of the roads, he found himself able to warm a little to the unformed scrap of a girl he was ordered to wait upon. After all, she gave him no trouble and put on no airs. In the evenings, at camp, when he'd feared she would get bored and troublesome, she seemed content to spend long hours with paper and brush – writing, always writing, he observed with a smile and a shake of his head, marvelling at her patience.

And it was true, she did write. Her sworn mission was going well. Her memory was clear and un-crowded. Shu-chen would deliver the messages she wrote to the agreed places along the roadside, and everywhere they found new ones, chalked on walls or marked where they could easily be seen, addressed to other women further up the road. These too she memorised and delivered, and so her journey went on.

She had not forgotten Song Rui, but the way she thought of him began to change in the course of the journey. It was as if the new things she was seeing gave rise in her to an extra layer of understanding, a burgeoning maturity which turned her feelings for Song Rui from a leaping flame to a warmer, broader heat, one that filled her so completely she felt she could look forward to the future without fear. Even her excitement had grown into something almost serene.

She gave little thought to the barbarian travellers a day behind her on the road. The Captain of the Guard assured her they were giving no sign of trouble.

On the eighth day of their journey, Antioch's party came to an ancient town that the local people called Sha-fen. The centre of the town stood on a steep hill and was circled by the remains of ancient walls. Yang declared that these had been built long ago by a robber-king, a young man who through his daring had seized a kingdom many miles wide. As the caravan swayed closer, Yang told them the tale. It was said this bandit came to hear of a beautiful girl who worked in chains in the house of the fire gods, who were known for their great cruelty. Moved by her plight and inspired by the tales of her beauty, he had gone disguised to the house where she was held and had stolen her away, bringing her back to his palace as his bride.

When the gods discovered this they were outraged, and fell upon the town with a great army. But finding they could not storm his stronghold, they decided instead to send a messenger to the young lady in the guise of a nightingale. The messenger found her in the garden at dusk and sang to her a song so beautiful that the robber's bride could not help but listen. Little by little she followed the bird as it weaved its spell around her, past the inner and outer walls, singing all the time, until she was seized by her tormentors and carried away to a far-distant land where she was returned to her former servitude.

On discovering his beloved's disappearance, the young king took off his robes and allowed his city walls to fall into ruins while he wandered the world, following the songs of nightingales wherever he heard them, in the hope that one day they might lead him to his bride.

The boy heard this story with wonder and was greatly affected by it, even though Antioch shook his head and tutted aloud at the superstition of the foreigners. And for all his master's grumbling, the boy's excitement increased again when the caravan was led through the crumbling walls to an ancient caravanserai at the heart of the old town, surrounded by a thronging market that reminded him more of Damascus than any place he'd seen since leaving the shores of Arabia.

That same night a message reached them from an old man of the town, a physician and philosopher who wished to see for himself the unusual travellers he'd been told about. Being prevented by infirmity from leaving his own home, and having heard the party was to move on again at daybreak, he begged Antioch to visit him that very night, an invitation the old scholar was happy to accept.

He was accompanied on this visit by Venn and the boy, Yang the merchant having business in the town. They set out when the light was already fading. Away from the lanterns of the market stalls, the night was darker still, and they found the physician's quarters down a narrow alley in the heart of the town where only the faint glow from the windows lit the rutted path at their feet. It was a tiny, narrow house, dark inside as well as out, lit only by dim rush lamps that cast a jittery, yellow glow. The physician seemed almost as ancient as the town itself, wizened and shrunken to the size of a child, his few strands of grey hair pulled tight behind his head. He sat in a low room amid a confusion of unlikely objects, all made stranger by the movement of the shadows: the skull of a crow, the paw of a great striped cat; an orange stone the size of a hand containing in its translucent depths what seemed to the boy to be the tooth of a dragon. In the gloom of the surroundings it was hard to be certain.

Their host welcomed them with a joyful cackle of laughter, for he was a very old man who had outlived his sons and had few visitors. He was waited upon by a small child, a girl of five or six years of age but who brought them steaming drinks on a tray almost as big as herself. These drinks were the first of many, for their visit lasted long into the night. The physician was delighted with his guests and studied them in wonderment, asking question after question, wanting to know precisely who they were and where they came from. Venn's mastery of his language made him clap his hands in glee, his smile revealing his pink, toothless gums. His pleasure increased further when he learned the reason for their journey, for he maintained that he too had a great interest in the mysteries of the world and had made – in his own small way – a study of them. Did they know, he asked, that in certain provinces the great bones of ancient dragons could be found still littering the hillsides? It was said that, if pounded into dust and mixed with the blood of a tiger, they would make a man invulnerable in battle.

Inspired by this, Antioch described for him the unicorn, the great monoceros that was fabled in his own land but so rarely seen. Had the old man heard tell of such a creature?

'Yes, yes,' he replied gleefully. 'These beasts are not wholly vanquished, although they shun the habitations of men. They too are greatly valued. Their horn is prized much higher than gold. Some say it has the power to make men young again.' He laughed. 'But what gift is that? To choose the blindness of youth over the wisdom of age! To forget all the knowledge we've so painfully acquired! Ha! I would not be young again! No, no!'

As the evening wore on, as the heat from the lamps and the lateness of the hour began to work on him, the boy found it harder and harder to follow everything that passed. He grew drowsy and a little confused, trying desperately to stay awake by fixing his eyes on the physician's face as it rocked in and out of the lamplight, the shape of his skull picked out by the shadows. It seemed an age before he realised Venn and Antioch were on their feet and ready to depart. And the final act that passed in that narrow house seemed to him dreamlike too, a scene he might have easily imagined as he dozed there in those early hours. As Antioch said his goodbyes, the old physician rose and hobbled into the shadow, returning with something cupped on the palm of his hand. In the better light the boy could see it was a tiny bag of shimmering green silk, tied at the neck with a thin golden ribbon.

'Take this,' he urged. 'It is a gift to you. I have no use for it, although I prized it dearly once and thought to gain great knowledge through possessing it. No, do not open it,' he went on, as Antioch made to look inside. 'The powder is too fine. It will disappear like mist into the air.' He looked at all of them then, and the next words were said with a flourish. 'It is the horn of the beast we spoke of. The unicorn, you call it. Less than the weight of a wren's egg but more than you could ever need. Take care with it, for I did not tell you its true power, as told by my forefathers and passed down to me.'

He looked around, then wagged his finger happily.

'The power of unicorn horn is to banish memory. *All* memory, mind. They say five grains of this, dissolved in liquid, will smooth the mind and leave it unblemished, like new-spun silk. Ha! A fearful, terrible gift! What man would ask for that? To cast away the very thing that makes us who we are! I have never dared to try it, nor offer it to any man. And that is not why I give it to you now. I give it to you because of its great value. It is light, easily concealed, yet at market it would earn you many pounds of gold. You have travelled far, and to return will not be easy. Take this to any physician in any town, and he will know it for what it is. In exchange he will give you all the help you need. Yes, and send you on your way in comfort!'

The last image the boy had of the physician was of a stooped figure framed in a doorway, a hand raised to wave them on their way.

When they left, the dew was falling and the town slept. No stars, but the tiny servant girl went before them, leading the way with a glowing lantern that threw long shadows down the turning streets. As they neared the place where their wagons lay, she led them into a dark street funnelled between blind walls, and it was there Venn noticed the writing. He called out sharply and gestured for them to stop. At first the boy could make out nothing unusual, but Venn beckoned the child to lift the lantern higher and then the boy saw what had made the interpreter stop so abruptly: ten lines of slim, wispy characters running down the walls in columns, a message freshly chalked on the black stone.

'What is it, Venn?' asked Antioch, his voice a little hushed as if he had sensed the interpreter's great interest. 'Is it writing? What does it say?'

Venn seemed not to hear. The boy watched his eyes moving down the columns, his face puzzled.

'I don't know,' he said at last. 'Only once have I seen something like it, and then only a fragment . . .' He turned to the small girl who had guided them and said something to her in her own language. The boy watched her eyes widen as if frightened by this sudden attention but in reply she simply shook her head, then gestured for them to continue. Venn however stood his ground, studying the message again, his eyes narrowed.

'It's no matter,' he said at last, stepping away to break the spell. 'I'll come back tomorrow at daybreak and make a copy then. For now let's be on our way. I know the captain wants to strike camp early.'

But when Venn returned at first light, the streets empty but for the trailing wood smoke of early fires, he found his journey wasted. At first he thought he must have mistaken the street. Then he searched further, thinking that perhaps he had not gone far enough. But the truth was simpler. The message that had caught Venn's eye was gone. Not a trace remained. The wall had been wiped clean.

It might have meant nothing. They might have forgotten all about it. But two days later, making camp on the outskirts of a small, straggling village, the boy tugged Venn's sleeve and pointed. There, on the panels of a ramshackle hut, were similar characters, chalked in a similar way. The long grasses almost covered them – it was only by pure chance they'd caught his eye. But from that day onwards, because they knew to look, they found such messages by the roadside nearly every day. They would find them on the sides of houses or scrawled on the walls of pigsties or marked on the hurdles used to pen stock. They learned to seek them only in places that were subtle and discreet, where a stray glance was unlikely to find them. The boy came to recognise the narrow characters. They put him in mind of the straggling legs of mosquitoes – and yet still somehow had a grace and elegance of their own.

Some days they found none at all. Sometimes the messages were very short. But always, wherever they found them, they would quickly disappear, removed by an invisible hand. Venn learned to carry paper with him and was diligent in his copying. Once he showed the writing to one of the soldiers who accompanied them but the man merely shrugged.

'Not ours,' he grunted, using the form of words which in those parts was applied to anything unfamiliar or unrecognised. It expressed a calm, dismissive unconcern for anything that was not a part of the speaker's daily life. After that Venn did not ask the guards again.

The mystery of these disappearing messages added a new element of interest to the boy's journey. But ten days after leaving Sha-fen, another incident occurred, one that wiped them from his mind. Before it, his mistrust of Decius had been instinctive and ill-defined. After it, he had every reason to believe that he and the others were in great danger while travelling with the cold-eyed general.

ζ

I did not come to Málaga by chance. The ports along this coast were once the wonders of the world, with ships arriving here from Egypt, Syria, Byzantium and beyond, and goods of every sort piled high. Now things have changed. Córdoba and Seville have fallen to the Christian kings and they have closed their ports to unbelievers or made their laws so harsh that Saracens and Jews can ill afford to trade there. But Málaga remains a trading city, still strong in Moorish hands. They taught me as a boy to hate the infidel. Now, with age, I see that there are honest men of every faith and villains of all races. And to this port they all still come, where Christians trade with Moors, Jews with Greeks, from the far ends of the Mediterranean Sea or further. And so come I, for here are men who have with their own eyes seen the Coromandel Coast and the Peak of Adam, or the strange tides that ripple round Hormuz.

But others also come. Spies from the Christian courts, Berber preachers, outlaws fleeing papal law, beggars, scholars, craftsmen, thieves. A man soon learns to watch his tongue with strangers. And yet the man who followed me today seemed none of these. It was the hour before noon and from first light I'd been abroad, waiting for a barque due in from Libya. Wearied by the heat, I'd turned for home: this man followed. I marked him as he did so, for I haven't lived this long and not learned to feel a stranger's eyes upon me. But he made no move to close on me and so I let him follow. He reached my door a minute after I did, knocked once, then waited.

He was a big man, broad and powerful. A man of fifty, quietly dressed, his cloak dark, without insignia. Confident. A man to be obeyed. His face was weathered, with a small scar across his chin. He smiled as he entered and offered me his hand, his brown eyes seeking mine.

'They tell me that you're English,' he said, his words in formal, courtly Latin. His voice was deep, his accent hard to place. A Florentine, perhaps, but I wasn't certain.

'From the city of Lincoln,' I told him, and brought him further inside, out of the glare. When I offered him a seat, he took the larger chair.

'I have heard of it,' he replied. 'The Lord Aldred says it is a fine city. You know him? He was once my guest in Rome.'

I shook my head. 'I am a merchant. I trade in wool, from the ports of England to Flanders. I am not an acquaintance of great men such as he.'

He pursed his lips to blow away the difference, as if to say that lords and merchants were all as one to him.

'Well, it is not of trade or English lords I come to speak. My name is Quintus Fabius, once of Siena, now a humble servant of the Church. I am here by order of the Holy Father.'

'A papal spy.' It was an observation, not a criticism.

He shrugged. 'You can call me what you like. It is my business to know what happens here, and in all the flea-bitten ports along this coast. They are places people come to meet who are nervous of meeting under the eye of the Church.'

I nodded, but did not altogether believe him. His name was one I had heard before, but not as a simple Church informer. I had heard it spoken with respect. This was a man of influence, a powerful man.

'And what can I do to advance the interests of the Church?' I asked him, my curiosity quite genuine.

He settled himself more comfortably into his seat. 'They say you're here to seek your son, a page who sailed with Antioch. Well, I am here to offer any help I can. The loss of a Christian force in Saracen lands is not to be ignored. Although it is some years now since Antioch's party disappeared.'

'All expeditions disappear,' I told him. 'They vanish over the sea or beyond the horizon. That is their nature. Those who remain can only wait, and pray for their return.'

He accepted that with a flicker of his eyebrow. 'Very well. But in this case it is a long time to wait.'

'You think so? Perhaps a father sees things differently.'

'You really hope to hear of him? After all this time?' His eyes searched my face. 'But perhaps you have received some news of him that brings you here?'

'No,' I told him evenly. 'I have heard nothing. All these years, I have heard nothing. So now, before I die, I am doing what I should have done before. I am trying to find out what I can.'

Fabius studied me carefully for a moment longer, then stirred and nodded.

'Yes, I can see that. Tell me, how came your boy to be in Antioch's service?'

Outside, the afternoon was lying white and unforgiving on the town. I could almost feel it press against the shutters. But inside, in the semi-darkness, the room was cool and time was slow. Why not, for once, speak freely of my son? Was that not why I'd come? I rose and poured wine for my guest, then allowed myself to remember the bishop's hall in Lincoln, the small boy beside me, the priest ahead of us. I can still feel the leaden pain I carried with me that day.

I tried to explain to this unannounced visitor that in my country it is the elder son who inherits his father's interests and the younger son who must find a way of his own through the world. I tried to explain how blessed I felt when the bishop took an interest in my boy. He was so bright, with such quick wit; it was easy to see that he would make a scholar. When Bishop Richard offered to place him with a famous man of books who was visiting Flanders, the honour was too great to be refused. I had never heard of Antioch of Sicily, but all who knew him said he was both kind and learned. And such preferment opened paths for my boy that no younger son of a merchant would dare to dream of. What was my pain in losing him compared to this? What was my sorrow against his future?

Opposite me, the Pope's officer listened in silence. Behind him, one window remained unshuttered. It faced the north and through it I could see the mountains. Their blue intensity made the green summers of the Lincoln meadows seem distant and suddenly strangely improbable.

'I have no one to blame but myself,' I told him.

Fabius stirred in his chair then. 'Come, sir. None of us can read the future. You knew nothing then of Manfred's mission, I presume?'

I shook my head. 'I knew nothing of Manfred. Antioch wrote to me the following summer to tell me he was to undertake a journey. My son was in his care. What else could I do but let him go?'

'And what of Count Decius? What did you know of him?'

I looked at him carefully then. His eagerness had betrayed him.

'That is the question the Catalan asked,' I told him. 'Is it really *Decius* you seek? It would seem you want my help, but are not prepared to pay for it with the truth.'

My visitor looked up sharply. 'Someone else has been asking questions? Who was this man?'

'He told me his name was Raymond. He said he was an agent for the Count of Mirande.'

'A thin man, a little taller than yourself?'

I described him as best I could and Fabius seemed to relax. 'The man you speak of is Raymond of Nava. I have seen him in the town. He is fallen on hard times and finds what patronage he can. But in his visit to you, I'm sure he was representing no one but himself.'

'And what did he hope to gain from me?'

'He asked you about you son?'

I nodded.

'And what did you tell him?'

'That I received no word from him or anyone with him since they sailed from Italy.'

Fabius digested this, his head back.

'Raymond of Nava is after money,' he said. 'That is the only reason he came to see you. You see, one member of your son's expedition was a wanted man. All these years on, he is still considered dangerous. Any information that leads to his discovery would be well rewarded.'

'You mean . . . ?'

He took a breath that made his great chest swell.

'Come, the day grows hot and it is cool here. My affairs will wait a little longer, and it is only fair that you should know the truth. You have, after all, suffered for it. To explain why popes still fear him, I had better tell you a little more about Count Decius . . .'

In the hours after noon, the town falls very still. Work halts, and the air grows slow and heavy with the heat. The streets empty and you notice much more the buzzing of the flies. Ships that put in now tie up and wait, for the stevedores will not unload until the glare softens and the raw heat relents.

I listened quietly while the Pope's representative told me about Count Decius. There was authority in his voice, and after so many months of waiting here alone there was comfort in his presence. He was a man who knew much more than I, through whom perhaps I might yet find my answer.

'Count Decius,' he began, 'was born into a family of soldiers. He was never rich. They say the title dates from the Great Crusade where his forebears served with distinction. His family lands were in Lombardy, but he left them when still young to begin his own military career.

'From there he grew into one of the most feared commanders in Europe: unsmiling, callous, cold, fanatical; he tolerated nothing less than total obedience in those around him. And then of course he had those strange eyes. We see a man's humanity in his eyes. Decius had none. But he proved a brilliant soldier. By the age of twenty-five he led his own battalion and his fearsome reputation was established. In his skirmishes he showed no ounce of mercy, no moment of doubt. His reputation was written in blood. His troops grew famed for their efficiency in hunting down their enemies. None were spared. For Decius, orders came first.'

Fabius paused and drank a little wine, and while he drank my eyes wandered to the open casement, back to the distant outline of the mountains. I thought of my son somewhere in the great wilderness beyond my charts. Those fleeing soldiers hunted down by Decius . . . Was that his fate? To be slaughtered by some cold-hearted lord who cut him down without a thought? Was that his life? Or was he now a soldier too, learning cruelty in the service of that callous leader?

My visitor cleared his throat and drew me back to the shadows of my sparsely furnished room.

'For many years Decius was a soldier of the Pope. He served in Italy and in the Cathar wars. But he changed sides and that is when he grew dangerous. He disappeared for a little, then re-emerged in Sicily with the usurper Manfred.

'That was at the time of the Emperor Frederick's death. Manfred was at war with the Pope. We don't know how he drew Decius into his service, but the count became his closest ally. In all Manfred's battles he was vital. The campaign Decius fought on the mainland was hailed as brilliant, even by the generals he fought against. Unaided, with a tiny band of men, he secured Manfred's power there against all odds. Time after time his small force surprised enemies and outwitted those sent against him. He showed more brilliance and cunning than any other soldier of our time. Perhaps the papacy feared him more than it feared Manfred himself.'

A heat haze was beginning to rise from the roofs of the town, blurring the outline of the mountains beyond. I remember thinking how blue the sky was: a blue more deep and brilliant than even the swirling mosaics in the city mosque.

'Yes,' Fabius went on, engaging me with his eyes, 'the empire is broken now, yet its cause still has supporters. But there is only one man left who could unite them. So that is why we wish to find Count Decius – to make sure he cannot again plunge Europe into war. That is why the reward on his head remains a prize that would change a man's life.'

'But Decius would be an old man by now,' I reasoned. 'Why would you care where fate has taken him? What possible danger could he pose?'

Quintus Fabius smiled in reply.

'In war there are two things one learns to fear. One is genius, because faced with genius you are never truly safe. The other is hatred. Because when someone really hates, they never go away. Decius is made of both in equal parts. Let us just say that we would rest easier if we knew what had become of him.'

'And you really don't know?'

'No more than you. Possibly less. In the years since he left Genoa, we've sent many agents to follow his tracks, but none has been successful. After Basrah, who knows? It is as if the sea engulfed them. And yet the rumours persist – of a mysterious Frank seen on the road in Khiva, a man wearing a cross in the wilds beyond Tashkent. So let us imagine that after all these years he and the followers who went with him are not dead. And let us imagine that someone brought word to you of where they could be found. Then your way would be clear to do God's bidding. Show us the way to Decius and we will bring your son home to you, with the blessing of the Pope upon his forehead.'

ζ

A Messenger

There was no moon. The forest that surrounded them was black and boundless. Somewhere a road twisted away to the plain below, but the night had engulfed it, rubbed it from the map. The camp where the boy lay was no more than a dark smudge against the trees. Beyond it a small lake cut into the forest, sickly still, deeper and darker than the night itself.

Afterwards the boy realised it was no coincidence, that vanished moon. The darkness was calculated, a black cloak pulled over the pale smear of a conspiracy. On moonless nights, he realised, the soldiers always slept well. Decius saw to it that an extra ration of rice wine was called for, a riotous act of gaiety that became him strangely. And when the camp slept, he alone sat watching, dark eyes soaking up the night.

That night the boy should have slept too. He had been allowed his share of wine, had grown first warm, then weary. But he did not sleep or, if he did, only in unsettled snatches. Then, when the darkness was at its deepest, he found himself awake, alert and listening. All was still, but something had startled him. He guessed from the cold air on his cheeks that the night must be well advanced. Nothing seemed to stir, but he lay and listened, his body taut.

When the sound came it was close to him: the faintest click – a man's fingertip tapping on an awning. Then nothing. Another tap and nothing. Only on the third did the boy hear an answering signal, followed by the soft shuffle of an awning being lifted.

One of the guards? A late sentry reporting? The boy knew it was neither. There was something furtive in the signal, something hushed and deliberate. And the sounds had not come from the place where the guards slept. They came from Decius's tent.

He didn't ask himself why, or consider the danger to himself. Instinctively, without any conscious thought at all, he slipped from beneath his blanket, under the flap of his canvas and slithered, still on his stomach, the eight or nine paces that separated him from where the general slept. He hadn't been mistaken, he knew at once. The voices were low, sometimes indistinct, but he could hear enough. A council was in progress.

There were three voices, three men conferring. He recognised Decius and Yang the merchant. The third man's voice was strangely hoarse and spoke a language the boy didn't know. The merchant was translating.

'I have earned my payment,' he heard the stranger say. 'My lord has received your message.'

Decius's voice was cold. 'And you're sure you travelled undetected?'

'Of course. It is as I told you. I travel unseen on either side of the border.'

'And you found the Tartar lord we spoke of?'

'Have I not told you? I am his man. Wherever he is, I find him. The Lord Tendiz is encamped outside the border post of Shanjan.'

'And he listened to my proposal?' The boy thought he detected a note of anxiety in Decius's voice.

There followed a rustling sound, as if the stranger was settling himself more comfortably.

'He heard your proposal, General. But he heard it with disbelief. "Who are these people to ask such a thing?" he said. "Are they kings? Are they great lords? Do they think the Lord of a Thousand Tribes will negotiate with pedlars and ruffians?"'

The boy could sense the mockery in his voice, even though the words meant nothing until Yang translated. His speech was followed by silence. When Decius spoke again it was slowly, deliberately, with the voice of a man restraining his anger.

'I always deliver what I promise,' he growled. 'I can show your lord and his master the way to wealth beyond their dreams. And in case they do not believe what I have told them, I shall send them a token – proof of the prize they are offered.'

'A token?' The man's voice quickened with interest.

'Something that will dazzle your lord. Even the Great Khan himself will never have seen the like.'

The man's reply was hesitant as if Decius's forcefulness had half persuaded him. 'But you travel in carts,' he reasoned. 'You are herded along the road like geese driven by peasants. Why should my master listen to a single word from such as you?'

Decius laughed, a dry hacking sound, cruel in its disdain.

'Come, Yang, hold up the lantern.' A light flared inside the tent and the boy flinched as the shadows shifted. 'You will go back to the Lord Tendiz and tell him of this.'

Decius's hand was raised close to the light and the boy could see it clearly in silhouette. Between his third and forefinger he held something the size and shape of a plover's egg. He said nothing else but the boy could sense that the atmosphere had changed. The tension had grown tauter, more brittle. The boy waited for it to break.

In silence, the man's arm reached out and took the object, then he bent his head to study it.

'It is . . . exquisite.'

'It is more than that. It is the finest ruby you or any of your countrymen has ever seen. And it has a companion. Look.'

Something else passed between the two men. 'You see? The two are equal in every respect.'

Decius waited while his visitor studied both stones.

'Now listen carefully,' he went on, his hand retrieving one, leaving the other in the man's possession. 'You will present that stone to your lord as a gift from the barbarians who travel in carts, and you will invite him to reconsider my offer. Oh, and you will tell him about this . . .'

The suddenness of Decius's next movement took the boy by surprise and he shrank back as the flap of the tent was flung open. Decius emerged and stood for a moment, studying the darkness. Had he turned even slightly he might have seen the boy, but his face was directed towards the waters of the lake. He waited only a moment, while his two companions stumbled out behind him. Then he raised his arm and, before anyone could move, sent the object high and irretrievably into the lake's dark centre.

'There,' he said. 'Tell your lord how commonplace such objects are to me. And bid him come to us himself. We shall speak no more to servants.'

The Waking Lamps

She would have studied him anyway, of course. There could be no doubt about that. He was a barbarian and a novelty, shocking in the brute size of his frame and the coarseness of his features. She would have observed him as she observed the others, pleased by the sight of such strangeness, enjoying the perplexing mixture of horror and excitement that proximity to such a creature engendered.

But the first time she truly noticed him, it was for none of these reasons. It was because of one simple gesture which took her by surprise and made her think of home.

The two caravans that were scheduled never to meet came together on the evening of the twentieth day of her journey. The cause of the meeting was a fallen tree across a ford, an obstacle that left the wagons helpless on one bank while peasants from the nearest village were fetched and set to work with ropes and axes. Forced to pause in a broad and open clearing by the river, the Captain of the Guard reconciled himself to complications. By late afternoon it was obvious the tree would not be moved that day. A few minutes later the caravan containing the foreign travellers had rumbled into sight.

The captain sent word telling them to stop where they stood. It was the best arrangement he could hope to achieve but, even so, the two encampments faced each other no more than a hundred paces apart.

That was when Ming Yueh caught sight of the barbarians for the first time. She was peeping out at the world through the gaps in her wagon's awnings when three of them, finding their progress blocked, urged their horses forward. They paused only thirty paces or so from where she was watching and from that distance she could see their faces clearly. One was young and very slight, with hair so pale it seemed to her ghostly and unsettling. The second was more disturbing still: features cruel as a hawk's, and eyes that said nothing. A little behind them rode a third, a man of middle years – brown skinned, hair cropped, his face creased about the eyes. This rider lingered longer than the others, his gaze working steadily across the scene in front of him, his brow furrowed as if he were searching for something. Then, as he moved to turn his horse, he reached up and ran the tip of one finger along the line of his eyebrow. It was a meaningless movement, instinctive, without purpose, but it produced in her a reaction so profound that for a second she was quite bewildered.

It was a gesture she had known from her childhood. It took her back to a place so vivid that she could still recall the flickering shadows and the heavy scent from the burning lamp. For so many years the ritual had been the same. From her early childhood, whenever she woke in the night and saw a light still burning in her father's study, she would rise and go to him. She knew if she did not he might easily work till dawn. She would find him always amongst his ledgers, and when she entered he would look up at her so blankly, his head so full of worries that he seemed to have no idea who she was. And then he too would reach up and run his finger down the line of his eyebrow – the same finger, always the third on his left hand – and he would smile and she would know from that gesture that he had drawn a line beneath whatever matter occupied him. His deep thinking was concluded.

For that same gesture to be repeated by another, and in just such a way, surprised in her a flood of feeling for her father that she scarcely knew was there. His image was suddenly in front of her – that awkward, wordless man she hardly knew – and she thought again of those countless nights when she would tiptoe into his presence and watch him wipe away his preoccupations with that unthinking stroke of his finger. For the first time since leaving, she wondered how his house would feel without her; imagined her father alone, with no one to interrupt his work. And in that instant she could almost have given back her dreams and wished herself at home again.

But the moment passed, leaving her confused and embarrassed. It was shameful to be so affected by such a creature as the one in front of her – a barbarian scratching himself, nothing more. But the concentration in that foreign, angular face was not unlike her father's concentration, and it occurred to her for the first time that those strange travellers must have worries of their own, their own fears and hopes. Perhaps they were not, after all, the thoughtless brutes they were considered. It was a surprising thought and she looked on the retreating figure with interest. Not until he disappeared amongst his own wagons did she continue the consideration of her own affairs which had been interrupted by the arrival of the foreigners.

At that stage in the journey, her emotions were mixed. Over half the messages brought by her from Zaiton had been delivered safely, and so too had many new messages received along the way. These were from women exiled to the villages of Zaiton's hinterland, women who watched for any caravan containing a female traveller who might carry their words onwards. She would find their messages already waiting for her, chalked in places by the roadside, and she would memorise them as she passed, growing swift and adept with practice. She was proving a good messenger, she knew, and the thought made her proud.

However, behind her pleasure lay a shadow of uncertainty. Although she was many days into her journey, she had received no word from Song Rui. Of course, she knew she shouldn't really expect it: sending messages to her when their meeting was now so close would have been both indiscreet and unnecessary. Yet she hoped for one nevertheless, some small token that he thought of her. Her faith in him was strong, but such faith can be a burden to carry, especially when the shadows gather at the end of a wearying day.

It was in the shadows that Venn first saw her. Not her face, for no man but the Captain of the Guard was allowed to see that. Not even her figure or form, for she was hidden from his gaze. He could see nothing but her silhouette.

It was dusk, the night the two caravans met. Earlier he had ridden forward with the others to stare at their fellow travellers, but he had seen nothing – only the canvas of their wagons and the comings-and-goings of their camp attendants, building fires and fetching water. The messages he was finding by the wayside were still at the forefront of his mind and he had begun to work on them like codes or ciphers, looking for patterns, searching for repetitions that might suggest to him their meaning. He had become convinced that many of the characters resembled those that occurred in the local script, the common writing of Zaiton. It was as if someone had taken that script and somehow stretched it, changing the slant and the angles and distorting the curves to make something new and unique. And then they had added other things and put them all together in a different way. There were characters he did not recognise at all, symbols that seemed to resemble nothing in any of the languages he knew.

And who were they intended for, these messages in such strange characters? What caused them to appear? They stayed close to the line of the road, that much was clear. Nowhere in his forays away from the highway had he found any trace of them. The conclusion seemed obvious: they were all intended for a traveller on the Lin'an road. Not for his party, he was sure, but for some special recipient up ahead, after whose passing they were quickly wiped away.

That was why he surveyed Ming Yueh's caravan so intently. He knew little about the members of that party, only that an army captain was escorting a woman to the Emperor's court. And his first view of that caravan told him nothing. It lay neat and orderly in the afternoon sun, patrolled by soldiers like those who guarded his own caravan, peopled by servants anxiously preparing dinner.

But that changed with sunset, when the shadows of the mountains reached out across the plain and touched both caravans with the chill of darkness. Then the lanterns came alive, pin-pricks of light magicked out of the gloom. Venn watched them appear, one by one, from a little hill beyond Ming Yueh's camp where he had wandered on his way back from the river. It was a scene of great serenity, this slow lighting of lamps, part of an ancient ritual played out whenever humans faced the night together. The greatest loneliness he'd ever felt had not been in the empty places of the world, where no human foot would follow his for months. Far greater, he knew, was the loneliness of the traveller, alone upon the road when the day fades to dusk, who passes at a distance the warm lights of a village.

Venn had known that loneliness himself. Sometimes he had even sought it out. Yet that night, watching the lights appear below him, he felt again the familiar yearning of the traveller.

He might have sat and watched the lights far longer if his eye had not been caught by the move-ment of a shadow, there, in the heart of the other camp. At that hour of the evening attendants were hurrying from wagon to wagon, busy with errands, serving food or laying beds. But the movement Venn had seen was above all that activity. In the centre of the camp a wagon taller than the rest stood draped in golden silk. Behind the silk a low light burned, and it was this light that cast the shadow which had caught his eye – the pale silhouette of a woman, kneeling.

By contrast with the campfires the lamp was not bright, and its pale glow left the figure indistinct. From where Venn stood he couldn't guess her age or height and certainly nothing of her features. Indeed it was not the woman herself that made Venn stare at all, but the motion of her hand, the careful motions of brush-strokes moving over paper. Writing. At the centre of the camp, someone was writing.

In one sense, it shouldn't have been a surprise. Venn knew it was not uncommon for women of a certain class to keep a day-book, a record of their thoughts and feelings. But there was something in that sight, there, at that time, which turned his thinking about the wayside messages completely on its head. He had assumed the messages were intended for someone of importance travelling by road. But now he saw with a rush of understanding that the opposite might also be true, that it might be in the villages that the recipients were waiting; the important traveller he'd imagined might in reality be no more than a humble courier, posting messages along the way. Perhaps it was not a sequence of separate pronouncements he was seeing, but a dialogue – information moving up and down the road in stages, one village to the next, carried by the caravans that passed.

And carried, surely, in secret, for much care was taken to remove all record of them.

Venn looked again at the woman framed in silhouette, her body motionless but for the movement of her hand. He watched her for a long time, his brow furrowed, until eventually the lamp behind the gold silk was extinguished and the night air made him shiver. Then he shook himself and, reaching up, ran one fingertip along the line of his eyebrow, before retracing his footsteps to where his own camp stood, quiet now and shrouded in darkness.

On The Road To Lin'an

Decius was anxious, the boy was sure of it. Ever since the night by the lake there had been a tension in his manner that the boy had not seen before. Through the many months of their journey, he had shown nothing, betrayed nothing, as if inside him lay a dark void where no emotion stirred. But now there was a new-found urgency in his manner and he scanned the hills through which they passed with eyes that never rested. At night he sat awake and watched the darkness.

The delay by the river seemed to gnaw at his patience, shaping his anxiety into something sharper and more defined. The boy watched him examine the tree trunk that blocked their way, summarising the situation at a glance and immediately turning away, his eyes to the hills once more. On returning to their camp he went straight to Antioch's tent.

'We shall be here three days,' he told the scholar. 'I will use that time to ride out and see the lie of the land. The guards are busy and will not think to stop us, and you must reassure that captain that we mean to return.'

Antioch was sitting at the low table that travelled with him and served as a lectern for his books. The boy could see that for all his high spirits the hardships of their journey were beginning to tell on the old man. His face was greyer than when they had set out and the wiry vigour of his Sicilian days, if not gone, was certainly diminished. But his eyes retained the fire that the boy remembered, a passion that seemed to be reserved increasingly for his study of the bestiary.

Now, after a long day on the road, he looked up at Decius with his face clouded by weariness. 'You do not wish to rest? Very well, Count. You must do as you think best. I am sure Venn will make your peace with the captain.'

'I shall take Venn with me, to speak for me,' the other man replied. 'I have asked Yang to stay here and attend to your comfort.'

The old man showed a flicker of interest. 'Venn, not Yang? Will Yang not expect it?'

The general shook his head, already beginning to take his leave. 'It is unknown country, and dangerous. I will be happier with Venn by my side.'

And so Venn found himself for the first time alone in Decius's company. They took with them little but their rugs and some blocks of dried meat that could be placed on hot stones and warmed by the fire. Their bundles fitted easily behind their saddles, but at the hour of their departure the boy saw that Decius was leading up a packhorse with its saddle bags also filled.

'I thought the count would travel on campaign rations,' he whispered to Venn, a certain scorn in his voice. 'You are travelling much lighter than he is.'

At first, Venn said nothing but looked where the boy was pointing. Then he looked down and smiled. 'We shall see,' he said, and tugged his mount into position, waiting for the order to depart.

At first the two men headed away from the road, until the trees hid them from sight. Then they wheeled left so that they once again faced Lin'an, and crossed the river without difficulty some half a mile upstream of the other encampments. Decius set a demanding pace, straining as fast as the slow-footed packhorse would allow. As soon as they could, they regained the road. From then on, they rode always towards Lin'an.

They rode in silence, through an empty landscape of jagged mountains fringed with pines. At any sign of other travellers they left the road and waited until they passed, but generally the way was theirs, for this was the mountain road and less frequented than the longer, smoother road that kept the plain. They continued in that manner all day, past empty miles of forest, under bare peaks, pushing on until the road dimmed in the dusk and the horses began to stumble. Then Decius called a halt and led Venn off the highway, setting camp deep in the woods where any approaching foot-falls would sound crisp against the crust of the leaf mould.

Throughout the day the two men spoke only of practical matters. It wasn't until the fire was lit and the rations consumed that Decius chose to break the silence. His question, when it came, took Venn by surprise.

Throughout the day, Venn had been watching his companion, observing how he worked, the way he picked a route and gave his orders. For all his suspicion of him, he had been struck by the general's skill, how well he paced the horses, how he instinctively found the least visible line of movement. And Venn could see he was listening all the time. Even when giving orders he was listening. The stories of Decius's efficiency as a soldier were easy to believe. And that day had proved to Venn he was a soldier still, a soldier with a mission, still following orders. Ever since their landing in Syria, Venn had suspected that the Count's purpose was not the same as Antioch's. Now, looking into the brooding darkness behind those eyes, Venn was sure.

That is why the question Decius chose to ask that night, beside the fire, caught Venn so very much off guard.

'We have come a long way together, interpreter, over many months. There is something I would like to know. Tell me, who have you left behind?'

Even the tone surprised him, for it contained none of the count's usual coldness. No kindness either, Venn was quick to realise, just curiosity – the tone of someone accustomed to understanding others because it was his business to do so.

For a moment he did not respond, busying himself with the dying fire.

'No one,' he replied at last, his gaze meeting Decius's.

'No wife? No child?'

'Neither. I have lived a restless life.'

The count's eyes never left his and, faced with that strange darkness, Venn found himself wondering if perhaps he was wrong, if perhaps the freak of birth which made those eyes so black served only to hide feelings that were like any other man's.

'There was talk of a woman in Genoa . . .' Decius did not offer to say more.

'I knew a woman in Genoa, yes. She's unlikely to be there now. She was a traveller, as I am.'

'You still think of her?'

Venn reached down for a twig and stirred the fire again. 'There are many I think of. Yet here I am.'

To his surprise, Decius nodded and when he spoke next his voice was changed. 'It is as I thought. Your loyalties are to yourself.'

To Venn's well-tuned ear there was condemnation in the statement. He recalled that Decius's own loyalty to Manfred was renowned.

'No,' he corrected him. 'I have loyalties. Not to kings or princes, perhaps. Not family loyalties either. But loyalties nonetheless.'

'Loyalties to God?'

Venn shook his head. 'I have seen too many gods.'

'To who, then?'

Venn let the twig in his hand fall into the fire, then took up a larger stick and pressed one end into the flames. 'To those who honour me with their trust on journeys such as this. I am true to them in my own way.'

Then Decius surprised him again, taking the stick from his hand with unexpected gentleness and continuing to stir the flames. 'I pity you, Venn,' he said softly. 'Your life is built upon words. So many of them. To have so many words pass through you, it must be like a river that washes everything else away.'

Again Venn found himself off balance. 'And you, General,' he asked, trying to right himself. 'Who have you left behind?'

But Decius's face remained expressionless, his eyes on the fire. 'Haven't you heard, interpreter? Has no one told you?' He withdrew the stick from the fire and held it up, its tip glowing red, still licked by a pale blue flame. Very deliberately Decius laid this end of the stick across the palm of his hand and slowly, calmly grasped it. The flame went out with a hiss. Venn's eyes ran from the hand to the general's face but its expression never altered.

'Haven't they told you, Venn? I have no feelings. Ask the remnants of the Pope's force which survived my attack on Reggia. No feelings, no mercy, no remorse.'

But as Venn watched him turn and settle for the night, the smoke still acrid in the air between them, he could not be sure. After all, he had travelled widely. Men with callused hands but feeling hearts were not unknown to him.

The next day was like the first. They set off before it was light, covering a league or more so quickly that Venn feared for the safety of the horses. Shortly after dawn they reached a point where the land fell away dramatically and before them, still many miles away and far below them, lay the city of Lin'an. Balancing between mountains and lake, in that clear first light it seemed almost untouchable in its beauty. The early sun picked out in gold its temples and its towers.

'Our destination, Venn,' the general murmured. 'Does it make you afraid?'

His companion followed his gaze. 'I have seen great cities before. Why should I fear this one?'

'Because if you do not fear it even a little, you're a fool. Great power in the hands of a great tyrant. It's a dangerous combination.' Decius continued to study the distant city as if trying to commit to memory an outline of its shape.

'They say that the Romans once destroyed the city of Carthage,' he went on, 'that the Greeks annihilated Troy. And God is said to have wiped from the earth the Cities of the Plain. You know the stories? Tell me, do you believe that such acts were for the good? Could it be right to raze a great city such as the one below if in doing so you could put an end to boundless suffering?'

Venn looked at him astonished and saw that Decius's eyes were meeting his, waiting for an answer.

'I'm an interpreter,' he replied. 'I concern myself with the shades of meaning between one small word and another. I do not sit in judgement on the fate of cities.'

Decius smiled then, a grim shadow of feeling running across his features.

'But your little words do just that, don't they, Venn? They order the acts that set in course events that can never then be undone. They make it all happen. And people die in agony because they will not say the little words required of them. Or they die because they say the wrong words, or just because they've never been taught the words that will save them. The power of kings is nothing to the power of those words you deal in.' He turned away as if to spit. 'You know that better than anyone. So don't tell me about the humility of your calling. Your trade is fire, Venn. The fire that burns us all. Remember that. And you are here on this journey because you have come to need its heat.'

The interpreter did not reply, he merely pointed. Below them, half a mile away but moving quickly up the mountain road, a column of cavalry had emerged from the trees and was rising towards them. Already Venn could make out the imperial banners above it, could almost sense the urgency of the rider at its head.

Song Rui arrived at the camp in a chaos of dust and horses' hooves, the serenity of the encampment scattered by his cavalry.

He arrived just as she had dreamed he would, laughing, urgent, glowing with health and strength, and all her fears and doubts were resolved. The long wait for his summons vanished to nothing. He arrived and took her in his arms, then held her away from him and told her she was beautiful.

And it was true. The passage of time had turned youth into beauty and poise into grace, and Song Rui was startled by the slim loveliness he beheld. He had remembered her a naïve girl of the provinces, sunburnt and a little scrawny, awestruck by tales of the Emperor's court and intoxicated by dreams of freedom. Song Rui had met many such girls on his travels, girls destined to blossom and wilt in obscurity, all facing the same inescapable fate. It would begin with the ritual haggling as families agreed prices. Then came the sale: the rituals and the joining of hands and a night of yielding. And then, worse than anything that went before, the unrelenting servitude of marriage. They would fade quickly, he knew, broken by their labours and their subservience, by the casual contempt and cruelty that was their lot, by the inevitable and interminable series of confinements. And through it all, no prospect of alteration and nothing to look forward to, even their love for their children tempered by the certainty of parting. Their daughters would be torn away from them just as they had once been torn from their mothers, and the cycle would begin again.

Song Rui was not an unfeeling man and he pitied them their fate. But what could he do for so many? In return for their adoration he gave them kindness and honesty of a sort, and memories of nights both true and tender to cherish through the empty years.

In the year that had followed his departure from Zaiton, he had come to think of Ming Yueh as one of those many young women. Back amongst the trappings of his real life, the qualities that had enchanted him began to fade against the bright colours of the city, leaving only a vague awareness that his young admirer had been unusual for her fire and determination. But he had made a promise, and after all it would be diverting to introduce his Zaiton moon to the pleasures of the night. Song Rui considered himself neither dissolute nor selfish, but he was a young man of warm passions and by no means immune to the pleasure of sensual anticipation.

But seeing her as she was that day, flushed by his unexpected arrival, a stab of emotion surprised him and made him wonder for a moment if his plans were not, in truth, a little unfeeling. The brightness of her eyes when she saw him, the smile that changed her face from quietness to radiance . . . These were things he could not fail to be struck by. Then, when he held her in his arms and felt her body pressing close to his of its own volition, his doubts were swept away by a pulse of desire that allowed for no doubt. His judgement had been good. His rewards awaited him. And he would make sure she did not suffer by it.

At Song Rui's insistence, the Captain of the Guard rearranged his encampment. His men were ordered to the perimeter while Song Rui's cavalry pitched their tents at the centre of the camp, around the main wagons. Then they set about watering their horses in the river and gathering material for a huge bonfire. Song Rui explained that they had been ordered north, to the frontier, and would be away six months or more. This was the last night when his troops would be at leisure, and they would mark the occasion with a feast before the rigours of the road embraced them. He did not care that the diversion was in defiance of his orders, he assured her. Was love not more urgent than honour? Was beauty not more demanding than the dictates of men? The next day he must leave her. But that night there would be feasting and music and his men would drink her health.

So the arrangements were made and as dusk fell the celebrations began. Antioch and the boy watched from beyond Song Rui's perimeter and felt stirred by the energy of the spectacle. The sudden arrival of imperial troops had encouraged Antioch. Was it not an indication that they were nearing the Imperial Court? It seemed to Antioch to bode well. The boy thought so too, and watched with admiration the easy grace of the finely armoured officers.

That night the bonfire burnt so high that Venn and Decius saw a brightness in the sky from where they lay in the leaf mould, still half a day's ride from the camp. Nearer than that, the flames brought villagers out of their houses to wonder at the profligacy of the young general who had passed by earlier. There was music too, and the laughter of Song Rui's soldiers grew louder as the blaze grew high, disturbing Antioch when he tried to sleep, thrilling the boy with its wildness.

At the height of the celebration, Ming Yueh heard Song Rui's footsteps approach her carriage and tasted again, stronger than ever, the raw longing she had felt that morning in his arms. When Song Rui parted the heavy silk hangings and stepped inside, he was surprised by the quiet certainty with which she welcomed him, her lack of any protest or pretence. And later still, as the leaping flames threw twisting patterns on the silks around them, he found himself touched by the tenderness with which she gave herself, containing as it did no feigned surrender, none of the desperate wish to win favour that he'd come to know so well.

In fact, when the camp was silent and she lay asleep against him – when the fires were out and their bodies were touched only by the starlight – he realised he felt none of the usual, guilt-edged triumph of taking. Only a curious sense that the woman beside him had sought from him – and had obtained – something that he had not altogether expected to give. What did that make her, he wondered? Had he been deceived as to her innocence? But her breathing was so even and her face so calm, so perfect in its peace, that he ceased to trouble himself with the question. She was truly beautiful, he thought. He must find a way to make her happy.

Often at the start of a mission he found it hard to sleep. He lay still until the stars above the wagon began to pale in the sky and then, with the scent of the dawn beginning to rise out of the grass, his thoughts turned to the duties ahead of him and the opportunities they offered. Then he began to feel that rush of energy which always seized him when a new mission beckoned. He must make double-time that day, he thought, to make up for the folly of this wild diversion. Were his men strong enough? Were his horses fresh? Yes, on both counts. He knew he had it in his hands to mould his future, and he would not fail. Before the stars were quite gone he had left her carriage and was busy with his preparations.

Venn and Decius returned an hour or two after Song Rui had departed. They slipped quietly into Antioch's camp, unnoticed by anyone but the boy, and found the place much altered. The neat camp set by the Captain of the Guard had been wrenched apart by the passage of Song Rui's men, its wagons scattered into ragged positions, and a huge scorched circle marked the centre of the previous night's festivities. A small contingent of the captain's men was at work restoring order. The rest, the boy told them, were occupied with the teams of villagers still working to remove the fallen tree.

Decius made his report to Antioch in a few, terse sentences. They were ten days' journey from Lin'an, he said. The road was rough but free of obstructions. The land between the mountains and the city appeared fertile and heavily populated. They had avoided other travellers and had gone unseen.

Venn's report to the boy was rather different. He told him of the steep gorges and the rivers in spate, of the dark forests that clung to the mountain slopes. He told him of the plain beyond, embroidered with waterways, leading in the distance to a city of palaces built on the shores of a great lake. And he spoke of the moment at the furthest point in their journey when he had been made to wait while Decius rode ahead into the trees. He had been gone an hour or more and never said wheré he'd been. But on his return it was clear to Venn that the saddle bags of his packhorse were empty.

ζ

It can be hard to see the truth in the faces of strangers. I sit here tonight and watch the people pass. A boy brings me wine. He knows me now for I sit here often. He smiles when he sees me and calls me *master* and I feel I have found a friend. Yet when I leave, I know he does not think of me. The young live in the present, and their lives are still to come. Love scarcely troubles them. It is a beast that bites harder the older you become.

There is a man I know here, Ibrahim, a Jewish trader from the Maghrib. He deals in cheap fabrics or whatever small goods come his way. I have exchanged some words with him to tell him of my son, but when I speak to him he never lets his eye meet mine. A timid man, eager to be gone. I did not think to find a friend in him.

But three days ago, he came to me by the harbour. There was, he said, a merchant who'd arrived that day from Kairouan, someone who perhaps could help me. If I would deign to follow him . . . He waited, his eyes never rising above the buttons on my chest.

I agreed to go with him. What options did I have? I live on the scraps of knowledge that strangers throw me. If there was danger in going with him down narrow streets to a place

I did not know, I did not think of it. I have little to steal, little to lose but my memories — and losing them would sometimes seem a blessing.

But Ibrahim the Jew, for all his nervous manner, was acting in good faith. I followed him to a dirty alley and thence, through a low doorway, to a beautiful courtyard where a fountain played. Beyond, a flight of steps led to a large apartment, richly hung. It was clear that such rooms did not belong to Ibrahim.

He urged me to sit, then slid shyly from the room. Shortly after that I heard a rustle of garments and footsteps approaching from the room beyond. Then the door opened and the merchant of Kairouan stood before me.

True beauty lies not in the flesh but in the spirit. I have always believed that, and I have never been one to lose myself in the curve of a waist or in the promise of a smiling eye. But the woman who stood before me now was undeniably beautiful to look upon. And let there be no mistake, this was no young girl made lovely by the blush of youth, this was a woman of thirty years or more, tall, striking, strong in her features. Her hair was dark and within her own apartments she wore it loose, in thick, curling tresses. Her eyes were dark too and it was not some tawdry playfulness that made them striking, it was the sympathy in them, a depth that said here was a human creature both strong and kind.

I've heard some say that she is haughty, and in the prosecution of her business she must sometimes seem so. But I shall never say that. I have met no one like her.

I rose to greet her as she entered.

'Good day, sir.' She welcomed me solemnly, without a smile. 'You are the English merchant Ibrahim has spoken of? I welcome you. My name is Leah Bathsheba, or Leah of Kairouan. Please sit.'

She seated herself on cushions facing me and waited while a male servant brought refreshments on a copper tray, an Arab drink of mint and mountain honey. Then she looked at me, a long, hard look, as if deciding what to say.

'I had not planned to see you, sir. It does not help my business to involve myself in matters other than my own. This is a lesson my people have learned over many generations. The affairs of Christians are, in particular, to be avoided. But Ibrahim persuaded me. Many years ago, he lost his only son in a shipwreck off Malta. Many times he has urged me to tell you what I know, and finally he has prevailed.'

She spoke softly and with great care, with the formal speech of a merchant, for whom courtesy and manners ease the flow of goods as surely as a following wind. She told me she was a widow acting in her husband's business. In her religion, I knew, it was not unknown for a woman to behave so. She had been married young: her two sons were both old enough to act on her behalf, one in Egypt, one in the trading posts beyond Byzantium. Her husband's family was a large one, and through them she had a chain of contacts stretching to Baghdad and beyond.

'From one of those I learned a little about the people that you seek. A cousin of mine had dealings with them and, though the years have passed since then, you will see why I remember his story.'

She paused and for a moment her eyes wandered to the latticed window where broad green leaves filtered the light. 'My cousin for a time was based in Greater India, in a port we know as Quillon. It's a busy place, where merchants come from Java and from Sinim. It was there he met Count Decius and the old man who travelled with him.'

'In India, you say?' I tried to recall my charts, tried to place the port of Quillon.

'That's right. It's a changing post in the south, on the Malabar coast. Travellers who wish to travel east to Sinim must change ships there, for only local craft may enter the great port of Zaiton.'

'And you say that they were both there, Decius and Antioch?' My eagerness for news was overwhelming. I felt my body shiver and my ribs were tight around my heart. 'Forgive me if I seem demanding but no certain word of my son has ever been reported after Basrah. Even agents of the Pope found nothing.'

She returned my gaze a little sadly. 'I cannot say for certain that your son was there. I only know that when my cousin met them, their party was intact and healthy, and no disasters had befallen them. They had leased their ship in Basrah and a merchant of my race had travelled with them all the way to Calicut. In busy ports he would speak for them, as his was a familiar face in those parts. Perhaps that is why enquiries after a Christian party were not successful. After

Calicut, they continued to Quillon. It seems they found trouble there.'

She sat so calmly there in front of me and spoke so firmly that the events of which she talked grew vivid, as if they'd happened in a neighbouring port and in the last few days. It is hard to see him there, my small boy, in a land so strange that I cannot even imagine the faces of its people. But there, in Leah's room, that day, it all seemed very close.

'I do not know the details,' she went on, 'but there was a brawl and a man of Quillon died. The captain of the troop of soldiers was arrested. The penalties there for foreigners are very harsh and a sentence of death was passed. My cousin heard of it when the man they called Count Decius sought him out. He'd been told my cousin had influence with the officials there and begged him to use it. My cousin took pity on the strangers and did what he could. It ended when the count paid from his own pocket the sums needed to save the officer's life. Out of gratitude to my cousin for his intervention, the count presented him with a ring from his own finger. He told him it had once before been given as a reward for mercy and that he hoped one day perhaps it would be given so again.'

I nodded in reply, though in truth I found this tale of Decius difficult to reconcile with what I had been told by the Pope's officer, Quintus Fabius. Was the relentless soldier he described the sort of man to reward mercy in others? Perhaps Leah's tale had altered in the telling. Or perhaps the Indies had worked a change in him. I put the question out of my mind and attended again to my hostess.

'My cousin wore the ring,' she continued, 'and in his travels many people noticed it. But it was not until he came to Venice that his troubles began. There he was approached by someone we call a man of the crowd, the sort of man who is paid to inform on others. There are some in every port, watching and listening. My people have learned to recognise them, whatever the guise. This one was fascinated by my cousin's ring. He wanted to know all about it, where it had come from, who had sold it to him. My cousin told him it was a gift from a Christian lord. He would say no more, but the man pursued him, intent on discovering the full story behind it. He even offered to buy the ring but my cousin would not sell. Shortly afterwards my cousin disappeared. He was not seen for three days. When they found his body floating in the lagoon it was naked. From the marks on it, we knew that he'd been tortured before he died. And the ring he wore was missing, along with the finger on which he'd worn it.'

I looked at her in horror. 'But who would do that? And why?'

To my surprise she smiled at my question.

'Those are not questions that greatly concern Christian judges. A Jew was dead. That was all.'

I shook my head, horrified by her calmness.

'You think the ring led to this?' I asked.

'Yes,' she said. 'It was no common robbery.'

'But why?' I asked again. 'Was it of great value? Or was there some other meaning to the ring? What did it signify?'

She shrugged. 'I have told you what I know. The significance of the ring is not my business. We did not expect justice for my cousin's death. We merely learned to be more cautious.' With that she rose to her feet and hastily I did the same. 'I cannot see how what I've told you helps you find your son,' she carried on, 'but Ibrahim insisted I should speak of it, and he is a good man.'

I thanked her, and then, perhaps because of the kindness in her eyes, perhaps because I didn't want to leave her cool, calm room, I found myself talking. Since my arrival in this town, I've listened much but talked little. But there was in Leah of Kairouan something that opened paths within me I had thought long closed. I am an old man and a fool. But she never let me think so. I found myself explaining things to her I had hardly understood myself.

'The people of this town,' I told her, searching for the right words, 'they think my son is dead and that I cannot accept it. But they are wrong. I know there's little chance my son still lives. Too many years have passed. But until I *know*, I cannot rest. And if he sleeps, I need to know his fate and how he met it. When I close my eyes at night I feel the pain of the wounds I imagine on him. I feel his pain a thousand times in a thousand different ways. I cannot sleep for his agony. I came here to find the truth – if that is possible – in the hope that I can reconcile my heart to what befell him. Perhaps then I shall rest. They think I pray my son is still alive: in fact I only pray that, if he died, he died without great pain, and that he did not die alone.'

Then Leah of Kairouan took my hand in hers and I felt the strength in her fingers. Her touch was cool. I remember it still. But when she spoke, it was of something very different.

'Your Count Decius . . .' she said. 'I've said that his affairs are not my business. But in Granada, in the street of the letter writers, there is an old man by the name of Ichabod. Go to him. I think he will tell you more about that ring.'

ζ

An Encounter

Three days before they arrived in Lin'an, Venn went looking for the woman he had seen only in silhouette. It was an act he had contemplated many times since the night when he had seen her writing, that first night when the two caravans had come together. Since then he had found his eyes drawn to her wagon whenever he was close to her camp and he would sometimes catch a glimpse of slim fingers holding back the drapes to open a peephole into the world outside.

But for many days he kept his distance, redoubling his efforts to understand the messages he'd collected. In one village he found an old woman selling strips of fabric. They were intended for young girls, she told him, to hold back the hair during family ceremonies. Each strip was embroidered with symbols and she explained how each one had an ancient meaning: this one for gold, she said, this one for luck; this one for health or children or an end to suffering. Venn listened avidly and bought every one the woman had to sell. The boy watched him over many nights, studying the neat silver stitching, copying the designs onto paper, drawing them over and over again before he reached a result that seemed to satisfy him.

While Venn kept his own counsel, in the caravan ahead Ming Yueh fretted. From the morning Song Rui had ridden away, the serenity she'd found in the daily routines of her journey was lost and never returned. The farms and meadows of the Zaiton plain had given way to an unforgiving curtain of dark pines, and the change seemed reflected in her mood. The high peaks above the pines made her shiver. At such a height the air still held a breath of winter in it.

The atmosphere in her caravan had changed too. The soldiers of her escort seemed sullen and dissatisfied after their encounter with Song Rui's cavalry. She did not know it, but by posting them as sentries at his feast Song Rui had slighted them. They were an infantry troop, not household flunkies, and his action caused a lingering resentment. Now they were eager to reach Lin'an so they could take up an assignment more fitting for fighting men.

And she could not pretend that her own mood had not changed. Song Rui's arrival had been a moment of the purest, most perfect joy — a moment when the dreams of twelve long months had been fulfilled. Never had she imagined anyone more brilliant, more dashing, a man whose every movement spoke of daring and charm and of easy, instinctive authority. And he had come there for her. She knew that. She had seen the pleasure in his face when he first saw her and had felt the surge of feeling in his arms when he held her body close to his. She was his now, betrothed in all but name, and not a moment that had passed between them had been anything but the perfection she had dreamed of.

But then he had ridden away and his departure left an emptiness behind it. It was the second time she had watched him go from her life, and to her surprise it was infinitely harder – crueller – than the first. After such dark, tender intimacy it felt like daylight on a wound, revealing with unforgiving clarity the jagged edges he had left behind. And try as she might, she could not conceal from herself the depth of the cut. It was as if she'd already seen him ride away a thousand times. She began to understand that with him every perfect homecoming would always be a prelude to departure.

Suddenly, for the first time, she feared her arrival in Lin'an. She had always imagined him waiting for her. Now, although he had made arrangements for her welcome, she knew she would arrive alone.

Then came the day when the barbarian accosted her. Every morning she and her maid would withdraw into the woods to bathe. It was a carefully organised event. The Captain of the Guard would identify a place – a pool in the woods or a stretch of stream – where she would be able to swim with absolute discretion. At the appointed hour his men were placed around a discreet perimeter to ensure she could not be disturbed. With such arrangements, she knew, it was not possible for any man to come into her presence by accident. As soon as she saw him in the shadow of the pines, she knew he had come looking for her.

She had sent her maid ahead and was returning to camp alone when she sensed his presence. He was standing only a few yards from her path. She almost called out when she saw him, out of shock, not fear, and stopped abruptly, uncertain what to do. If she shouted the guards would come running and his end would be swift. After all, he was a barbarian and almost certainly dangerous. But surely his presence was an accident? He could not know it was a crime to approach her, a crime merely to stand there alone in her presence. She must send him away, she thought, away from the guards. Then she could make her escape and no harm would be done.

It was with some such thought in mind that she opened her mouth, but before she could speak, the intruder had raised a finger to his lips and was shaking his head.

'Softly,' he said. 'We must not be heard.'

The words astonished her. They were spoken in her own tongue, the language of Zaiton, and the delicacy of their pronunciation seemed impossible from such coarse lips, from such a brute of a man. She would have been less surprised had he growled at her like a beast. But instead of the guttural grunts she had heard the barbarian travellers exchange, he spoke well and she realised his voice was a pleasant one. And when he finished speaking he ran his fingertip along his eyebrow in that way she recognised and suddenly his face was not grotesque and coarse as it had been, but the face of a man like any other man. A face as complex and uncertain as her own.

He was speaking to her again now, carefully, still in her own language, telling her his name, telling her about himself and about his journey. Then she watched in astonishment as he produced a fragment of fabric from his pocket and held it out to her.

'I understand the danger,' he told her. 'I know I must soon be gone. But first, please look at this. I have seen the messages you leave. You write in a script I have never seen before. Some of it comes from here, does it not? Look, this symbol here means sorrow. I have seen it in the messages you leave behind you.'

She stepped back from him, her thoughts in chaos, and the stranger seemed to sense her alarm for he too stepped back.

'My apologies. I have frightened you. But I mean no harm. It is a script for women, is it not? One that has grown out of the embroidered charms. Is that why the men do not understand it? Because they have never taken notice of those symbols and their meanings?'

She said nothing and for a fraction of a second he thought she was poised for flight. But she steadied herself and with visible effort allowed her eyes to meet his. She had never seen such eyes before: somewhere between blue and green, like sky over the sea at twilight.

'Who are you?' she asked. 'Who has told you this?'

'I have told you who I am,' he replied, 'but perhaps I was not clear. This is my trade. Words are my living.'

'What do you want of me? I know nothing of these messages. You are mistaken.'

He shook his head. 'You know I am not. But I have my answer.' He returned the fabric to his pocket and turned to go but paused, looking back over his shoulder. 'When I understand this script of yours, I shall be satisfied. Your secret will be safe with me, I promise you.'

With that he was gone. She remained where he left her, standing very still, half expecting to hear a cry as the guards discovered him. But no alarm was raised and the silence returned, broken only by birdsong and by the movement of the trees. She stood and let it flow over her, calming and caressing, until her confusion had passed. The worst had happened. The very worst. She had led a man to the secret of their messages. And she didn't even know how. What if he were to announce what he knew? The age-old secret might be torn apart forever. It would be a disaster like no other.

And yet she found she was less frightened than she should have been. Was it because the man was a foreigner? After all, few would give him credence. Or was it because there was something in his expression as he took his leave that somehow took away her fear?

When she returned to the Captain of the Guard he noticed how quiet she was, how very still, and thought she must be thinking of her lover.

Venn's return that morning was marked only by the boy, who had been looking out for him.

'Safely back, as promised,' Venn smiled, bending to gather up his things. Around him the camp was preparing for the new day's journey.

'What happened, Venn?' the boy asked. 'Did you see her? What did she say?'

'I saw her, yes. It is as I told you. The writing is a secret of the women here.'

'And the woman herself? What was she like? Was she very proud?'

The interpreter shrugged and busied himself with the knots of his straps. 'Yes, proud in a way. Brave, too. I gave her a shock but she scarcely let it show.'

'And in her person? Is she very beautiful? They say she is going to marry a great lord.'

'She's young. Tall for one of this country.' Another shrug. 'I couldn't say. But she has a bright light in her eyes. That is what you notice.'

*   *   *

Seven days after Song Rui's visit she could still feel the echoes of his embrace. She could still remember how she felt when he touched her, she could still hear him say her name. But he was gone as if he had never been, and the marks he had left behind were a puzzle to her now, symbols pointing to a meaning that had somehow slipped between her fingers. That night, when she lay down to sleep, his image did not appear before her as it had done so often before. Instead her dreams were troubled by the recollection of a great brute in the woods who somehow spoke to her in words she understood.

The Emperor

Lin'an, the lake city, city of poets, girdled by pleasure gardens, bejewelled with palaces, pitted with brothels; part fantasy, part mystery, part dense, steaming slum. A city that had outgrown itself, so tightly squeezed between the lake and the mountains that beyond the public squares and avenues its streets narrowed to fetid alleyways. There, dwellings jostled for space so fiercely that they leaned upon their neighbours or climbed over them, until they stood three or four storeys high, cutting all light from the passages below. Fires were the scourge of the city, taking hold in seconds, blazing for days. But in their wake the houses grew up thicker and faster and the city began to sweat in the heat once more.

It was the canals that let the city breathe, threading through its cramped sinews, bringing water and the flat-bottomed boats that crowded in each day to sell and carry. Even the narrowest canal created space for daylight. East of the city lay the great tidal river which brought in the massive rice boats, but the city did not face the river, it faced the lake. That was the Holy

Lake that lay to the west, cupped between the knuckles of the mountains, mirroring their peace and tranquillity: clear, cool, sacred. The city's eye to the heavens, a balm for its overheated brow. And, of course, jealously guarded, its purity maintained by imperial decree. Only the very privileged might float upon its waters or live upon its shores.

Antioch's party was not allowed to approach the lake. They were made to skirt around it on the old mountain road, the water a blur of silver below them. A mile before they reached the city they could make out the roofs of the royal precincts and the great outer wall that enclosed them. Within that wall, Yang told them, lay palaces and gardens that spread for three miles or more, down to the pleasure gardens of the southern shore. Few were allowed to enter them, he said. Commoners such as themselves were allowed no further than the great Hall of Petitions that stood beside the main palace gate.

But in this Yang was proved wrong, and in a most spectacular way. Their arrival at the Imperial Court was welcomed with the most solemn ceremony, and they were given the sort of welcome an ambassador from the southern kingdoms might have envied. For it happened that the previous year another visitor had reached the Imperial Court, a Syrian scholar who had travelled with the caravans east from Damascus and after two years of journeying had found a way to

Lin'an. His arrival had caused a stir, for he was a mathematician and astronomer and was able to demonstrate to the Emperor's own scholars certain devices for astrological measurement that were completely new to them. In addition, as a man who had travelled through the lands of the Khan, his reports of what he had seen there and his observations of the enemy's deployments were considered of the greatest value. Such was the impact of his stay that an unusual vogue had developed in a land not generally welcoming to strangers. For that particular season, foreigners were in fashion.

Which is why, when Antioch's caravan was first sighted, officials of the court rode out to make them welcome. To the astonishment of the Captain of the Guards, Ming Yueh's caravan was forced to wait at the roadside while the shabby wagons of the barbarians were hurried forward and guided directly to the palace precincts. The last Venn saw of his mysterious message-writer was her wagon on the roadside, a little uneven in the mud. As he and the boy rode by, the silk of the hangings stirred, but whether moved by the wind or by a hand within, he could not tell.

That evening the Emperor was in a jovial mood. There had been a double execution in the morning, an event that always put him in a good humour, although on this occasion he found himself less cheered by it than usual. A young courtier, a man prominent in the palace secretariat, had died alongside one of the Emperor's own concubines. The girl had been a gift from the Lord Rustum, sent to him only six months previously. In truth he had not greatly taken to her – a silent, tearful creature who after the initial thrill of subjugation had never greatly aroused him. And because he had no feelings for her other than a vague antipathy, the young man's offence had caused him more surprise than anger. To risk one's life for such an uninteresting trifle seemed simply inexplicable and made him worry for the judgement of his civil service.

Still, it was unpardonable, and there was no question that they must die. They had been witnessed passing notes and under interrogation the woman had confessed as much. There had been no bodily contact between the pair, no physical contamination of the Emperor's property, otherwise the sentence would have been much harsher. As it was the two died facing each other, skewered by the same blade in one stroke, living barely long enough for either to witness the other's disembowelment.

Nevertheless, the proceedings left the Emperor dissatisfied. He was a sentimental man who found the disloyalty of concubines particularly hurtful. Did he not give them every luxury? Why could they not be satisfied with that? The thought that one of them might, of her own volition, cast eyes upon a pimply clerk depressed him.

But by the evening, his mood had changed again. He was an enormous man, not tall, but very broad and amply padded with fat, who when seated covered a much greater area than any two or three of his courtiers. He liked to eat, and over a hearty meal he put the reasons for the morning's execution out of his mind, reflecting instead on its intriguing repercussions. The head of his secretariat had been put firmly in his place by the incident. He had come to the Emperor and begged for his life, apologising for his subordinate's indiscretion by shedding real tears upon the Emperor's feet. The Emperor had been merciful, sensing his interests lay that way. By sparing the man he had bound his loyalties to him more closely than before. As a result he reckoned that any dissent among his secretaries was likely to be rooted out with greater rigour than ever.

And as for Lord Rustum who had sent him the girl in the first place . . . Anything that gave the Emperor ammunition against that particular courtier always made him happy. Rustum was unruly, sullen, a walking impertinence. He ruled his lands in the west like his own personal fiefdom. But he was necessary too – a good soldier and a barrier against the Khan's influence in the western deserts. Managing him took skill and patience, and the Emperor enjoyed the challenge. By evening, the girl's treachery was making him smile. When Lord Rustum returned to court later in the year, he decided, a subtle sanction would be needed. The thought of devising it put him in excellent humour.

That is why he received the party of barbarians so warmly. He was in a mood for amusement and reports told him these were true barbarians, unpolished and ungroomed, from the distant lands where the sun set. He received them in his personal state room with the twenty members of his council around him, and the visitors did not disappoint. They proved a motley group of oddities: a hideous old man, all bones and angles, as coarse-featured as all his kind; an oversized soldier with monstrous eyes that made the Emperor shiver gleefully; a boy with shockingly pale hair; and a brown-skinned servant, with hands roughened like a ropeman's, who was said to be their interpreter but who stood a little apart and said nothing. The half-caste merchant from Zaiton who translated for them was less entertaining. The Emperor had nothing but contempt for such half-breeds.

But overall their uncouth appearance, their wild looks and their outlandish garments were every bit as fascinating as he had hoped, and the tales they told of their homelands entertained the whole of his court. They spoke of their cities as though they were great marvels, yet spoke of rushes on the floors, of filth in the streets, of endless wars between the cities, of bloodshed, ignorance and hunger. No paper, no porcelain – no silks or spices but those they gleaned from foreign merchants at prices that made the Emperor's courtiers laugh. Why, in such a land their common shopkeepers would be as rich as lords! But then who would choose to be a lord in a land so bereft of comforts?

The interview lasted over an hour and concluded only when the Emperor grew weary. 'But there is much more I wish to ask them,' he declared. 'They shall stay here as my guests until we have learned all we wish, and we shall show them every comfort.' Then, when they had been led away, he added to his chancellor: 'But mind you keep a close watch on them, for they look murderous brutes. And when they are gone, be sure to burn everything they've touched. I don't like the smell of them.'

Later that night the Emperor inspected a young woman called to court by one of his generals, who wanted her for a plaything. Nothing wrong with the young man's taste, he concluded. A bit tall, perhaps, and a flash of fire in the eyes that did not bode well, but neat and nicely put together. After some thought he ordered that she should be accommodated in a garden house by the lake until the general's return. He had originally promised that she would be housed in the women's quarters of the palace itself, as an honour to the general in question. But rumours had reached him recently – one spy had spoken of an unauthorised detour, another of a feast requisitioned in the Emperor's name but without his permission. So instead she would wait in the Garden House, which would not yet be fully aired, and she could blame her lover for her isolation and for any chills she suffered in the meantime.

All in all, the Emperor had enjoyed an excellent day.

In Lin'an

At the Emperor's insistence, Antioch's party were guests at the Imperial Court for three months. To the boy they were months where his wildest dreams of comfort took shape and wrapped him in an embrace so bewilderingly luxurious that all the hardships of the road, the bitter thirsts and the raw salt sores, began to seem less real than the softness of lark down or the scent of musk roses in the cushions on which he slept. Many years before, his father had taken him to see the arrival in Lincoln of a great lord and his retinue, who came there as guests of the bishop. So wealthy was this man, his father told him, that his lady slept every night in silken sheets which were carried on ahead of her wherever she went. And now the boy did the same, and never failed, each night before he slept, to stretch out and glory in their softness, wondering how he would ever convince his father that he had slept on silk far finer than any that had ever yet been seen in Lincoln. And if a sort of gentle, dizzying delirium took hold of him, he saw it also reflected in the eyes of Yang the merchant, elevated now to the post of official interpreter; and perhaps even in Antioch, who was waited on by the court's wise men and spent his days in disputation and debate while eager servants tended him. It was as if the lotus charms of the Emperor's court had, in all three of them, put aside all thoughts of Manfred's mission.

Even Decius seemed changed, the boy decided. The tension and suspicion of the road seemed less rigid in him now, and he would spend his evenings seated quietly on the palace terraces as the twilight firmed into darkness and thousands of floating lanterns were set adrift on the lake below. Sometimes the boy wondered if beneath that calmness the general might simply be watching, waiting for something unguessable to happen. But it was impossible to tell. His face betrayed nothing.

Venn was quartered apart from them, in the servants' hall, but he too was made comfortable. He spent his mornings with the boy, walking in the palace gardens while Antioch studied his books. In the afternoons and evenings, when Yang was appointed to accompany Antioch to all appointments, Venn was free to explore beyond the palace gates. His favourite hour for this was dusk. At that hour, wrapped in a cloak and slouching a little to disguise his height, he could walk the streets in shadow and avoid the attention of the crowds.

Lin'an was a city that did not sleep, and at dusk, when the daily market stalls were packed away, street pedlars took their places, setting up great metal pans over low fires and selling quick-cooked meat and vegetables on plates of leaves. The taverns and the eating houses became lively and the crowds boisterous, filling the narrow streets with noise, and jostling for spaces in the most favoured haunts. The smells of the cooking mixed with the scent of the great red-flowered creepers that twisted over every courtyard and which, by night, opened their petals to breathe a heavy, languid perfume into the darkness.

This scent twisted itself around whispering lovers and gossiping traders alike, and Venn would let the sounds of the place wash over him and resolve themselves into fragments of meaning.

'She knows nothing, I promise you. . .'

'I asked for twice that price and got it!'

'She trusts me.'

'Never! Please! You must not.'

'Walk away from him. He will understand nothing else.'

Venn found these fragments comforting. Everywhere he had ever been he had heard the same. This was no foreign land, it seemed, no lost empire of strange beasts. Just a place of towns and villages like any other. Whatever Decius plotted, he could do little to alter that.

Then, one evening, a voice from the darkness called his name.

At first Venn thought he'd misheard. Then he assumed it must be the voice of someone from the palace – a servant, perhaps, or someone acquainted with him – and he looked around, expecting to see a smiling face and a greeting. But there was nothing, only the crowds passing down the narrow street, too busy with their own affairs to see or notice him. When it came again it was low as the faintest whisper but it was clear and Venn could tell it came from the deep shadow of an alleyway close beside him. There he made out a figure as cloaked as he, someone pressing back into the darkness.

'Stay in the light,' the voice commanded, speaking in the language common to both Lin'an and Zaiton. 'They are watching you. The Emperor's spies. Wherever you go.'

Venn looked away and gazed into a nearby tavern as though wondering whether to enter. 'I have nothing to hide from them,' he said.

'I do.' The voice was still a whisper. 'I have a message for your master.'

'For Antioch?' Venn asked. 'For the scholar?'

'For the lord with murder in his eyes. Tell him there is a boathouse on the southern shore of the lake. It is set under trees and it has the shape of a rat carved into its gable. Tell your master this.'

Venn sensed movement in the darkness as if the speaker was preparing to leave. 'What of it?' he asked quietly, still looking at the tavern. 'What else should I tell him?'

'Nothing else. He will know when.' With a rustle of garments the figure was gone.

Venn walked for a long time after that. He allowed his feet to find their own path while his mind turned over the meaning of the message. It was many minutes before he paused and looked around him and when he did he found himself in a small, deserted square he had not seen before. Above him the outline of a moon hung low in the sky and it was then he began to understand. By his calculation, in only a few nights' time there would be no moon at all. Another moonless night for Decius to receive messages. That was why no date needed to be given.

As he stood and considered this, a lamp was lit in a room above him. Some of its light fell on the wall close to where he stood and picked out a frayed paper marked in an unusual hand. Without intending to, without searching for it, Venn had found the Women's Wall.

The women's script learned by Ming Yueh was not widely known in Lin'an but there was a small number of women in that city who had made the journey from Zaiton, or whose mothers had made it and had passed their knowledge to their daughters. This little community was disparate in both geography and rank, and few of its members ever met. They knew each other only by the messages they posted – for the first women from the port city to arrive in Lin'an had established a certain wall in a certain market as the common place for messages. And in Lin'an the location never changed, perhaps because in such a tiny group the continuity was important, perhaps because it helped newcomers from Zaiton to find the wall more easily. It was this location which Venn had chanced upon on his night wandering, and it was to this location he returned the following day, an hour before sunset, while there was still light to read by.

Before that, as soon as he awoke, he had sought out Decius. He had found the general in his apartments, elegant rooms of green silk painted with the images of birds and blossom. Venn had not spoken to him in Latin but in a peasant patois of the Sicilian west, a rough tongue laced with Moorish slang that few could understand who had not themselves lived in the lands around Selinus. When Decius heard it spoken, it seemed to Venn that for an instant a flash of fire appeared in the depths of those dark, impassive eyes.

'What tongue is that? I have heard it used before,' he replied in Latin. 'What do you mean by using it with me?'

'You understand it?' Venn replied, persisting with the dialect. 'If so, it's safer. We do not know for certain who is listening nor what they understand.'

Decius nodded slowly. 'I understand a little. I had a farm once, a villa in the hills . . .' His speech trailed away to silence, and Venn nodded, as if to say he had heard as much in the general's way of speaking.

The two men walked in the Winter Garden, a place still lovely although its season had passed. It was laid out in the expectation of snow, and its trees and shrubs were chosen to blossom when the landscape was bleakest. In spring the garden was little visited except for occasional hurried officials going between the Chancellery and the Lake Temple. When it seemed they were alone, Venn – still speaking in the peasant dialect – told the general of his encounter in the alleys of Lin'an. His message delivered, he fell silent.

'Well, Venn,' Decius asked after a pause, 'what are you thinking?'

'I am thinking that you value the lives of your companions no higher than you value your own.'

A silence followed as the two men continued to walk.

'That is all?' Decius asked. 'You have no questions?'

The interpreter shook his head. 'None whose answers I cannot guess. You have always shown a great interest in reaching the lands of the Great Khan. What you propose to do there I do not greatly care. But I have a request.'

'Go on.'

'Two requests. First, that you will be careful of their lives – Antioch's and the boy's. Whatever your quest, they did not ask to be a part of it.'

'And second?'

'That when you go to the boathouse you take me with you, not Yang.'

Decius stopped then and turned back to look at him. 'Why? You do not trust him, then?'

'I trust myself more. He has taken a great liking to the life of a courtier. I assume that what you promised him in Zaiton to gain his co-operation will prove less attractive than the favour of an emperor.'

In reply, the general turned away towards the mountains.

'Very well,' he said, 'but know this. You are right in thinking I have business with the Great Khan. It is something I must do. And if you and the others have to die for me to do it, I won't hesitate. Not for one moment.'

That evening Venn waited until the rest of the party was at dinner before returning to the place where he had seen the writing. He took great pains to follow his usual pattern, wandering for half an hour or more apparently without direction, before allowing himself to chance upon the square he sought.

In that half-hour, his hopes were not high: he had seen for himself in the course of his journey how swiftly messages in the special script were removed from sight. But what he found that day amazed him and kept him anchored in the square until the light had gone, afraid that what he'd found might have vanished by morning. Because, instead of the one message he'd anticipated, he found dozens; some new, some older, some so old they were faded almost beyond legibility; all of them unobtrusive against a background of old bills and messages, tucked away in the darkest corner of the square. And better even than that, he saw at once that they were posted in pairs, as if each original was paired with its answer.

Never before had Venn had so much of the script to work with. Before that day, his understanding had been gleaned from short samples with little context. The sight of so much writing laid out in such a way changed everything. He could see at once that certain words and phrases used in one message were mirrored in the response and with that came a certainty that the unknown characters would at some point yield up their meaning. All he needed was time. Time to make copies, and to do it with discretion. Time to sit and work through each line. Then time to practise, to master what he'd learned. He knew already that he would scarcely sleep until he had done it.

As he made his way back to the palace that night, he was filled with the thrill of discovery. The feeling was not new to him, but never before had he felt it with such force, for this was something he had never known before. A script known only to women. A language hidden beneath the noses of the men who ruled them.

Did such a thing exist elsewhere? He had never even heard rumours of such a thing. What new meanings and constructions might such a tongue contain?

No, he knew he would not sleep. Because for Venn, as Decius sensed, understanding new tongues was not just a trade to live by, but something more important, more profound. And something simpler, perhaps, than finding a language of his own.

ζ

The road to Granada is not an easy one. It winds into the mountains through raw, rock-hewn heat, heat that closes around the traveller like a curse until the great peaks ahead disappear into a simmering haze. The asses stumble on paths strewn with stones and the dust rises at every footfall to choke your lungs and creep into the crevices of your body. The summer is not the time for such a journey, and I am not the age for it. Since coming to al-Andalus I have clung to the edges of the sea like a cormorant, nervous of the land.

Meeting Leah Bathsheba changed all that. Two days after we met, she came to take her leave. She was heading south, to Africa. Had she been anyone else, I might not have followed her advice. What business had I with any of it? If Count Decius owned a ring, and if that ring was later stolen, did that help me find my son or lay his ghost to rest? In Málaga there is the hope that any day a traveller might land and tell me what I need to know, someone who'll say, *yes, I knew your son, he was a fine boy who became a fine man.* Words with which I could die in peace. But if I leave the coast, there is no one left to watch for me. I might easily miss that crucial meeting.

And for what? To jolt my bones on a bitter journey to a strange city, seeking a man who may know nothing in a matter that did not concern me.

And yet I went. What else could I do? The threads that hold me to the past are thin as lines of silk. When one touches my hand, I must treat it like gossamer.

So I hired a guide and asses, and all the paraphernalia of a journey, and set out for the great city of the Moors. I confess that, for all the hardships, there were times travelling through groves of oranges and lemons, high above the heat of the plain, when I did not regret the towns of the coast with their flies and the heavy stench of people. But mostly as I travelled I thought of my son. If Leah was right, if nothing ill had befallen him, he had travelled with Antioch beyond the tip of Greater India. What thoughts were in his mind as he travelled? What did he make of his companions? Did he know enough of men to be wary of Decius? Did he recognise the brutality in his face? The figure of Decius seemed to grow in my mind as I travelled. What manner of man was he really, this soldier who'd had my son's life in his hands? And then my thoughts would turn again to the road ahead of me. Perhaps Granada would answer my questions.

To do justice to the glories of that city is beyond me. Suffice it to say that for splendour and for order, for a sense of life well lived, I had never known the like. The street of the letter-writers was as Leah Bathsheba had described it: a narrow alley that twisted steeply down the hill, at times no wider than two men abreast. In that street dwelled many scribes who for a fee would take down letters for those who could not write.

On Leah's recommendation I had hired a guide-interpreter for my visit to the city, a Berber who knew the place well, a man she trusted. He helped me in my search. The man we sought went under the name of Ichabod. When we enquired after him we were told he was still alive, still working – though suffering now from poor eyesight – in a small room near the poorer end of the hill. And it was there we found him, as old as they said, toothless and shrunken in his frame. Around him were the fragments of an impoverished existence: a prayer mat and a mat for sleeping, some blankets and, on a low table, a crust of bread beside a water jar. Nothing else. He was dressed in the garb of a Moorish scribe and his wrinkled skin was brown, but the eyes that peered at me as I entered the room were the palest shade of blue.

He must have heard me exchange a word with my guide as I approached, for he spoke before I had time to address him.

'Ah, a traveller from the north!' he chuckled. 'I recognise that way of speaking, though it is many years since I've heard it. The worst Latin in the world, we always used to say!' He chuckled again, then narrowed his eyes shrewdly. 'You want a letter written in the Arab script, perhaps? I may be old but I am the only one you'll find here who can take dictation in your English tongue direct to court Arabic. Or to French, Greek, Syriac, whatever you prefer.' He mumbled to himself and, reaching beneath his sleeping mat, began to pull out parchment and quills. 'I may be old, but I remember tongues that the young ones here have never even heard!'

There was nowhere to sit so I remained standing. He pushed aside the remains of his food and kneeled at the table, preparing to write.

'Forgive me,' I began. 'It is not for a letter I have come. I have come to ask a question.'

His face fell. 'A question? You do not wish to give dictation?'

I felt a pang then, a sharp jab of sympathy for this old man with his failing sight for whom a piece of work could mean so much. I moved closer and lowered myself to the floor across the table from him so that he could better see my face.

'I have no need of your writing skills today, master,' I told him. 'I come to ask your help in a different way. I have travelled many miles to see you. A merchant named Leah Bathsheba sends you honour.'

He nodded, and grew calmer. 'Leah the Jewess? Yes, I know her, although it is many months since she was here. But my memory is good. Far better than my eyes. For what reason did she speak of me?'

'She spoke of you because she knows my son is lost. He sailed abroad some years ago and has never returned. She knew something that she thought might help me. She told me of a certain ring, a ring of unusual design. She told me you would know more about what its pattern signifies.'

He nodded again as he listened to my words, but this time he did not smile.

'Ah, yes. That ring. That is what I spoke about with Leah.' He paused, his weak eyes drifting past me to a point elsewhere. 'The white and the black. The eternal struggle.' When his eyes returned to mine, they were full of an old man's tears.

'Leah told me that ring was worn by a Christian lord,' I told him, 'a man who travelled with my son. It is a fragile hope, but by learning more of him I hope to learn more of my missing child.'

He nodded but his eyes were still looking past me and I wasn't sure how much he'd heard. Then he looked at me again.

'These are painful things you ask me to recall. I'm not sure I have the heart to speak of them.'

I remained silent then and waited while the old man gathered himself. Eventually he spoke again.

'I cannot say for certain what that particular ring was meant to mean. But I have seen one like it. When I overheard the Jewess describing it one day in the bazaar, I could not help but speak. The ring that I saw was given to a young general. I was there when he first started wearing it.'

The letter-writer paused there for a long time, his eyes downcast. But then he lifted them to mine and they seemed to see me clearly.

'You have heard of the Cathars?'

That question again. The one asked by the Catalan, Raymond of Nava, when he came to me in my rooms that starry night; the same one asked by Quintus Fabius, the Pope's man, when his visit followed Raymond's.

'Yes, I have heard much of them recently. Heretics, I'm told.'

The old man's face clouded. 'They were a people who worshipped God in their own way. Remember, sir, I am not of your faith.'

'My apologies. I know nothing of the Cathars.'

Ichabod seemed to consider before replying. 'True enlightenment is not mine to give. But I might perhaps tell what I have witnessed, things that will not sit well with the teachings of your church.' He made a vague gesture with his hand. 'Sir, please be comfortable. I have no refreshment to offer you, but only a few steps away there are stalls and a tavern. I could fetch you wine, or food perhaps. You say you have journeyed far to be here.'

'Please, master. I am impatient to hear what you would tell me. Let me send my own attendant . . .'

I signalled to my guide, a compassionate man of quick understanding. When he returned I was pleased to see that he had bought food and drink to feed the old man for a week or more. But our host scarcely noticed his return. For by then he was speaking of another time, a time when he was a priest of the Holy Church and when Christ's armies were besieging Montségur.

A time when he stood beside Count Decius.

I listened to him in silence, scarce able to imagine the things he told me.

ζ

An Envoy

It had been Antioch's good fortune to arrive in Lin'an in the spring, at a time when the Emperor's affairs seemed to be prospering. By summer, things had changed.

First there was news from the north, brought to his daily council by his councillor-in-chief, Jao Sidao, who had served as first minister since the start of his reign. The Emperor did not much like Jao but he trusted him implicitly. Jao had grown old supporting the cause of the Emperor's family. He would almost certainly die in its service. But now he brought bad news. An enemy force under the Tartar general Bayan had crossed the border and had routed an imperial army sent against it. Having achieved their victory, Jao told him, the Tartars had retreated to their former lines, taking with them everything they had been able to seize or steal.

'A foray, then?' the Emperor asked. 'A raid to test our strength?'

Jao nodded.

'And who was responsible for this defeat?'

The old minister licked his lips, which to his great concern were permanently dry, despite the daily application of rose oil. 'General Wen led our army, my lord. He fell in the action and did not survive. They say he was hacked to pieces where he lay.'

'He was in luck. I would not have shown him such a merciful death. Who else?'

'The young man Song Rui took over the command. I'm told he rallied the infantry to stand again and the next enemy charge was broken. Then he fell back in good order to the line of the river north of the town.'

'But a retreat, nonetheless,' the Emperor snorted. He was angry that such news should spoil his day. He had planned to spend the afternoon in the company of a courtesan from the Dali coast, a woman reputed to have several unique and remarkable accomplishments. But now his mood was spoiled and he knew he would get no pleasure from her. And when his comfort was disturbed, he liked someone to answer for it.

'They say Song Rui prevented a rout, my lord,' Jao told him softly. He liked the boy and, besides, the supply of competent generals was beginning to run low.

'On whose authority did he fall back?' the Emperor went on. 'Am I now to praise my generals for their efficiency in running away?'

At this point the other man in the room coughed discreetly. Qin Gui, the Emperor's spymaster, was an unattractive man, unusually small and rather sickly looking, yet said to be the possessor of unusual and energetic sexual appetites, an aspect of his character that rather intrigued the Emperor, who frequently wondered if the rumours were true.

'My lord,' Qin began, 'I have had word from an agent in the enemy camp who tells me that the Tartar general had every hope of a crushing victory before Song Rui's intervention. Now he is cursing most heartily that the old fool Wen did not live long enough to oversee a complete disaster.'

The Emperor considered for a moment. 'So Song Rui lives. I'm glad, I confess, because I'm quite fond of the young man. To have him killed would pain me. But he must be taught a lesson. I want him stripped of his command and brought back here.'

'My lord . . .' Councillor Jao fidgeted and licked his lips anxiously. 'We must not weaken our position in that region . . .'

'I know, I know!' The Emperor waved the objection away. 'Never fear, we shall restore him in due course. But it will do him good to kick his heels here for a little as a reminder that he is not invulnerable.' He turned to his spymaster. 'What else do you have for me?'

'Nothing in the south or from the mountains, my lord. All seems quiet.' He paused. He was a man of sallow complexion with eyes that shifted around the gazes of others. 'In the west, they say Lord Rustum intends to take a wife. The daughter of a chieftain of one of the border tribes.'

'A wife? Without my blessing?' The Emperor was outraged.

'He travels to Lin'an as we speak, my lord, to pay his annual tribute. No doubt he will raise the matter then. He will be here within a fortnight.'

'I see.' The Emperor's eyes narrowed. 'Then I have time to consider my response. Are we done here? Jao, you will see that the necessary orders are given to the armies in the north?'

The councillor bowed. 'Yes, my lord. One other matter, my lord. The foreigners. Are we to keep them much longer? The old man drives our scholars to distraction with endless talk of birds and beasts. The soldier Decius sits and broods and lets it be known he is a fighting man, impatient to see service. The others grow fat, and the half-caste visits brothels.'

But the Emperor seemed cheered by this. 'A barbarian in my service? Why not? We could create a battalion of bears and unleash them on the Tartars! I shall consider it. As for the rest, it is time they were gone. Make preparations to return them to Zaiton. Tell them they are to be gone within twenty days.' He rearranged himself on his seat and a look of almost wolfish satisfaction settled on his features.

'Now, I have changed my plans for this afternoon. I will not see the courtesan. Instead I think it would be appropriate if that young woman of Song Rui's were sent up to me. I think he has a debt to pay.'

Lin'an, it seemed, was not the city she had dreamed of. On every day of her journey she had felt hope growing inside her. Surely any place, however good, however bad, would be preferable to married servitude and a life lived in subjugation? She had not dreamed of comfort or ease. In fact she had welcomed the thought of hardship, if that were the price to pay for having the freedom to dream.

But on finally reaching the Imperial City, all that hope seemed to drain from her. The fresh mountain wind and the scent of the pines were gone. The music of the harnesses, even her awareness of the barbarians on the road behind them – all came to an end. But nothing took their place. She waited and nothing happened.

It hadn't seemed that way on her very first night in the Imperial City, when she had been told the Emperor wished to see her. She had often imagined her first audience at the Imperial Court – the great audience chamber; the figure of the Emperor high on his throne, the brightness of his robes almost dazzling; the ranks of courtiers standing deep around the walls of the room as she entered and made her obeisance. In all her imaginings she had seen Song Rui beside her, making the presentation. She had felt his great energy lifting her, his freedom of spirit carrying her through. She had felt the promise of his love.

But instead she had been shown into a small room hung in red silk, without furniture of any kind. A door had opened and a short man, enormously fat, had entered. There was no retinue. He was accompanied only by a much smaller companion whose eyes never met hers but flicked slyly all over her body. Confused, she had not known to kneel until the small man commanded it. No sooner had her forehead touched the floor than the Emperor himself had ordered her to rise, had told her to position herself in the light so he might see her better. Then he had inspected her, walking around her in smaller and smaller circles until she was certain he was going to touch her, and all she could think of was how to fight the revulsion, the horror that rose in her at the thought of his fingers on her skin.

But he did not touch her, not that day. And he did not speak again. His inspection over, he swallowed noisily then left the room. His sallow companion followed him out, pausing only for a last glance down the length of her body.

After that she and her maid were shown to the Garden House, one of the many summer houses that stood in the palace grounds along the curve of the lake. The lavish goods and gifts that her father had assembled in Zaiton did not accompany them. She never saw those again. That night the two women huddled close together, daunted by the silence that fell upon the lake by night.

And that was how it continued. The Garden House had once been the summer quarters of a famous courtesan and there was nothing mean in its proportions or appointments. But it was a secluded place, surrounded by its own exquisite gardens and enclosed by a high wall. Ming Yueh was made to understand that it would be improper for her to venture beyond this without the specific permission of the Emperor.

Yet for all her isolation, she was well looked after. Every morning an army of servants from the palace would descend upon her residence to bathe and dress her, and to try what they could to bring her appearance into line with the latest court fashions. Lavish meals were prepared for her and nothing she needed for her comfort was ever refused. Her maid, Shu-chen, would come and go on her behalf, bustling between the Garden House and the palace or running errands in the markets of Lin'an.

It was through Shu-chen that she made herself known to the Zaiton women living in Lin'an. In the course of her journey, the maid had become as expert as her mistress in reading the script and committing it to memory, and when necessary was able to copy messages quickly and reliably. She had soon located the Women's Wall and brought back reports of any new messages that appeared there – the details of births or betrothals, pleas for deliverance from poverty or illness, news of deaths. In return Ming Yueh wrote messages of her own, telling her story and describing her plight, her love for Song Rui, her loneliness, her hopes for his return. The replies that followed were formal and very circumspect. They made her understand that her grand circumstances set her aside from the other women. She could sense their nervousness.

And then the Emperor called for her a second time, the day he'd heard of Song Rui's defeat in the north. After that she wrote no more messages. The palace servants barely saw her. Something that had made her bright was gone from her. For the first time in her life she was afraid.

Only Venn noticed. The women she wrote to were busy with their own lives. Visitors to Lin'an came and went, they knew, and a woman who resided in the Imperial Palace was unlikely to be a regular correspondent. They continued their lives without thinking of her.

But Venn noticed. His study of the script was going well. By studying the messages he had found the keys he needed, and where there were no clues he fell back upon his own peculiar gift, that special intuition for language which was never to desert him. Sounds, symbols, meanings . . . The mist began to clear and he went to the market square each day in the hope of new scripts to puzzle over. To avoid being seen in the act of copying he would memorise portions of new messages and carry them home with him. There he committed them to paper, and as his hand formed the characters their meanings began to appear to him, fresh, shining, as if newly minted. The act of writing seemed to summon them.

He had never before felt such excitement in a new language, for never before had a language felt so new. Yet for all his sense of wonder, he could not help but be affected by the meanings he was uncovering.

Every language, Venn knew, had its own heartland, the place where it had first grown up and where the true purpose of its eloquence still lay. He also knew that the less widespread a language, the closer it remained to that original purpose. He had travelled in the remote mountains of Ethiopia, where villagers who had no words for money could describe with the most perfect precision the tracks made by animals in the dust. The hunters of the Persian marshes could, in two or three syllables, convey the different patterns made by flights of birds during the great spring migrations.

But never had he found a language such as this, a language that seemed to exist only to express immeasurable sadness. As he read he found himself in a world that echoed with longing, where the words for love and pain were hard to tell apart, where loss and regret filled the air like sad music on a still morning. And through it all there was dignity and restraint. No ranting, no despair. Venn read and as his understanding grew, he began to glimpse something of the suffering the writers shared, something of their mute, enduring patience.

Among such writing, the letter which appeared a few days later took him by surprise. It was quite unlike the rest. The writing was so full of a special zest for living that he could not help but be gripped by it. It was a simple narrative, told crisply, with clear dates and names and places. And within only a few lines of its beginning, Venn had guessed the identity of its writer.

He had thought of her more than once since arriving in Lin'an. He'd been told she was to marry a great lord, and often when a richly hung litter passed through the crowds he'd pause to watch, wondering if it might contain his mystery scribe. But he reasoned that she was probably far from the city by now, living on the estate of a wealthy man, or spending her days in the pleasure gardens on the far shore of the lake. It hadn't occurred to him until that day that she too might be staying in the palace grounds, nor had he ever thought that her journey, like his own, was not yet at an end. But now everything about her journey was laid before him and he was touched by what he read. There was an innocence in it that moved him and, stronger still, courage and determination that lit up her writing.

Intrigued, he took to walking in the direction of the Garden House. There was a terrace near it which had a view of its gardens and from there he would sometimes see her, a tiny figure at a distance, walking with her maid. Sometimes, when he walked close to the high wall that surrounded her garden, he would hear her voice.

When her messages stopped, he waited, expecting them to begin again. When they did not, he took to walking by the lake more often. He noticed that he no longer saw her walking in the garden. This change worried him. Something must have happened, he thought. But he was not able to walk that way as often as he wished, for the date of Decius's next assignation was approaching and there were things to be done to prepare for it.

Venn had not intended to tell the boy about the message he had carried to Decius. He sensed there was danger for them all in the count's hidden plans and his instinct was to shield the boy as much as he could so that he might be spared the Emperor's wrath if Decius fell from grace. But it was not a hope he placed great reliance on. The Emperor, he knew, did not see the party of barbarians as individuals, and for that reason the fate of Decius would be the fate of them all. And if Venn wanted to make sure that Decius's meeting on the night of the full moon went undetected, he knew they would need someone to keep watch.

Other than the boy there was no one they could trust.

At the end of the month, when the moon was no more than a whisper of silver in the sky, Decius called Venn to his quarters. In the long green room hung with silk, where the painted birds sang in the painted blossoms, the two men stood together and spoke again in the rough patois of the Sicilian west.

'Tomorrow night,' Decius stated baldly, 'wait till an hour after the guard changes. We'll meet by the shore in the place I've shown you. Go carefully, interpreter.'

Venn nodded and prepared to leave, but the general stopped him. 'One thing more. About our friend Yang. He has it in his head that I carry with me some form of treasure.'

The two men did not need to exchange glances to understand each other. 'You surprise me,' Venn replied dryly. 'What of it?'

'Yesterday these rooms were searched.'

Venn looked around him at the immaculate order which prevailed and Decius shook his head. 'No, not in a way you would notice. It was nicely done. Nothing displaced by even a fraction of an inch.'

'Then how can you tell?' Venn asked, and Decius smiled.

'I know exactly how the patterns of dust lie in this room. If they stir, I notice. Believe me, they were here. But they found nothing. There is nothing here to find.'

Venn shrugged. 'I realise that. I was with you, remember, that day you rode off alone into the woods. So why do you tell me this?'

'Because I want you to know that our friend Yang is a danger. And I want you to understand . . .' For the first time in their acquaintance Venn saw the general struggle, unsure of his words, but in an instant he was composed again. 'It's no matter. We'll meet again tomorrow, by the lake. Bring the boy. And do not fail me.'

They did not fail him. They met him in the shadow of the trees where the pleasure grounds reached the lake. It was a precarious position. One movement out of place, one stumble, one alert pair of eyes looking out from the palace's dark windows . . . Venn knew their lives swayed uneasily in the balance. But the weather favoured them: a starless night, thick cloud, no dew to betray them. The lake lay black and still, so lacking in any feature or reflection that it might have been a void at their feet. The boy found himself hoping for a wind to ruffle its surface, something to make it show itself, to prove it was still there.

They had been careful to rehearse their way to the boathouse many times by daylight, when a stroll through the woods along the shore was no more than an innocent diversion. But in the darkness they found the landscape changed. Night altered the contours, stretched distances. As they moved through the trees the boy began to grow uncertain, convinced they had missed their way. But Decius led on without hesitation and the sound of him ahead was reassuring. Perhaps he has the eyes of a cat, the boy thought. Perhaps those eyes of his allow him to see in the dark.

The boathouse lay beneath low-hanging willows on a small hidden inlet. A remote place. They were already close to it before Decius signalled them to halt.

'I shall go ahead,' he whispered. 'When you hear me knock twice, join me. If I do not knock before you count to twenty, make haste and go back the way you came.'

He didn't wait for a response. The boy watched him go and counted. On the count of twelve they heard him knock.

There was no light showing in the boathouse, but two people waited there. The boy's eyes had grown accustomed to the darkness but he could make out little more than the black outlines of their figures. From Decius's familiar greeting he understood that one was the messenger he had seen before, that night on the road. The other was a stranger. The boy waited until Venn and Decius were seated before taking up his position outside the boathouse door. From there, in that night's seamless silence, he could still make out the murmur of Venn's voice, and when he heard the stranger introduced, his eyes opened wide.

'Count Decius,' Venn began, translating words spoken by the messenger, 'this is the Lord Tendiz, cousin of the Great Khan himself and his deputy in the southern provinces. He is here today as the Khan's personal ambassador.' Then, with a smile in his voice: 'He bids you welcome to his palace.'

Hushed exchanges followed and conversation turned swiftly to the ruby Decius had sent him. On this subject, the Lord Tendiz had many questions. Where did you get such a gem? How did you come by it? Are such stones so common in your land that you can cast them aside so lightly?

'Tell him it is but one example of the riches of Christendom, a tiny sample of the wealth that his great lord might obtain.'

'How do we know there are more such stones like that one? A single shoe does not prove a horse.'

'Those were but two of a hundred I carry with me. Each one is of a rarity and brilliance that even the Khan himself will never have seen the like. And this collection is his if he pledges to take the steps we ask. I will give you directions to where it is hidden. Remember it is but a small down-payment on the treasures that await him.' Decius paused to let Venn finish his translating. 'But these are just words,' he went on. 'As token of their truth, take this.'

A pause followed and a taper was lit, the messenger shading it carefully between his hands so that the light did not spill too far. A silence had fallen and when Tendiz spoke, his voice seemed hushed in awe.

'What is this?' he asked.

'The finest pearl you have ever seen.'

Even without translation, the boy could hear a note of wistful amazement in Tendiz's reply.

'I have heard of such pearls as this but I did not believe the stories. How came you by it?'

In contrast, Decius's voice was calm and measured. 'Such is the wealth of the Christian lands that such things are not rare to us. This one reached the coffers of a society of men entrusted with great wealth who, in turn, entrusted it to me. And now I have found a use for it. Let the Great Khan see it and know what wealth awaits him in the west.'

'So now we come to it,' the Tartar lord mused. 'Explain again your purpose in coming here with these promises and these tales.'

There was a pause before Decius replied and in that brief interval the boy felt a shiver run through him, as though somehow the silence itself was sinister with meaning.

'The request is simple. I wish to travel to the court of the Great Khan and beg his aid. The lands of Christendom lie divided. The men who rule there are petty tyrants, cowards who rule by murder and assassination. Above them all is the Pope, and the grasping bishops who do his bidding. I come to beg for a fire to purify what is foul and corrupt. If the Great Khan would unleash his might upon the Christian states they will fall to him in days, as once they began to fall to his grandfather. My master seeks only this: that the power and authority of the Pope and all he stands for is dismantled forever.'

'And how will your master benefit by this?' Tendiz asked.

When Decius replied his voice was flat.

'My master will gain nothing. He asks this knowing he will never live to see the day. Nor will his sons, nor any of those he loves. And yet it is his will. When I have the Great Khan's pledge, I will lead you to the gems I carry with me. But you must remember, what I give him now is nothing to the wealth you shall discover in your conquest of Christendom. A dozen kingdoms will be his, their stores to plunder, their leaders to enslave. Let him turn aside from this kingdom of Lin'an. Let him direct his armies to a greater prize and one more easily won.'

'And your master would call this fire down on his own people? His fellow believers?'

Decius didn't waver for an instant.

'My master is decided. If your lord carries away the last copper coin and leaves the fields a desert in his wake, it will be a blessing on the generations who follow, for there can be no hope for the future unless the land is scourged of the evil that reigns there now.'

And although those words themselves made the boy shudder, their real horror lay in the icy certainty with which they were spoken.

The rest of the evening seemed to the boy to pass in a haze. He was aware of Decius still negotiating, insisting on a sign from the Great Khan to prove he had the will and wherewithal to deliver what Decius asked. In reply Tendiz told him there was a fortress near Shanjan held by the Emperor's army. He mentioned to Decius a day and a time and told him to wait until then for the sign he sought. Of what else passed, the boy remembered little, and he remembered still less of his return to the palace. He knew Venn had stayed with him until he reached Antioch's chamber, but he couldn't remember if they had spoken at all about what they'd heard, or if they had, what they'd said about it. On reaching his bed he fell almost immediately into a restless, troubled sleep.

The next day, Song Rui returned to Lin'an.

ζ

'I have not always been as I am now,' the old man began.

The room in which we sat was dark, but as the letter-writer told his story, what little light there was fell on his face and reminded me of the stained-glass patterns I'd seen in great cathedrals. If there was an angel in him, that light found it out. And now that he had decided to speak, he needed little prompting.

'I was born on the coast of Normandy. My father was clerk to the lord of that region, a position of great privilege. My brother was to follow him but I was bound for a place in the Church. It was a great honour for which my father paid in gold.

'Think of it, a boy of seven and the world already closed to me by divine prohibition. Any urge I had that was like the urges of others was a double sin, for I was God's child, and I would do his bidding or surrender my immortal soul.

'I cannot say what effect such a childhood had on me, for I have known no other. Indeed I was scarce aware of being a child at all. I only know that by the time of my manhood I was an ordained priest and assistant to the chaplain of a French count. I think by then I was already different from

185

others of my calling, for my mind asked questions. Yes, questions of men, but worse than that, questions of God. And when, much later, I was taken to join the crusade against the Cathars, I found the questions in my mind grew louder. But however loud they were, it appeared God could not answer them.

'The Cathars, sir, believe our world is a battleground where God and the Devil compete for mastery. Worldly things, they say, are the creation of the Devil, and so to achieve a perfect grace they must renounce them all. That way they seek to live a life that's perfect in its godliness. I did not know this then, of course. I only knew that they were heretics, doomed to eternal damnation if they were not made to recant. We were told many things of them: that they worshipped Satan, that fornication and sodomy were virtues in their eyes, that they gave their daughters to be violated by their fellows. To save their souls we had to bring them to repent.

'Perhaps I believed that once, but it was not long after reaching the Cathar lands that a secret part of me had begun to doubt. Soon after I arrived, there was brought to me a woman, a baker's widow, who had been renounced by her neighbours as a believer of the heresy. She did not deny it and her fate was clear. She was to be burned the next day if she would not first recant her beliefs. I spent that night in the cellar where they'd thrown her, using every argument I'd ever discovered to bring her to the light. She was a simple woman of no learning. All she could reply to me was that our

Lord had worn no golden robes. She could not believe that he would have clad his bishops in such riches.

'I explained she must recant. I described to her the torments of the fire. I told her how the hair burns first, how loud the screams become when the flame begins to lick against a heretic's skin. I asked her if any teaching was worth such mortal agony. She looked me in the eye. *All my life,* she said, *I've lived humbly in this place. Your fire will only take me to a better one.'*

The old man paused there and looked around as if remembering my presence.

'A better place,' he said again. 'Look.' He pointed to his open doorway. 'There are no burnings here. And this place is not the only one. Egypt, Syria, Persia. Yes, in these places people starve and steal and suffer, but they do not burn.'

The old man's head began to nod and he seemed to fall into a reverie. My interpreter, back with us now, met my eye and stretched to shake him, but I waved him back and waited while the moments passed.

'What happened next?' I asked eventually. And slowly, bit by bit, he told me.

'I watched her burn,' he said. 'She didn't scream or beg for mercy. But the stench of her burnt flesh lodged in my nostrils. Of course it was not just her. That smell was one we lived with day by day. Many years passed before I could wake without feeling it still clinging to my skin. But with time the horror began to pall. The routine of daily arraignments, daily executions, became so wearying that the Siege of

Montségur came as a relief. This at last was proper battle, with an armed foe arrayed against us and acts of valour in the field that would blow away from us the poisonous air we breathed.

'Montségur was the last Cathar stronghold and as such could not be allowed to stand. It was a fortress built at the summit of a huge, rocky outcrop, defended on all sides by cliffs and steep ravines. To storm it seemed impossible and so an army under the Archbishop of Narbonne settled at its base and laid a siege.

'The garrison opposing us was led by Roger of Mirepoix, a lord of that land who offered sanctuary to all people regardless of their belief. No one in that region had forgotten the siege of Beziers, where the entire population was butchered, heretics and believers alike. Since then the people there have learned that a wall between them and the Pope's armies is a desirable thing, and that the mercy of the crusader is not a rock on which to build high hopes.

'This Roger was said to be a Catholic by faith and yet I came to think that he was in truth a believer of the heresy because of his stout defence of the heretics within his walls. I'd seen him once, some years before, and his ring that day had caught my eye. It was unusual in design. Later, one of the heretics told me that the black and white are a reminder of the good and evil at work within the world.'

I interrupted him then, eager to make sure I understood. 'So the ring that Leah described to me was a Cathar ring?'

The old man pursed his lips. 'I cannot say that. I can only say I saw a similar ring worn by one of the defenders of Montségur.'

'Then there is no mystery here. We know Count Decius fought the Cathars. The ring was probably seized as plunder.'

Ichabod the letter-writer looked up at me.

'Count Decius did not deal in plunder.'

His certainty astonished me. 'You knew the count yourself? Or had you merely observed him from a distance?'

He met my eye and his gaze was steady. 'I knew him well. Perhaps better than anyone. Of course, everyone on that campaign knew who he was. He stood apart from the rest, in every sense. But I knew him, sir, and he was the only leader of that whole campaign for whom I felt the smallest seed of respect.'

I raised an eyebrow then. 'And yet he was ruthless, was he not? They say he showed no mercy to the heretics.'

The letter-writer's lips pursed in distaste and his manner grew suddenly formal.

'Perhaps, sir, you do not trust an old man's memory? I tell you, Decius was a man I could respect. I don't know who has been speaking of him to you, but I was there. I knew him. And I give you my word, he was not the man you say.'

I do not know what I expected to learn in Granada, but it was not this. This was the opposite of what I'd been led to believe. Even years ago, at the time of Antioch's mission, Decius's reputation was well established: unsmiling, cold, a harsh disciplinarian and feared by everyone. I wondered for a moment if perhaps the letter-writer was a fool, with a memory as uncertain as his eyesight. But before I could consider that, he carried on.

'Remember,' he said, 'I was not a young man at the Siege of Montségur. I say that so you know that I was not easily impressed. I encountered a great many Christian lords in the years before I burned my habit and became a fugitive from the Church. By the time of the Siege of Montségur, I had come to feel disgust for everything my masters stood for. But not for Decius. He was different.

'He was still a young man then, perhaps ten years my junior, but his youth was scarcely noticed for he was a dour and forbidding individual. He seemed to have had no child-hood. In the same way I had been made a priest, he had been made a soldier: he had been commanding men at the age of fourteen. His reputation around the camp was fearsome. Other officers were wary of him and his men stood out from the rest. He allowed no indiscipline. He expected orders to be obeyed. When one of his men was discovered looting a Cathar farm, he had him flogged in front of his fellows.'

'So that is how he won your respect?' I asked. 'By making sure his troops observed proper discipline?'

'Far from it,' the former priest insisted. 'That was only one face of Decius. Eventually I saw another.'

Outside his shadowy room, people were busy living their ordinary lives. This was the hour when the men of the town would gather at tables in the shade of orange trees and let the heat of the day slip past them. Somewhere nearby a mule brayed as a boy berated it. I could almost smell the heat on the street outside. But in the old man's presence, these things faded. He had taken me back to a darker time and place. He spoke of mud and fear and fever, of lives squandered and innocence lost. Beneath the precipice of a great fortress, an army wallowed in its own filth. He watched men die the most mundane and pointless deaths: an ostler from the kick of a horse, a blacksmith from a graze that turned to gangrene. A young boy teased by his elders was found hanging in the woods. Disease was rife. Young men with no training and no sense of what they fought for were cut down in fruitless sorties beneath unbreachable walls.

And in revenge for these miseries, and to keep their own soldiers from mutiny, the leaders of that Christian army sent patrols around the countryside to rape and steal at will. A good general knows that whatever befalls them, his troops must be entertained.

In the midst of all this, the priest found Decius. At first he assumed the soldier with the freakish eyes was the same as all the others. When he was summoned to Decius's presence one day, he thought it would concern some trifling matter of the count's welfare. The officer who came for him was on horseback and brought with him a spare horse.

'The commander begs you to come in haste,' he said. 'He is not far from here.'

'On what business does he require me?' the priest dared to ask.

'I cannot say. Only that he begs you make haste.'

They rode from the camp without acknowledging the sentries, the soldier dragging the priest's mount behind his own. After a short ride they came to a farmhouse. It was one the priest knew for he had passed it many times.

'In here,' the soldier pointed. 'Quickly.'

Inside the priest found a scene of destruction. The furniture of the room had been overturned and broken, and from somewhere out of sight he could hear a woman weeping. Following the noise, he found an old man on a low bed, the sheet that covered him stained with blood. Next to him, the man's wife was sobbing. Behind her, most memorable because it was most remarkable, stood Count Decius.

He looked neither at the woman nor at her husband, but shifted awkwardly, clearly uncomfortable, his eyes on the floor. He looked up when the priest entered.

'Quickly,' he said, using the same word as his soldier. 'Hear his confession. It is what he most desires.'

He left them then, and the priest spent an hour by that bed, comforting the farmer until his hour came, then offering words of consolation to his wife. When at length he emerged, he found Decius gone but the same soldier waiting for him.

'The commander orders you to attend him tomorrow,' he said, and then, as he helped the priest onto his horse, he added: 'Until you speak to him, do not speak to others of what has passed here.'

The priest's interview with Decius the following day was short. He found the commander in his tent. When the priest entered, Decius dismissed his attendants and spoke to him alone.

'I wish to explain to you what you saw last night,' he began. 'Of course, your job as a priest is to do as you did, without questions, without explanations. But you might wish to be cautious in speaking of your night's work. I tell you this partly for your sake, and partly because the reputation of my men is important to me. I wish to make it clear that what you found last night was not their work.'

Again, the priest said nothing and the commander looked at him with those strange, intent eyes.

'By sending for you last night, I disobeyed an implicit command. You assisted me in doing it. I do not seek your complicity in this, you understand. I am not afraid to state plainly what I did and to face the consequences. You must act as your conscience dictates. But as some blame might be attached to you, I feel it only right that I explain.'

The priest listened as Decius described to him how his troop had come across the raided farmhouse. They had heard the woman's cries and found the husband bleeding to death by his own hearth.

'This farmer had assisted us when the siege was first laid,' Decius explained. 'He sold us meat and grain, and then, when food became scarcer, he had been forced to sell us the remainder of his livestock, and then his stores of seed corn. Without these he would have nothing to start again with, for the archbishop's gold will not run far here, where every animal is already sold or stolen and where a single fowl sells for what was once the price of a charger. But he had no choice but to sell to the archbishop's men, holding back only the very barest of supplies to feed him and his wife. Yesterday the archbishop's men came for those. The old man refused to yield them up and when he resisted, they ran him through. By his resistance, they argued, he revealed himself an enemy of Christ and a supporter of the heretics. They left him to die without absolution, for how could he be absolved until he had admitted and recanted his heresy?'

Decius turned his dark eyes full on the priest. 'So, by sending for you I was defying the archbishop's judgement. Worse than that, by my actions I was showing I did not believe the man was a heretic. And if he was not that, then his death was an act of murder.'

At that the priest nodded. 'Yes, I understand. It is no light thing to defy the archbishop. However, your concern is unnecessary, I assure you. The night was dark. I chanced upon a dying man, I cannot remember where. By tomorrow I will have forgotten him. In this place I see many dying men.' He paused. 'But there is one thing I do *not* understand.'

The count appeared cautious. 'And that is . . . ?'

'Why you went to such trouble. Were you so concerned for his mortal soul?'

Decius shrugged. 'Armies are built on discipline and order. There are rules. Sometimes the rules are harsh but we must enforce each one, for if one is flouted how does a soldier know which others are to be obeyed? So yesterday there were acts of theft and murder committed in breach of military orders. It is important that my men see these are not condoned and that the army has a duty to make good any damage done by its men. I was able to offer his widow gold but what value was that to the old man? He begged for a priest. And so I sent for you.'

'I see,' the priest replied. 'And tell me, Commander, these armies, with their rules and their discipline, what purpose do they serve?'

The count looked up at him sharply, as if for the first time seeing the man within the priestly habit.

'That is not a question I advise you to ask too widely,' he returned. 'This is a time when a wise man doesn't ask questions. But since you ask, let me tell you something. I was trained as a soldier from the moment I could walk. They taught me everything except why. And that, priest, is a question every soldier must answer for himself.'

ζ

Song Rui

Word of Song Rui's imminent return reached the Garden House early in the day, while a white mist still lay on the waters of the lake. Shu-chen brought the news, running breathlessly from the palace, shouting it out almost before she reached the door. He would be there that night, the palace gossip said, or at the very latest the following day. Either way, she complained, it wasn't much time for them to prepare. Did people think that a lady's wardrobe planned itself?

Ming Yueh listened to her outrage and smiled, but try as she might she could not hide her suffering. She had yearned for his return through so many days and nights but now the prospect of it filled her with anguish. She had such things to tell him . . . She wasn't even sure what words to use, though since her second audience with the Emperor she had thought about little else. But at least the waiting was over. He would be by her side, and she would no longer be alone. If anyone could soothe her, he could. That in itself was a consolation.

By dusk he had not come, and she paced her terrace in frustration, refusing to retire, refusing to allow the lamps to be dimmed for fear he would not find her. And then, towards midnight, they heard hooves and shouting, calls for lights, the cries of ostlers. She knew it was him.

She stopped pacing then. She wanted him to find her calm and ready to receive him. She remembered how he had found her that day on the road from Zaiton. She would be like that. She would find that innocence again, and that certainty. She would hold him without words. The morning would be for talking.

But he did not come. Not that night, nor the following morning. With each hour that passed she felt something dying inside her, but whether it was hope, or pride, or simply the memory of the feelings she had felt during their night together, she wasn't sure. Whatever it was, she knew its passing left her empty, like the hollow dolls her father had once brought her. They had been poor things, those dolls. She remembered how easily they had broken.

By midnight there was still no word from him, no sign that he remembered her. She cried then, for the first time since she'd met him. But only a few tears which she quickly choked back, resolving that the following day she would send Shu-chen to him with a message. He would come then. Surely he would come then.

*　　*　　*

As a blood relation of the Emperor, Song Rui had attained high rank at a young age. However, he knew in his heart that no appointment he'd ever received had been undeserved, and his career had certainly been a brilliant one, a series of successes both on the field of battle and off it. He was not yet thirty. Until the most recent action his star had only risen. He had no experience at all of dealing with reverses.

And now his world had collapsed around him. Everything was lost – his position, his honour, his pride and his reputation. To be relieved of his command in front of his men, to be brought back to Lin'an under guard – the humiliation still burned in his cheeks. How could he ever lead those men again? How could he expect them ever again to rally at his command? He was shamed forever, a laughing stock.

And the injustice! That was perhaps what burned most deeply and most painfully within him. The Emperor's order to recall him had left him astounded. He had expected praise and honour, not disgrace. Had he not saved the day? Had he not turned back the last charge of the Tartar cavalry? And done it with beaten men, too, foot soldiers who only moments before had been in disarray. He would tell the Emperor that, and more. He would show him that he still had pride *and* honour.

In the midst of such turmoil, he could think only of how to retrieve what was lost. He didn't think of Ming Yueh at all.

The Emperor had known his young general would be angry and he was enjoying the prospect. For two days after Song Rui's return, the Emperor refused him audience. When eventually the young man was summoned, it was not for a private meeting with the Emperor but to a full imperial council, to answer charges of cowardice and disloyalty.

However, two days of waiting, two days of being treated as a man disgraced, had affected Song Rui in the way the Emperor had anticipated. Out on the frontier, with the enemy pressing him, with his men looking to him for leadership, it was easy to forget that the rules in Lin'an were different. But back in the palace the courtier in him gradually resumed control and he thought carefully for the first time about how much trouble he was in. The alternatives were stark. He might still win back the Emperor's favour, in which case he could hope someday to be restored to his position. Or he might lose it forever, and with it everything that he most desired. He had known the Emperor for too long to expect logic. He had watched generals executed for losing battles in which the odds against them had been overwhelming from the start.

Strangely, the prospect of death unnerved him less than the thought of disgrace. He was too young to understand its meaning. But the thought that his days might ebb away in exile filled him with despair, and worse even than that was a prospect he dared not contemplate. He knew of men – young men like himself – who had lingered fifteen years or more in chains in the Emperor's gaols, knowing each day that they would never again feel daylight on their skins.

So his performance before the Emperor was a great deal more circumspect than it might have been. He explained his actions clearly, gave reasons for his decisions and begged the pardon of the court for leaving the field with his life. He humbled himself and promised to give his life in the Emperor's cause if only they would allow him back. It did not come easily. There were times in his performance when he wished in all earnestness that he really had died on the field of battle.

Then, to his immense frustration, he was told that he must wait for a decision. The Emperor, speaking to him directly for the first time, ordered him back to his quarters and told him he would learn his fate within seven days. And, after all that, when he returned to his rooms with his pride bruised and his self-respect in tatters, he found Ming Yueh's message waiting for him.

He did not visit the Garden House until the following day. He went reluctantly, reflecting that it was only honourable to wait on her but knowing that in truth he wished her gone. The Song Rui who approached her door that day was very different from the one she had first met, more different still from the one who had taken her in his arms that dizzy morning on the road from Zaiton. The act of begging for his future in front of men he despised had affected him deeply. That day he had tasted his first defeat. He had been brought down, humbled. The taste of it was still bitter in his mouth. He did not think he would ever be free of it.

In such a mood, the days when he first courted Ming Yueh seemed a distant memory, an irrelevance in a tale that ended in tragedy. Even the visit to her carriage seemed the act of a different man – a happier man who had since been vanquished forever. He had summoned her to Lin'an on a whim because she was brave and determined and, in her own way, beautiful. The thought of showing her the things she had dreamed of seeing made him feel pleasantly benevolent. He couldn't deny that he had looked forward to making her his mistress, that even during his last campaign he had thought often of their night together, the way she had given herself to him. The thought aroused him and he had looked forward to more.

But now he wanted her gone. She reminded him too much of that other life, that time when there was nothing he could not do and could not be. The promises he'd made then were now beyond his power. He was not the omnipotent, dashing young man she thought him. He was no more than the Emperor's lackey. In time she would hear how he had begged for his life.

No, before that happened he would send her back to Zaiton. She would be none the worse for her journey to the capital and no doubt a husband could still be found for her, some callow merchant's son who knew his place. The arousal he had felt for her once was gone completely. He wanted to be alone, or back with his men, rebuilding the reputation that had once been his. He had no room for her in this new future of his.

She hated him that day. She had never felt the deep, hot, twisting blade of hatred before. She had never felt anything even approaching it. But that day in the Garden House as he stood before her, cold, head bowed, explaining to her how his circumstances were altered, *then* she hated him.

Their meeting didn't last long. He greeted her with a formal bow and told her that she must go, that he would make arrangements, that the situation in Lin'an was such that it was impossible for her to remain. He explained that his standing in the Emperor's eyes was much diminished, hinted that perhaps, should his fortunes ever recover, then the two of them might meet again. She did not speak. He gave her no opportunity.

Instead she heard him out in silence. Only when he had finished, when he stood waiting for his release, did her anger break through.

'This is it? This is all you have to say to me?'

She had been standing by the long window that faced out onto the lake and the length of the room was between them. But now she advanced on him, her eyes hard, her faced raised to his. She stopped only when they were a pace apart.

'Is it?' she repeated.

The force of the question made him take a step back. He'd expected tears or pleading, possibly even a pouting, kittenish dismay, all to be followed by the inevitable, disheartening haggling over the practicalities. What would people say? How would she travel? What would she tell her father? Instead this fierce passion astonished him and he hesitated.

'There is nothing else to say,' he told her. Then, suddenly indignant, he flared up at her. 'I'm telling you, I'm ruined. Tomorrow I might be in chains. I might be dead. Don't you understand?'

She laughed then, full in his face, her eyes never leaving his. Then she turned her back on him and returned to the window.

'I understand,' she said. 'Yes, I understand.'

She said nothing more, and he waited, confused.

'So you will go?' he asked at last.

'I cannot go!' She turned and spat the words at him, the contempt in her voice so raw he felt it sting. 'Can't you see? Don't you realise? Have you no idea how these things are done?'

He looked back at her, uncomprehending. His lips were parted as if to speak but he had no idea what she meant or how to reply.

'The Emperor came to me while you were away. To punish you. Do you understand?'

In his confusion Song Rui did not. He merely shook his head, trying to take in the implications. 'What happened? Did he speak of me?'

There was no mistaking the disdain in her face then: she had to turn away to steady herself. Out on the lake in front of her a tiny boat with an orange sail was the only object disturbing the blue. Where its prow broke the water, the light sparkled. When she shut her eyes the image remained clear behind her eyelids. She paused before opening them, waiting for her breathing to steady.

'He told me your future was in my hands. That if he found me . . . agreeable . . . then it was in my power to return you to your fortunes.' She laughed again, a bitter laugh that her father in Zaiton would never have recognised. 'Oh, never fear, you will be back with your soldiers in no time. The Emperor has given his word. You see, I *was* agreeable. Very agreeable. But I am no longer yours to dispose of. I cannot go home just because you bid it.'

'I will go back to my men? He told you that?'

That was the moment when she hated him most. She wanted to walk forward and strike him across the face, to scream her pain at him so loudly it would pierce his soul. But before she could do either, the hatred began to drain away so suddenly that it left nothing behind but contempt. She watched him move away from her, to the side of the house, still working out what meaning the Emperor's words had for him.

'So,' he said, without looking up. 'So that is to be my punishment. It is like him. It is his way of asserting his power. He uses you to show me that nothing is mine. Only what he lets me have. And now he's made his point he will be content. I am doubly humbled in the eyes of the court. But he knows it is not in his interest to keep me from the front for long . . .' He looked up. 'But what of you? He plans to keep you here? To be chosen by the Emperor is a great honour . . .'

To her astonishment, she found herself studying his face as if for the first time. It was not a cruel face. His callousness, she knew, was unintentional, for all that it sliced a jagged blade through her soul. But there was nothing in that face – nothing – that spoke to her of remorse or compassion, no glimmer of understanding; not even the beginning of a realisation of how she suffered.

'The Emperor has other plans for me,' she told him, her voice cold. 'You are not the only one at court he wishes to punish through me. I am to be married to the Lord Rustum at the Emperor's command. They say he is a proud man as well as a cruel one. The Emperor considers it a great joke that Rustum should be married to a merchant's daughter who has already been his plaything.' She paused and swallowed hard. 'I knelt at his feet. I told him I would do whatever he asked of me. I thought of you and I was agreeable to everything.'

He stepped forward to comfort her then but she wouldn't let him. She shrank away from him and ordered him to go. She would not look at him, would not reply to his questions. He lingered for as long as he felt able, aware now that he had been remiss in not thinking of her. He was honest enough to feel guilt when someone suffered for his actions and there, in her presence, he now felt it most acutely.

But when eventually he yielded to her demands to leave, he couldn't help but feel a lightness in his step. Whenever he thought of her he would feel guilty, he told himself. It would be a great fault if he did not. But he was a young man with a talent for putting aside things that troubled him, especially things he was powerless to alter. And in the coming months he would be busy. After all, he had an army to rebuild, an empire to defend. Urgent matters were afoot and he must get back to work as soon as he was allowed. And when he thought of her the following day it seemed more and more clear to him that her position was not disastrous. He knew a little of Lord Rustum's reputation but he was, after all, one of the great lords of the kingdom and no merchant's daughter would ever dream of such a match as that. Better surely than a life of subservience to some bloodless merchant's son who would beat her regularly to prove to her that he could. Yes, he thought, he was sorry she had suffered on his account, but no one could tell him that it might not have turned out worse.

She watched him go and felt again that emptiness inside her, as if the rich soil which had once nourished so many dreams was now cracked, brown earth. When she looked out at the lake, the orange sail was still there, brilliant against the blue. She thought of the place she was to be sent: a place of dust and unfeeling winds, with a lord famous for his cruelty. Then she cried again, alone, facing the lake. Not for Song Rui this time, but for herself.

Compromise

Five days after Decius's secret meeting, the sign promised by Tendiz was delivered. Word reached Lin'an that a certain fortress near Shanjan had been attacked by the Tartar armies and had fallen within hours. The speed of the move had taken the defenders by surprise, the garrison had been caught off guard and the bastion had been overwhelmed, its defenders massacred. On hearing the news Venn went straight to Decius. There was a look on his face as he burst into the green silk-hung room that Decius had not seen before.

'So you have your proof,' he began without preamble, making no attempt to keep his voice low or to adopt the Sicilian patois. Decius, looking up in surprise, realised that the interpreter was truly angry.

'They say the Tartars killed them all,' Venn went on. 'Not just the soldiers, even the peasants who'd taken shelter there. Children. Families. All to prove to you that the Khan is powerful and without mercy. Are you pleased with your work here?'

Decius looked at him. 'The attack was coming anyway. You heard him tell us that.'

'And you are still prepared to unleash this savagery on your own lands?' Venn's voice was raised, the first time Decius had ever heard it so. 'For pity's sake, Count, this isn't like Manfred's treaty with the Moors. They were honourable men who would agree terms and stick to them. But this is a fire you cannot control. Once it takes hold it will devour everything. Manfred and his family too. No one will be spared!'

Venn knew his anger was showing but he didn't care. He had travelled in lands where the Tartars had once been, where even two generations later the fields were unsown for want of labour to till them. He remembered the silence of the empty landscape and the abandoned homesteads that punctuated it, their walls still black from the burning.

Decius looked at him and shrugged. 'Manfred must take his chance. It is the only one he has.'

Venn shook his head. 'That can't be true. Go back. Use the treasure you speak of to raise an army in Europe.'

'That cannot be.' Decius rose to face him. 'Where else can I find a power great enough to destroy a pope? To destroy all he stands for. And I don't just mean this pope, Venn. After him there would be others. The corruption has taken too deep a hold.' He shook his head. 'No, Manfred's plan is to destroy it all, forever. To break the papacy, to tear apart the Holy Church so it can never be rebuilt. That is what I am sent to seek,

Venn. Not just an army of mercenaries to ride with Manfred.'

Venn looked at him, his anger beginning to cool into disbelief.

'That's insane. It will never be.'

'Why not, Venn? You think God will not allow it? Perhaps you think the great stinking beast we call the Church has his special protection? Like it did in Egypt and in Syria? They were Christian lands once, remember. You think the Church in Rome is so different? You think it is loved by all those it keeps in poverty and ignorance? You think all those it suppresses will rise up in its defence?'

Both men were standing now, facing each other. Venn wondered that he had ever thought Decius's eyes incapable of emotion. At that moment they were blazing with a strange, dark fire.

'But a Tartar invasion . . . So much innocent blood . . .' Venn murmured. 'A man must hate in the very depth of his soul to think like that.'

'I have every reason to hate.'

'And Manfred? He really wants this?'

Decius's eyes moved to the green silk hangings. 'Not at first. For many years Manfred sought only to live in peace and watch his children grow. He has three young sons, you know. He thought if he could end the wars he might live to see them grow into men. But would they give him even that? Never, for Sicily is not his, it is the Pope's. His estates are not his, they are the Pope's. Everything is the Pope's. All right, all justice. Anything that can be sold is in his gift. And it comes down to this: Manfred's father was the Pope's enemy, so Manfred must die, his sons must die. For vengeance is everything. Who cares at what cost?'

Decius shook his head and Venn followed his gaze to the silk paintings that surrounded him. It seemed an irony that Decius's rooms were so exquisite. It was as though the two men stood in a glade of impossible beauty, where every bough bore perfect blossom. An Eden before the fall, where birds of every colour came to sing.

'If I could give my life to save Manfred's I would do it,' Decius went on softly. 'There was a time when I was alive, Venn. Alive like other men. But no longer. Something inside me died. When that happened, Manfred took me in. I wanted my life to end, but I saw in him something good. I saw his love for his wife and sons. So I carried on for his sake.

'And now he's doomed, Venn. He knew that when he sent me here. Charles of Anjou was arming against him. And after Charles would come another, then another. However many victories fell to him, he knew it was a war he could not win.'

Decius shook his head again, his eyes still on the birds in the blossom.

'Most likely he will be dead by now, for he dare not be taken alive. Either way, he will never see his sons grow to be men.'

A long silence followed, neither man stirring, neither looking at the other, until finally Venn spoke.

'And you are determined to do this for him?'

Decius looked back, the fire dying from his eyes. 'I have no other purpose left to me. Nothing else for me to do.'

'I cannot be a part of it,' Venn said.

'Very well.' Decius nodded. 'You have your conscience. But I will go ahead regardless.'

'And how will you negotiate without me to translate your words?'

Decius smiled then, but his eyes were blank once more. 'I will find a way. Besides, the seed is planted in the Great Khan's brain. He has the ruby and the pearl already. When he sees the rest of the treasure he will be beside himself with lust for more.'

'What if I go to the Emperor today and tell him you are plotting with his enemies? You'd never meet the Khan, never get to show Tendiz where to find the other gems.'

Decius nodded. 'Yes, I have thought of that. I'm not proud of my answer.'

'Which is?'

'Anything you say against me will implicate Antioch and the boy.' He paused to study Venn's reaction before he carried on. 'We are all of the same party. You really believe the Emperor will make a distinction? To him we are all dispensable.'

Venn felt the blow thud into his stomach. He couldn't deny its truth.

'Or you can wait, Venn. I have told the Emperor's counsellors that I wish to fight for him against the Tartars. They say the Emperor approves of the idea. When I get the chance, I will slip over the border to the Khan's people. I will make it seem I've been lost in action. No one here will be any the wiser. And the Emperor will have no objection to the rest of you heading home in safety.' Decius paused. 'It's up to you, Venn. You choose.'

Song Rui left Lin'an the following day, with orders to win back his honour through brave deeds. Ming Yueh received the news in silence and showed neither sorrow nor self-pity, leaving it to her maid, Shu-chen, to lament their plight alone.

When the dust of his departure had settled outside the palace gates, two strangers presented themselves at the Garden House. They were accompanied by an officer of the Emperor's personal guard. The interview – if it could be called that – was not a pleasant one. The two men said nothing to her but spoke between themselves in a language she didn't understand, while the guard barked orders at her according to their signals. She was made to kneel while they inspected her, circling around her until one stopped and grasped her face between his fingers and forced her to look up at him. His was a hard, unfeeling gaze and she read in it nothing but contempt for what he saw. Then he pushed her face away so that she lost her balance and fell to the ground. He turned and walked away without a word. Thus was she introduced to the man she was to marry.

But the incident barely seemed to ruffle her. She was not afraid, for nothing could be worse than what had already befallen her. And besides, she had a plan: she would return to Zaiton. She would escape the court and go home, and there she would say to her father all those things she had never said to him. This time she would find the words. Then, whatever punishment awaited her, she would not care. Nothing could be worse than the fate currently planned.

The next day Shu-chen was sent with a letter for the Women's Wall. In it Ming Yueh described the events that had befallen her and begged for help. Did anyone know of a caravan returning to Zaiton? Would anyone help her make her escape? She told them all she knew about the character and reputation of Rustum and she threw herself upon their mercy.

Venn saw the message only a few hours after it was posted. By then the morning haze on the lake had succumbed to the blazing insistence of the afternoon and Venn found the market square nearly empty, the business of the day completed in the first, fresh hours after dawn. Against the older, sun-faded messages, her letter stood out.

Although his dealings with Decius had left him much to think about, its contents shocked him and stirred him in a way he hadn't expected. There was something in the way it was written that reminded him of those other letters, the ones that spoke of abandoned hopes and dreams. Her letters had never been like that. But now she seemed resigned. She would risk everything to see her father once more and after that she would surrender to the death that awaited her.

All through the rest of that day he was unable to put the letter out of his mind. He returned to the Women's Wall later to read it again, trying to find in it some spark of the determination he had always found in her writing. But the more he read, the clearer it became that she had no thought of permanent escape. Her flight to Zaiton would be her last act of defiance. After that she would let the Emperor's justice take its course.

And that was something Venn could not contemplate. He knew more than he wished about the Emperor's fondness for devising new punishments. Looking out over the shimmering innocence of the lake, his mind would fill with images of horror, of calculated torments visited upon the captured fugitive.

Then he would think again of how he had first seen her – that slim silhouette against the lamplight, the studious figure bent over her writing. Most of all he would think of the joy that had shone through her messages like the energy of a stream in full spate. She had not witnessed as he had the true ugliness of physical pain, had not heard for herself the sort of cries that come with unrelenting agony.

Perhaps it was a reaction against Decius's plans that moved him. Or perhaps something in the new script he was learning had affected him in a way he couldn't explain. But that night he took clean paper and started to write.

The message astonished her. She found it early in the morning near the wooden veranda of the Garden House, carefully scrolled and attached by a white ribbon to a stone. She looked around, half expecting to see some sign of the person who had thrown it. But there was no one.

It was written in the secret script she knew so well, in a careful, competent hand that seemed to tiptoe down the page with exaggerated care. The execution of the script was good, she thought. Yet something in the writing was strange. At first she thought it clumsy, but as she read the message over again she decided it was simply different, the same tools she used but employed in a peculiar way. The result was a message that was somehow unvarnished, lacking finish to such a degree that it seemed almost brusque.

The message itself was a short one. The writer had seen Ming Yueh's words and urged her to reconsider. The wrath of the Emperor was certain death. She must find another way. She must think of a place where she would be safe, where loved ones could hide her. Only when she had a safe place to hide should she dare to run.

Her reply was even shorter. There was no such place. Her father was a merchant. He could do nothing against the might of the Emperor. He could not hide her. All she asked was to go to him one last time, or failing that to reach him with a message containing the words she had never thought to use. She did not want to die, she said. But she was to begin her journey to Rustum's court in three weeks' time, and any death was preferable to that.

Shu-chen pasted this message on the Women's Wall that evening. Next morning another stone lay by her door, with another message attached. This one was even more brusque than its predecessor.

'*This evening when the moon moves above the mountains go to the east wall of your garden where the willows cast a shadow. I shall be waiting beyond the wall. We shall speak then. Trust me. I can see a better way.*'

That morning, an hour after Ming Yueh found the note, Venn returned to Decius's apartments, where the general sat amidst his silken birds and watched the lake. The two men spoke for an hour, during which time Venn's hand stayed clenched throughout. Afterwards, when he returned to his room, the interpreter found his fingers were still pressed deep into his palm. This was unknown territory. And he had no one to translate for him.

The night was an airless one. Summer had turned its hot breath upon Lin'an, blighting its days and nights alike. So there was no relief for Ming Yueh when she stepped out into the darkness, only hot stones beneath her feet and the fragrance of white jasmine, heavy as the night itself.

But there was something in the peace of the lakeside gardens that promised ease. It was a peace woven from the tiny noises of the night — invisible insects, trees sighing, ripples on the sleeping lake. It was a noise that existed only when the palace slept: no people, no pain, just the soft, forgiving whisper that falls on human ears as silence.

She easily found the place by the wall where the willows hung their heads together, conspiring to create a perfect darkness beneath their boughs. There she stopped and listened, afraid of being observed, but also excited, for there was something in the air that spoke to her of hope — a faint, stirring scent of freedom.

And then she heard a movement beyond the wall and she knew she was not alone.

Speak first, she thought, for if it was a trap and she spoke first, she knew she would be lost.

On the other side of the wall, Venn heard her approach. He also hesitated before he spoke, afraid she might take fright and run when she heard the voice of a man. He wasn't even fully certain what had brought him there, nor what had moved him to seek out Decius that afternoon. He only knew her letters had spoken to him and he couldn't ignore her plight. When he finally broke the silence, his words were cautious.

'Your long life,' he began, using the greeting that was common in the marketplace. 'We have spoken before.'

The words rang through the night much louder than he'd intended. He could almost hear her flinch at their report.

'Who is that?' There was alarm in her voice, a blend of panic and bewilderment.

'My name is Venn. We spoke once in the woods on the road from Zaiton.'

He spoke the local language so well that she struggled to place him, imagining a servant from the palace or perhaps even a guard. Then, with a shock, she remembered the barbarian.

'You!' she gasped. 'Why are you here? You must go! Someone else is meeting me. You will scare her away.'

'I'm here to speak to you. That note you received . . .'

'You know of it? How is that?'

He paused then answered gently, 'I wrote it.'

The silence that followed seemed to last so long he was sure the moon had inched higher over the mountains before she spoke again. Her reply when it came was almost whispered.

'How?' she asked.

'I saw the letters on the wall. I studied them. It is a skill I have. Learning to read and write the language of others . . .'

On the other side of the wall she nodded, remembering the slight mistakes, the unusual phrasing.

'So you know everything,' she said. 'Everything about me. Everything that has been done to me. You read all that.'

He didn't reply but his silence was an answer.

'I was a fool,' she went on, as if the empty night was drawing the words out of her. 'I wanted to believe in him. I had no other hope.' And then, forgetting everything else, she found herself talking without reserve, pouring everything she had contained within her into the welcoming darkness. Whether the words were meant for him or for herself, or for the black sky above, she didn't care. All that mattered was to deliver herself of her inner anguish, to give it shape and form, and to find in words a conveyance to carry it away. So she talked, and her words floated out over the lake like fading lanterns until they disappeared into the darkness and were gone.

When she had finished, she waited. His reply came to her as if it were part of the intoxicating fragrance of that stifling night.

'It is arranged,' he said. 'Go meekly to Lord Rustum when you are told to. I and my companion will travel with you. Between us we will find a way.'

ζ

I had travelled to Granada in search of my son, but instead I found something of the man he travelled with.

What had I ever known of my son's companions? Antioch was a scholar – a good man, I believed. Of Count Decius I knew only that he was a hard man and a soldier. Of the army captain Pau, I knew nothing. And the rest were nameless, the simple soldiers whose stories were as lost as my child's.

Ichabod the letter-writer, one-time priest, fugitive, convert to an alien religion, changed much of that. That day in Granada on the street of the writers, he showed me the man Decius as few perhaps had ever seen him. Perhaps no one now remembers him as well as this old man with failing eyes, who holds loneliness at bay with the tales he tells to strangers.

That day in Granada his tale defied the long heat of the afternoon.

After their first meeting, the priest saw a great deal more of Decius. It was as if each had glimpsed in the other some grain of understanding that was missing in their fellows. They were not friends, the old man assured me, for Decius was not a man with friends. But there grew a mutual trust, and it was through this trust that the priest learned about Decius.

'Remember,' the old man told me, 'Decius was not a religious man. The detail of the heresy was not of interest to him. But he found those Cathars he had dealings with to be straight-dealing, honest people who did not attempt to cower or ingratiate. I tell you, these were qualities that appealed to the commander.

'And I could sense there was something else about him. It wasn't obvious. But at times I'd come across him with his eyes fixed on the horizon and a look on his face I couldn't fathom. In the end, I think I found out what it was. You see, just before he came to Montségur, Decius had acquired a wife.

'Yes, I see the surprise on your face. People used to speak of him as a man apart, a man without human feelings. Yet I believe he felt more fiercely for his bride, his Messalina, than he had ever felt about anyone or anything.

'He spoke of her to me one night, very late, the night the fortress surrendered. For some weeks before then, the fate of the castle had been certain, ever since our troops had surprised the defenders and grabbed a foothold on the ridge. With that the hopes of the inhabitants were ended, and they knew it. From that point on, small groups of frightened people began to leave the place, trying to creep out under the hood of darkness.

'Rumour has a way of penetrating the thickest walls. Somehow the defenders had heard that the commander of a certain section of the line was more forgiving than the rest. Soon Decius's men were discovering two or three parties each night attempting to cross their lines. Where other leaders set upon such groups with glee, greedy for plunder, the fugitives found that Decius's men were strangely inattentive in their watch. Groups passed unnoticed. For troops so thoroughly drilled, they seemed oddly prone to drowsing at their posts. With each night that passed, the number fleeing through Decius's lines grew, and as if in thanks they began to leave gifts and tokens as they passed: a pile of gold coins at the foot of a tree, a silver goblet under brambles.

'It's my belief that the ring which Leah Bathsheba speaks of was one such gift, something sent to Decius himself. And be in no doubt that he was in direct communication with the defenders, for I saw it myself. One night near the end he sent for me, you see. When I got there, he dismissed his guards and bade me follow him into the forest. It was a strange journey, I tell you, blundering from tree to tree in the darkness. He did not speak, and I knew him better than to ask questions. But he knew his way and walked quickly, while I tripped and stumbled behind him, staining my hands and knees with that heavy, sodden earth.

'We had walked many minutes through the forest, slightly uphill, towards the rock of Montségur, when we reached a place where a man was waiting for us with a small bundle by his side. The man was no more than middle years, I'll tell you that, but his cheeks were hollow and his eyes so tired that he looked much older. His chin was stubbled and he wore the clothes of a steward, ragged as if from many months of wear.

'He looked up when he saw us coming, but he didn't speak until Decius commanded.

'*Here is the priest,* Decius said. *Tell him what you have told me.*

'The man bowed slightly and turned to me. I remember thinking how his life was in our hands.

'*My name is Peter of Girona,* he said. *I have been sent by the defenders of Montségur to find the Count Decius. It is no secret that the castle must fall and many of us will die. Even if we are offered terms, the people of the castle will not trust them. They remember other towns, other times. Besides, there are some who would choose to burn rather than recant.*

'He paused there and picked up the bundle at his feet.

'*I have here the child of two such believers. They have vowed to die with the perfect, with the true believers, and they have trusted their son to me. But we all know that at Beziers not even the children were spared. So I have been sent to Count Decius to beg him to take the child and find him safety.*

'A silence followed then, until I saw the commander had turned his eyes to me.

'*What say you, priest? If you were to take horse this very hour and ride through the night, is there a monastery you could find that would take the boy and raise him? I can send enough gold to make them willing. You must be gone no more than a week. Your absence must not be noticed.*

'*Sir*, I told him, *there is a monastery near Pau where I might take him. It is an austere place, but it is more forgiving than the fire.*

'The count looked at the man with the bundle, who nodded. *Very well then*, Decius concluded. *Now go, Peter of Girona. And should anyone ever question it, tell them from me that you are a brave man.*'

The old letter-writer broke off there. The effort of telling so long a tale was tiring him, and the things he spoke of were painful to recall. When he did continue, his eyes were very distant.

'It was all so long ago, sir. But I tell you it is as clear to me today as if I lived it yesterday. At Decius's bidding I took the child and travelled to the monastery I had spoken of. In the confusion of those days, my absence went unmarked. When I returned I went straight to the commander.

'*Why?* I asked him, just like that, with no apology and no ceremony. *I have travelled for twenty hours a day asking myself that question. You cannot tell me this is about pre-serving your precious military discipline.*

'His eyes avoided mine then. *The Cathars were prepared to pay*, he said.

'I sat down opposite him then without waiting for permission. Perhaps I alone in that army camp would have dared to do it.

'*I don't believe you. You're not after money.*

'I looked into his eyes and he looked away.

226

'*You and I should not be here,* I told him. *Both of us know this slaughter is senseless. We must leave it behind and find what we believe in.*

'At that, he smiled. It was a most unusual thing for Decius.

'*I have found that, priest,* he said. *She waits for me in Sicily.*

'To say I was astonished is an understatement, I tell you. I had never thought of Decius as a man who felt affections. Certainly he was not the man to talk of them. But that night was a strange one. In my absence the defenders of the fortress had accepted terms. Those who would swear their allegiance to the Church would be allowed to leave with their lives, but nothing else. The rest would burn. There was a two-week truce agreed while the ultimatum was met.

'I don't know why he spoke to me of his wife and the story of their courtship. Perhaps because he would soon be with her. Or perhaps he wanted me to know he had found his answer. Or perhaps it was simply the hour of the night when we cleave most closely to the ones we love.

'A few days later he left Montségur. I never saw him again.'

ζ

The Road West

It was all agreed, and the Emperor was pleased. When the barbarians were told they were to be sent out of the country, the old scholar had caused a fuss saying his mission was not complete. The old man could have been whipped for such insolence, but because the Emperor found him amusing, and because he was a little superstitious about these ghostly foreigners, he had promised the scholar a fast ship back to the Indies with a purse of gold in his hand. He found his own generosity pleasing, and he enjoyed the idea that tales of his munificence would be carried to the other end of the world. Anyway, it seemed the old man was appeased by the promise.

And then, a few days later, the fiercest of the barbarians – the one with strange eyes – had approached the Emperor's counsellors with a renewed request for favour. He was a fighting man, he said, and a safe passage home had no appeal for him. He longed to use his sword again, to see action once more in the service of a great lord. He had heard that a small troop of soldiers was being assembled to escort a caravan westwards – through deserts and mountains, to the far corner of the Emperor's domain. The talk was of brigands and the danger of sorties by the Khan's men. The barbarian said he had a great longing to see these wild places and to face such dangers. He wanted to feel the heat of battle once more and to laugh in the faces of any who took arms against him. Send the boy and the old man on their way by all means, but let him see some action in the borderlands with a strong arm and a fearless heart.

This offer delighted the Emperor, who was much taken by the idea of setting barbarians against barbarians, and was confident that this bloodthirsty giant would cause consternation if unleashed upon the Tartars. The plan to send him with the expedition to Rustum's court was a good one too. It would do Rustum good to see the sort of men the Emperor had in his service . . . And after all, what harm could one barbarian do? There had been a rumour that this one carried treasure with him, but his rooms and belongings had been repeatedly searched and nothing had been found. Yang the half-caste, who had laid the information, had been given a whipping for his pains. So let him go, and let him take the interpreter. If they did well, so much the better. If not, if they caused trouble of any sort, they would be easily dispatched and their remains left by the roadside as a warning to others.

If Decius had been surprised when Venn approached him, he didn't show it. The interpreter's offer had been simple. The general would persuade the Emperor's advisors to let them travel west with Ming Yueh and, in return, once he was sure Antioch and the boy were safe, Venn would give him all the help he required in making contact with the Great Khan.

Decius had merely raised one eyebrow very deliberately.

'What, Venn? A compromise? You will risk the whole of Christendom for the safety of an old man, a young woman and a small boy?'

And then before Venn could reply, he had smiled.

'Don't look so pained, Venn. I don't condemn you. No, I smile for another reason altogether.' He paused and shook his head. 'You see, I have always thought there was something missing in you, Venn. And perhaps there is. But today you've chosen the harder of two roads. I wish you luck with it.'

Venn looked at him, uncertain what he meant, but Decius simply turned away in dismissal.

To the boy, the news that they were to be sent away from Lin'an and out of the Emperor's lands came as the most profound relief. His fear of Decius – and his fear that the general's fanaticism would bring doom upon them all – had begun to affect him. His sleep was broken by dark dreams of chaos. He saw his father's house in flames, the great cathedral of Lincoln sinking into ashes. Fire burst from the ground and consumed everything above it.

But now, it seemed, they were to be sent home under the Emperor's particular protection. The safe passage he promised them in a ship of his own navy would take them as far as the Indies, where it was an easy thing to find passage to Basrah. From there it seemed but a short step back to Antioch's villa in the Sicilian hills, where the thick heat would be weighing down the afternoons. Only a short step more would take him to the steep hill where his father lived. What a stir his return would cause, what excitement among those who waited for him! Sometimes he could imagine the feeling of his father's proud arms already around him.

But then he learned that Venn and Decius were not coming with him. He knew at once that this was not a whim on Venn's part. He could see that the interpreter was trying to protect him and Antioch from Decius's conspiracy by putting as much distance as possible between him and them. But even so, the prospect appalled him.

'Why, Venn?' he asked. 'Why cannot I come with you?'

It was a conversation Venn had dreaded. He could see the disappointment in the boy's face and hear the pain in his voice.

'You've heard Decius say he's bound for the Great Khan's court,' he explained, trying to sound cheerful, reassuring. 'Now he's looking for a way to slip across the border and that puts us all at risk. We were lucky the other night by the lake, but we cannot be lucky every time. And if Decius is caught, anyone still here will share his fate.'

'But why must *you* go away?'

Venn crouched down on his haunches so that his face was lower than the boy's. 'There is a caravan heading west – a long way west. It travels close to the Khan's borders. Decius and I will travel with it. When we are sure that you and Antioch are safely at sea, we will slip away over the border to make contact with the Great Khan. If we fail, you will come to no harm. If we succeed, I shall keep my promises to Decius and then head homewards too.' He smiled and placed his hand on the boy's shoulder. 'Who knows? Perhaps I shall reach Damascus before you. Perhaps you'll find me waiting there with a tale to tell and a drink to treat you with.'

But the boy had turned away from him and would not meet his eye. Venn could feel all the pain of betrayal in that small, rigid frame.

'There is something else, Benedict,' he said, more softly still. 'Something I must do. Something I cannot walk away from. Were it not for this thing, I swear I would not leave you. I would find another way.'

'What thing is this?' The boy did not turn to ask the question.

'I cannot tell you yet. For your own safety, I must not.' He smiled a quick, quizzical smile that seemed to tell of his own bemusement. 'In truth I cannot explain it even to myself. But if I do not try this thing, I don't think I can ever be at peace.'

And then, because he saw the boy was thawing, because he wished to lessen his pain and restore his pride, he carried on. 'And you, Benedict, you must stand by Antioch and keep him safe, and bring him home to Sicily for me.'

They were easy words to speak, simple commonplaces that were almost without meaning except as a charm to reassure. But the boy heard them differently and looked grave.

'Yes, Venn,' he replied. 'I will do that.'

When words are your daily currency, it can be easy to forget their power.

They spoke only once more before Venn left Lin'an. That was the following day, when word reached them that the expedition to Rustum's court was to leave at once. Amid the haste of preparation, Venn heard a timid knock at the doorway of his room. Looking up, he saw the boy watching him with such misery in his face that he stopped what he was doing and drew him inside.

'What is it, Benedict? No parting should be this sorrowful.'

The boy shook his head. 'No, it's something else. I've been meaning to speak of it for so long. Something I forgot. Months and months ago, back in Genoa. It's this.'

Venn looked down and saw that the boy was clutching something in his fist. When the pale fingers opened, they revealed an old coin of a sort he recognised.

'The harbour-master at Genoa gave it to me to give to you. But I forgot, and then I was embarrassed to admit my fault. And then after a while it seemed it wasn't important anyway, so I just put it to one side. But you should have it before you go, in case . . . In case we don't meet again.'

Venn put his arm around the boy's shoulder and drew him closer. 'Let's have a look, shall we?' Holding the coin up he saw at once the marks the harbour-master had made and smiled to recognise a code he had almost forgotten. Five stars of diminishing size, the middle one ringed, the next smallest marked with a cross.

The boy seemed to take some comfort from that smile. 'What is it, Venn?' he asked. 'Is it important?'

The interpreter shook his head. 'No, Benedict. It's nothing. Just a warning that we travel in dangerous company. But we have learned that for ourselves, have we not?'

*   *   *

They left Lin'an at dawn. Ming Yueh and Shu-chen travelled in the same wagon as before, but this time with none of the trappings or courtesies that had attended them previously. There was no baggage train, no dowry, just a dozen soldiers under a hard-faced sergeant from the western mountains who made it clear he had no interest in her or her comfort other than to see her delivered safely to her destination. Gone too was the courtly etiquette that had forbidden Ming Yueh to show her face. She was no longer a person of status travelling under imperial protection. It didn't matter that these rough guards could look upon her openly. It was the Emperor's way of showing she was of no value.

But it meant she was free to ride with Shu-chen at the front of the wagon and to speak and be seen as she chose, and after her seclusion in Lin'an this felt to her like a wonderful freedom. At camp her food was brought to her but in all other things – washing clothes, keeping clean – she and her maid were left to fend for themselves. This too was a relief, despite the hardship. She was happy to be treated as a nobody. It was how she wanted to be. She wanted to be forgotten, anonymous, no longer a piece in a game being played out by others. And having reconciled herself fully and completely to the prospect of her own death, she found an unexpected pleasure in watching the changing vistas and feeling the wind against her face again.

This surprised her. She had not been afraid to end her life, back there in Lin'an. She had been ready to join any caravan that would take her, and to run until she was hunted down. And if she had been dragged from it before she even left the city walls, if she had been executed there and then, in the dirt at the road-side, she would have felt her escape was complete. She had nothing better to hope for.

But her meeting with Venn had stirred something inside her. Perhaps it was his certainty, or the simpli-city of his words, or perhaps it was simply that the night they met was the sort of night that made one wish to be alive. She had returned to the Garden House still heady with the heavy scents of the garden. What did it matter, she thought, if she did as he said? She had the power to end her own suffering whenever she wished. But she did not want to die in Lin'an, within the Emperor's walls. No, she would undertake one more journey. She would feel bare earth beneath her feet once more. She would be guided by the hulking creature who ran his finger along his eyebrow when he was thoughtful, and who spoke to her so naturally out of the lips of a barbarian.

And he was as good as his word. When her guards first gathered in the half-light, he and his companion were with them at the palace gates, and when the column rolled out across the grand bridge into the city, they were still there, at the rear, riding easily as if comfortable in the saddle. The dark-eyed man showed no sign of seeing her, but the interpreter would acknowledge her glance with a short, purposeful nod of his head.

Venn and Decius also found it good to be on the road, riding the bright highways and shaking the dust of Lin'an from their feet. This journey was very different to the one which had gone before – no tents, no cooks and no supplies. They slept wrapped in their blankets and had to forage for their food alongside their new companions. The sergeant in charge of the escort was a man named Shuran who came from the furthest western margin of the Emperor's domain and who was used to fighting alongside men of many different sorts, from the sturdy hill men of Tibet to the slim, moustachioed Saracens of the Kabul plains. He and his men judged Decius as they would any soldier, and were content with what they saw. The two westerners were strong and did not tire easily. On foraging sorties, they played their part. It was enough.

At first Venn took great pains to avoid Ming Yueh. She would watch him going about the business of the day, riding the flanks, sometimes scouting ahead, translating for Decius when Shuran gave commands. Through it all he gave no sign to the others that they'd ever spoken and she began to enjoy his reticence. The sense of a shared secret eased the discomforts of a jolting road, and his occasional nod of greeting was met with a smile.

Venn rode each day with a growing lightness inside him. The meaning of their presence together on that wild road did not concern him. He simply felt the easing of a tightness, like the unclenching of a fist, and he welcomed it without question.

And it *was* a wild road, or it soon became one. A road very different from the meadows and the pine-crested mountains they had travelled through before. After Lin'an the way remained broad and busy for a week or more, an artery running through the farms and the orchards of the hinterland, spreading the city's wealth. It drew great crowds of traffic, from the litters of nobles to the crowds of barefoot pedlars heading to the city with baskets on their backs. After a few days more they came to a great river and crossed it, a river so wide it seemed more like a sea, where the wind made the surface choppy and their little boats had to dodge the deep-hulled ships plying east and west with heavy cargoes.

After that crossing they left the great highway behind them. At first they rode through further orchards, but gradually the landscape grew barer. This was the old western road, neglected for many decades, now sometimes chosen to avoid Tartar sorties from the north. It joined eventually with an old camel road, skirting the dusty plains, picking its way through the lower reaches of mountains where villagers cut narrow terraces to grow their crops. Further still and the terraces were left behind. This was goatherd country, sparse, brown, scented with mountain thyme, where the only trees were the clusters of holm oaks and the low jacinta bushes which gathered around water. It was a road of dust and hard, hot stone where the heat was dry and unforgiving. But the streams ran cold and spoke of high mountains ahead.

To Venn, this landscape was beautiful. It reminded him of the high uplands of al-Andalus or the rocky peninsulas of the Peloponnese, and with every day that Lin'an grew more distant he began to feel the air fresher on his face. Only at night, when he lay wrapped in his blanket looking out into the darkness, did he think of the boy, remembering the times they had sat together late at night. But he was counting the days in his head: so many days from Lin'an back to the mountains, so many days to Sha-fen, so many days till the boy and Antioch would be in Zaiton again. Then perhaps a week for a ship to be readied. In another month or so the boy and Antioch would be at sea once again, and on their journey home.

Ming Yueh wasn't sure how it happened, but even early in their journey it seemed to be understood that the two barbarians took special responsibility for her and her maid. Shuran's men had little interest in her.

They came from a warrior tribe where women did not expect consideration and were not shown it. But if the two foreigners were prepared to indulge the women, so be it. If they were willing to ride out with them in search of bathing pools at the hottest part of the day, when sane men rested, it was no concern of the others. The soiled discards of the Emperor inspired in Shuran's men only contempt, especially so when they were also the daughters of bloodless east-coast merchants.

At first Ming Yueh didn't know what to make of Venn's companion, a man whose eyes frightened her and whose lips rarely smiled. He seldom spoke, not even to Venn, and showed little sign of ever noticing her. But she saw that when Venn rode close to her, alongside the wagon, Decius did not accompany him; and when someone was needed to escort her while she looked for a hidden place to bathe, the general's eyes always turned to Venn.

And so Ming Yueh and Venn were effectively left alone for long parts of the afternoon, while somewhere below them Shu-chen fussed over her laundry and Decius waited in the shade. They were together in a landscape scented with thyme, where the bushes cast welcome shadows over the mountain pools. In such a place the realities of Lin'an – its fear and suspicion and thinly disguised cruelties – seemed to fall away from them like discarded skins, leaving them in a place untroubled by others, where the peace of the afternoon was theirs alone. They would wake each morning content at the thought of the day that lay ahead of them.

What madness was it that made her feel this way? She could not tell and did not try. Song Rui was not forgotten but now the thought of him brought no pain, only the residual ache of a deep and never to be quite forgotten wound. When she thought of him now she felt ashamed at the way she'd been so quick to trust him with the burden of her dreams. He had been no more than a bright, shining star above the desert, and she had yearned for him as a lonely traveller yearns for home. Even that night on the road when he had come to her wagon, when it felt for a precious moment that all happiness was hers – even that night was now no more to her than a bruise on her heart, tender when pressed, but fading, a little less painful with every day that passed.

She had not forgotten the Emperor either. That night when he summoned her, she thought he had destroyed her life. She thought she would die with the horror of it still fresh in her heart. But somewhere in the mountains, she began to change.

At first she simply noticed that sometimes she did not think of it. She found herself enjoying the rhythm of the journey. She began to feel stronger than she had for months. Her appetite returned. Her skin gloried in the sunlight. During the heat of the day, when the convoy rested, she would clamber up the rocky valleys, panting and hot, in search of pools where she could swim. And when she felt the shock of the cold water on her body, she would dive below the surface and surrender herself to its embrace. Sometimes she was almost ashamed of the pure joy that seized her.

Surely such emotion was not possible? Surely a used and discarded woman should feel her shame more keenly? But she did not. Somehow all the loathing and disgust she had felt for the Emperor had transformed itself into a tiny seed of triumph. The Emperor had failed. She had defeated him. He had tried to make her worthless, but he could not. It was not in his power.

And then there was the inexplicable contentment in having Venn close by. He would often ride beside her now – the thing had become commonplace and went unnoticed, an accepted feature of each day on the road. He would talk to her as a traveller addressing a lady whose path happened to cross his own. He never spoke of their meeting in Lin'an nor of the words of hope he had breathed to her that night. He had no need to, those words were with them both whenever their eyes met. They echoed unspoken in the silence that linked them. She was not alone, and in that itself she was happy. There was something in his quietness that soothed her, a telling contrast to the outpouring of words she'd shared with Song Rui.

When he spoke it was of the things that travellers talk about, of the dust and the winds and the state of the roads, or of how the gauze of cloud around the moon promised more hot weather. The words seemed less important to her than the way he spoke them. In return she told him the names of plants along the roadside and explained to him the special meanings given to each by the ancient poets: applethorn for longing, lily for forgetfulness, cassia for coming home.

In that way the little column edged westwards, further from Lin'an, into a landscape of its own, insulated from the rest of the world by the dry winds and the unrelenting sun and the jagged spines of the hills, silent but for the sound of streams rushing down from high places.

'Come,' she said. 'I can hear water. Follow me.'

And beyond the next ridge they came to a steep-sided gully, green with a riot of flowering bushes and low trees, fed by a waterfall that burst out of the rocks above.

'This will be a good place. Come on.' And she scrambled ahead of him, down the rough valley side. He followed slowly, wondering once again at her energy and at her sure-footedness. On the way from Zaiton he had imagined her a creature of idle refinement, carefully bred, tightly gowned, instinctively aloof. It had been something in her letters that had begun to change his mind, hinting as they did at her great zest for living. But he had never imagined her like this – an excited urchin in a rough smock, skipping over scree and thistles and mocking him for his caution.

'You see! I'm right again,' she called, looking back at him and pointing to something below her that lay hidden from him by a high outcrop of rock. 'This one's for me! You must go downstream and find yourself some muddy puddle to wallow in!'

When he caught up with her she had kicked off her shoes and was perched on a flat rock, her legs dangling over the edge. Below her lay a circular pool, twenty feet across, cut deep out of the rock by millennia of plunging water.

She looked up at him and smiled.

'You see? I told you so. I'm good at this.' Then she laughed and he felt his heart lurch with pleasure. 'Why do the rest of them not swim?' she asked. 'They are fools to miss this.'

'They are desert men,' he replied. 'They've never learned how.'

He looked down at her. One of her knees was raw, apparently grazed in her hasty descent. She followed his gaze and laughed again.

'Do you think the Lord Rustum will like a bride with cut knees, Venn? He is a desert man too, is he not? Perhaps in the wilds where he lives such things are considered beautiful in a woman.'

And then, quite suddenly, she became grave. 'I'm sorry,' she said. 'I should not joke. It is because you said it would never happen.'

Their eyes met and a moment of earnest meaning passed between them.

'I meant it.' Venn spoke calmly. 'It is a long way yet to Rustum's court. I promise you it will not happen.'

She raised an eyebrow at him. 'Since that night you spoke to me I have never asked anything more. I've never asked what will happen to me. Do you think that odd? That I've travelled all this way and never once wanted to know?'

He shrugged. 'I hadn't thought. But, yes, I suppose some would find it strange.'

'Not if they understood.' She smiled but her expression remained serious. 'If you are dying of thirst and you are offered water, you don't ask where the water came from. You just drink.' She paused. 'And that's what I'm doing now. Just drinking as deeply as I can.'

As abruptly as it had gone, the laughter returned to her face. 'Now, go. Go and find yourself somewhere to swim. When I've finished I'll wait for you by that big boulder.'

She watched him depart, picking his way down from the rocky platform that surrounded the pool until he dropped out of sight completely, lost among the leafy bushes that filled the gorge where the stream ran.

When he was gone she reached down and pulled her loose smock over her head, discarding it carelessly behind her. Then, naked, she tiptoed to the water's edge and lowered herself in.

The coldness shocked her, as it always did, and at first she had to bite her lip to prevent herself from crying out. For those first few moments the water seemed to press so tightly on her lungs that it threatened to squeeze her breath away and drag her down into its depths. But when that first crisis was mastered, when she had fought off the instinct to escape, the water lost its power over her and became instead her ally against the fierce heat of the afternoon. With a lithe twist of her body, she dived below the surface, into a green world where she could hear nothing but the roar of the current in her ears. Undeterred she kicked deeper, until all became silent and the water grew dark. Then she arched her back and curved up again, bursting into the sunshine with a gasp of delight. She felt clean again. The motion of the water against her bare skin thrilled her. It felt like a blessing from the high mountains, restoring her spirits and touching her soul. It made her body young again.

When she was cool to her core, she slipped back onto the flat rock and dried herself with the smock she had discarded. It was a garment borrowed from Shu-chen, who wore such things only in the countryside, and then only for the most menial and filthy of tasks.

But it suited her for these unwitnessed ventures into the hillsides where her fine court clothes were restricting and ridiculous. She found she liked the roughness of the fabric and the freedom it gave her to stretch and climb. It reminded her of her childhood in the water meadows.

That day, as she lay back and let the sun finish the drying, she felt a sense of perfect freedom descend upon her. Lying naked in the sunlight, smelling the scent of bruised mint rising from the pool's edge, looking westward at white peaks turning blue with distance, it came to her with a sudden rush of understanding that this was it, *this* was the joy she had been seeking. And she had found it without looking, on a rough brown mountainside in a place that had no name. Hiding in the water meadows to evade the traps of marriage; clinging to Song Rui in the hope of rescue; longing for the Imperial City and a place in society . . . Happiness was none of these things. It was this: a place in the world where she could swim naked and bask in the sun, where she was free to be herself; where there was no power bidding her to know her place. The Emperor had tried to rob her of all value and all dignity, but she had lost nothing. Nothing but her belief in his world and her fear of flying towards the sun.

Pulling on her dress and retrieving her shoes, she made her way down the valley, following the path

Venn had taken. A hundred paces further on, the path descended sharply and tumbled into another pool. She could hear Venn splashing somewhere below her. Slowing her pace, she crept forward through a stand of trees until she reached a rocky ledge that overlooked the place where he bathed. Filled with curiosity, she lay down on her front and watched.

His body was unlike those of the labourers she had seen on the docks of Zaiton. It was fuller than theirs and paler, broad in the shoulder with thicker, more obviously muscled arms and legs. And then as she watched him begin to rise out of the water she saw for the first time the great scar that disfigured the front of his body. It was impossible not to be struck by it, a huge cross, stark and shocking, as if the body that bore it had once been cut open like a beast being butchered.

But instead of repelling her, she found herself moved by the sight of it, filled with a sudden rush of tenderness. It was too shocking, too brutal. And it told her that this man who rode beside her had also suffered at the hands of others. She wondered what scars he bore that she could not see, that he did not show. She wondered if he too felt the mountain water made him whole again.

Venn had dried himself and was knotting the belt at his waist when he felt something sting his shoulder then bounce away down the rock. Looking up, instantly wary, he saw Ming Yueh's face looking down at him.

'I thought we were meeting at the rock on the hillside,' he called, hastily pulling on his shirt.

'We were,' she replied, watching his fingers work the fastenings. 'I just wanted to come and tell you I don't care.'

'What don't you care about?' His tone was light-hearted. He hadn't heard the seriousness beneath her smile.

'I don't care where you plan to take me to,' she replied, 'so long as it will be like this.'

He looked around, bemused, and so she went on. 'Just somewhere with the chance to swim in the sunshine and to laugh when I want to.'

She smiled again, but now he understood the earnestness in her voice.

'Only that?' he asked. 'Is that truly all you ask for?'

She nodded. 'And this. That if I could choose, I'd like it if you were there too.'

Back in Lin'an, the landscape was very different. The boy had watched his companions depart with a brave smile on his face and a sense of unutterable loneliness in his heart. The parting of the ways felt wrong, and with only Antioch and Yang for company he felt more alone than he had ever felt before. More alone than when his father had kissed him for the last time, that day in Flanders, his first day in Antioch's service.

The next seven days passed as the boy had expected, helping Antioch assemble their things and readying him for the journey. But on the night of the seventh day, instead of being woken by the sound of their wagons assembling, it was another noise that disturbed him – the sound of the palace gates opening and the thud of marching infantry. He knew it at once, even in the darkness – heavy-booted, tightly drilled, free of the jingle of loose armour that marked the local foot soldiers. And then he heard the commands – orders shouted in rough army Latin, deep and resonant, carrying over the cries of the gatekeepers and the hubbub of servants as they scattered to make things ready. Completely unexpectedly, Pau and his soldiers had arrived at Lin'an.

At first the boy thought it was some terrible mistake. They were supposed to be joining Pau in Zaiton. They were about to set off to do just that. Had some order been misunderstood? Or had Pau been sent all that way to provide them with an escort back? If that was the case, the soldiers would have to return the following day. Surely there had been a blunder?

But the following day, when Yang was sent to investigate, it emerged that there was no mistake.

The Emperor, it turned out, was a cautious man, suspicious by nature and ready to see conspiracy in every rustle of the reeds. Decius's proposal to stay behind and serve him had met with his approval. It did not in itself strike him as suspicious because he knew such men thrived on fighting. And yet, when he looked at everything together and imagined Decius travelling west while his companions went east, and all of them slipping away from his immediate control, the picture displeased him. These foreigners were becoming an irritation. Yes, he was eager to be rid of them, but perhaps as a guarantee of Decius's good behaviour it was more prudent to gather the rest of them where they could be properly overseen. And so he had ordered Pau and his men to be marched to Lin'an, and for Antioch's departure to be delayed. If all went well with Decius, they would be sent on their way. But if it did not . . . well, at least Decius's companions might offer him some sort of amusement.

To Antioch this change of plan did not seem greatly worrying, but the boy was immediately aware of the danger. He knew that Decius and Venn did not intend to return and, although they intended to make it seem that they had become separated from their companions by accident, he was not at all sure that the Emperor would greet such a disappearance with an even temper.

Worse still, he was worried about Pau. Back in Sicily, the boy had paid little attention to the young officer appointed by Decius to take charge of the men.

He had seemed a quiet, sullen fellow, given to keeping his own counsel and to keeping his feelings to himself. During the course of a long journey, the boy had come to wonder whether these suppressed currents ran more strongly and more dangerously than he had at first supposed. There had been times when he had seen Pau's fists clenched white when dealing with his men, and he had known that there was very real anger beneath the captain's impassive countenance. And then there had been the incident in India when a man had died and Pau had been charged with his death. The details had not been made clear to Antioch and his page – there had been talk of a brawl, of an accident – but the boy knew that it had taken all Decius's powers of persuasion to extricate them from the consequences.

And now he realised that Pau and his men had arrived in Lin'an in a dangerous mood. Their confinement in Zaiton had been uncomfortable and degrading, and when they finally came to march, they had been ordered to disarm. Pau had raged against such an indignity and for a time it had seemed they would resist any attempt to remove their swords. Only the appearance of a Saracen trader able to speak a little of their language had restored a degree of calm. He assured them that Lin'an was a city of unparalleled wealth and that permission for any foreigner to travel there was rare. Great riches awaited all those who did, he told them, and he urged them to seize the opportunity to go and make their fortunes. This was just sufficient to persuade them. But even so they marched in a state of such simmering resentment that the city magistrates felt it prudent to assign an extra body of soldiers to their escort.

To add to his concerns, the boy had noticed a change in Antioch. Shortly after Venn's departure the old man had been introduced to a philosopher of considerable reputation who was passing through the city from the north. Antioch had asked this traveller about the strange creatures that they sought, but to his great surprise the philosopher had dismissed the illustrations in Manfred's great book with a smile and a shrug.

'I have seen no such beasts,' he said, 'and I have travelled widely through all the Emperor's lands and through the southern kingdoms. You say your ancestors have written of these beasts? And yet there are no such living things in your country now?' The philosopher paused. 'Perhaps it happens that by chance, or through the efforts of your hunters, no beasts of these kinds have survived to this day. Sir, perhaps these beasts now exist only in the memory.'

Antioch met this reply with a snort.

'That cannot be,' he declared. 'The Lord stocks the fields and the forests for the benefit of men. His creatures feed and clothe us, or in some cases they exist to reveal to us an aspect of his nature, as the tiger shows Christ's fierce beauty and the unicorn shows his purity. Neither chance nor the actions of men can alter God's creation, for it is perfect and is meant to be.'

Such was his vehemence that the interview with the philosopher was brought quickly to an end. But for all that, in the days that followed, the boy thought Antioch increasingly pensive and downcast, as if the mission that had brought him so far no longer sustained him as it once had.

In the Mountains

Decius watched the two small figures, high above him, picking their way down the mountain. It was three or four hours after noon and the worst of the heat was beginning to subside. But it was still very, very hot. A bead of sweat ran down his brow as he watched. He found it painful to look up at them when the sky was still so blue behind them. Staring at bright objects always pained him. It was a weakness in his eyes – their strange pigmentation – and he had concealed it all his life. No soldier trusted a blind commander. So instead of looking away, he narrowed his eyes and squinted through the pain and saw that her hand was resting in Venn's. Only for a moment, as he helped her over the rough ground. But then, a few seconds later, their hands met again. There was much rough ground for them to cross, he thought.

A few hundred yards below him he could hear Shuran's men stirring from their rest, ready to resume the journey. Venn would have to hurry, he thought. And he would have to tread with care if there were to be no accidents.

For a moment he closed his eyes, but not because of the pain of the sunlight. An image had entered his head of Manfred of Sicily, an image of the two of them looking down from the walls of a palace to a garden where Manfred's wife and three young sons were walking. Manfred had turned to him, he remembered, and said to him with a sad smile, 'That is why we do it, Count. That is why we fight these wars of ours. For these days and that garden.'

Opening his eyes, Decius saw they were much closer to him. Venn had raised an arm in greeting and said something to the girl by his side. She smiled and replied, and then she too waved. If Manfred were standing there instead of him, Decius wondered, what would he say? What would he make of these days, this garden?

He did not wait for them to reach him before he turned and retraced his steps to the camp. When he next spoke to Venn it was about a poultice for horses.

Decius had never expected to love when he agreed to marry. His marriage was an advantageous one, arranged by an old general who had influence and an only daughter. The dowry had been generous. As well as gold there were lands in Sicily, a small estate in the hills with olive trees and lemon groves. Decius knew that an effective soldier needed somewhere to rest between campaigns: his motives were entirely practical – and never less than military in their precision.

But he had not planned on Messalina. He met her less than a year before he embarked on the Cathar campaign, some months after the formal agreement for the marriage was already in place. He was not a man who was easy to be with, he knew. He was curt and awkward with others, at ease only when giving orders to his men. He knew that his strange eyes made others uncomfortable in his presence. All his life he had watched people keep their distance. And he was not at all accustomed to the company of women. However, he wasn't concerned at the prospect of marriage. He understood that this was a business transaction and expected his bride to know the same.

He had known all along that she would be no beauty, and when they met he found himself confronted with an awkward, ungainly figure, skinny and without curves. Her hair was cropped short and her features were irregular, so that the neighbouring families laughed at her pityingly. She was, they joked, the old general's only lost cause. She had a hooked nose and a square, jutting chin. Later Decius would smile to himself whenever he thought of them.

His first thought on seeing her was that the general had struck a shrewd bargain: the monstrous-looking soldier with prospects and the ugly, unmarriageable daughter with money. The two were to be paired together and were to be grateful for what they got.

And then came the first occasion Decius was alone with her, out in the shady gardens. As soon as their attendants left them, she looked him directly in the face.

'They told me you were an ogre,' she said. 'Did they tell you how plain I am?'

Decius was taken by surprise and before he could speak, she smiled.

'Oh, don't worry. You don't have to pretend. I know I am plain. I see it every day. And I don't mind ogres. I've lived with my father for long enough to be used to them. He tells me you are very fierce.' And at that she laughed, though he was not sure why.

'I am a soldier,' he replied. He had said it before, but it had never before sounded so pompous to him.

'Oh, my father told me that as well. He considers it a great virtue.'

'And you do not?'

'To be *only* a soldier? No, that is not a virtue. But I do not believe it's the truth. No one is *only* a soldier.'

'I fear that is exactly what I am. Nothing more.'

'Really? Then look at that hillside yonder. What do you see?'

'I see a lemon grove.'

'What else?'

'A ridge with vines.'

She nodded. 'What else?'

'I see brown earth, green leaves. A blue sky above.'

'What does it make you feel?'

'Feel?' He looked at her in surprise, then looked back at the ridge and was silent for a time. 'It makes me feel grateful to be in such a place,' he said quietly. 'My life has been lived in harsher lands than this.'

She laughed. 'You see, you are not *only* a soldier after all.'

'I don't understand.' Her levity confused him and he began to feel annoyed.

'When my father looks at that ridge, he sees a defensible infantry position, with a strategic ridge for archers and a weakness at the rear where fortification would be needed against cavalry.'

He considered the hillside again. 'Well, yes, I can see all that too.'

'You see,' she said, 'not *only* a soldier. Come, you have passed my first test. Let me show you the orchard.'

With that she placed her hand on his bare elbow to guide him forward and there was something in the unthinking openness of the gesture, the butterfly softness of her fingers on his skin, that spoke to him in a way he had never before been spoken to.

That night, alone, he thought of the tiny hand that had pulled him along, and then of the small, plain, unwanted girl who found her fate so tangled with his.

Two shunned people together. Suddenly and without warning a surge of protective feeling flooded his heart. She had been confronted with a freak, a gaunt and graceless suitor who had seen only her plainness. Yet she had found in herself the courage and kindness to put him at his ease.

For the first time in his life, he felt himself humbled. He was in her debt. And Decius was a man who took his debts very seriously.

His stay in Sicily was extended first for one month, then another. Ostensibly this tarrying was to enable him properly to assess the estate he was to be given, but in fact he spent each day with Messalina, listening to her laughter and wondering at her brightness. In all his life, no one had ever treated him as she did. She bid him climb trees to fetch her fruit, and when he declined she attempted to climb them herself, until he, fearing some unseemly accident, would yield to her entreaties. Then she would shake the trunk as he climbed. She mocked him continuously for his seriousness and he found to his surprise that he enjoyed her mockery, for he had often been feared but never teased. And in the still evenings, she would lean her back against his chest as they studied the horizon, and listen to him talk. Yes, the silent, sinister general would talk to her for hours of the things in his heart, the things they would do together, the life they would lead. Through her he found the power of speech: she unlocked his tongue and turned his feelings into words. In that late Sicilian summer he discovered how to talk.

It was a summer of the most perfect love. He found a joy in having her beside him that he'd never thought could be his, and in her tenderness he found a love as startled and as breathless as his own. Sometimes he would think of the world beyond theirs, the clashing armies and the sodden fields, of the misery and despair that filled the world he came from, and he would stand and wonder at every immaculate sunrise.

By mutual agreement their marriage was brought forward, and when the ceremonies were over and the guests were gone and she stood naked before him for the first time, the astonishment he felt at her pale beauty was so great that she saw his eyes mist with tears.

He knew then that those feelings, that instant, would be burned into his heart until the moment of his death.

Decius had not waited long at Montségur after the citadel's surrender. On the day two hundred Cathars were burned beneath its walls, he had already left for Sicily, back to the bride who awaited him. On that journey he had vowed he would never leave Sicily again. And that he would never again raise a sword in anger.

* * *

Stranded in Lin'an, Antioch and the boy were growing nervous. With every day that passed, the heat intensified and the city became more oppressive. The Emperor's court took refuge on the lake, in pleasure boats and on barges, sometimes staying out all night, their music and laughter rippling to the shore. Listening to it, Pau's soldiers grew fractious and the boy grew more afraid.

On their arrival at the Imperial Palace, Pau and his men had been marched directly to the barrack house at the gate of the palace and confined there, their only exercise being the drill sessions that Pau insisted upon on the adjoining parade ground. Their arms remained under lock and key in the nearby armoury and it seemed to the boy that this indignity was having a disturbing effect upon the captain. The scowl on Pau's face had become a fixture, while outside, by the palace gates, the discontent among his men grew dangerously, like the slow murmuring of wheat before a storm breaks.

Precisely what he feared, the boy couldn't say. He knew that Venn and Decius planned to escape from their companions, but he was at an age when belief in human justice had not quite been extinguished by experience. Surely the Emperor would see that the rest of the party was not to blame? Even while he resolved to warn Pau of the danger, the boy knew it was not only fear of the Emperor's anger that filled him with foreboding. Each day he would feel a prickle of heat on his skin as he watched the Emperor carried on his litter from the lake to his bedchamber and would see Pau watching the litter's progress with a blank stare. He became gripped by a sense that what had once been neat and orderly had now become somehow brittle, as if the heat was stripping away all the certainties and revealing shifting foundations of resentment and distrust.

Antioch felt it too. The old man grew ever more restless, less and less content to spend the whole day with his books. The scholars and poets who had once sought him out had abandoned Lin'an for their estates in the country or else accompanied the Emperor in his expeditions upon the lake. Without the distraction of their company, he began to fret and to talk more and more about his lands in Sicily – his books, his library – until the boy began to think him feverish and worried for his health.

'It is time we were gone,' he would say to the boy. 'We have already waited here too long. We have collected some curiosities for Manfred and on the way home we will gather more. And who knows if the creatures of the book still exist? It is a question that troubles me greatly. Yes, it is time we were gone.'

Sometimes his agitation would persist despite the boy's soothing. 'I wish Venn was here,' he would say. 'Decius, too. They would know what to do. And I would be glad for us all to return together.'

Secretly the boy thought the same, and he wondered if there was a chance that plans would change, that Venn and Decius would come riding back after all. So while Antioch grew weaker and more feverish with every day that passed, the boy watched and waited, and longed for their return.

In the mountains, the heat was of a different sort – drier, harder, cleaner. Once again Ming Yueh had found good places to swim and this time Venn was the first to finish. He waited, drying in the sunshine, until her whistle summoned him. Then he climbed back upstream to where she was sitting at the water's edge, her long hair still damp, her smock hanging loose around her.

As he dropped down next to her, something fell from his pocket and struck the rock with a metallic ring. She trapped it deftly beneath her fingers before it could roll away.

'What is it?' she asked, and he leaned closer to her.

'An old coin,' he replied. 'It was sent to me long ago as a warning by one who wished me well. He was afraid to trust his message to speech, so he used signs he knew I'd understand. Look, you can see the marks he made.'

She held the object closer. 'I see the marks, but what do they mean?'

Leaning closer still he indicated the five stars.

'I think he meant each of these for one of the people I travelled with. This one is me, the one marked with a cross. That speaks for itself. You see, I'm the fourth in the line. Only one is smaller and less significant. By that one he means the boy.'

'And the circle? What is that?'

He smiled. 'The circle is used as a warning. Where he places it and how it is drawn shows where the danger is. By ringing one of the other stars, he was telling me to be cautious of another member of the party.'

Leaning back, he watched her trace the outline of the circle with her fingertip.

'It was good of him to send it,' he went on, 'but in truth it wasn't necessary. Decius's reputation as a dangerous man had gone before him. I already knew to be wary of him.'

She looked up at him then, her eyes a little puzzled and a little anxious.

'So he thought Decius was a danger to you?' she asked. 'Was he right?'

He reached out and let his fingers touch her hand. 'In a way. Decius has a dream. He wants to cleanse the Christian lands with fire. He believes they are corrupt beyond redemption. He would save his world by destroying it. But he means no harm to *us*. His is a greater calling . . .'

But he saw she was not listening. She was examining the coin again, this time with even greater intensity.

'This is wrong,' she said, still looking down. Then she said it again, louder, looking him straight in the face. 'See, he has circled the wrong star.'

She held up the coin and he took it from her.

'If you're the fourth star,' she went on, 'then surely Antioch must be the first, because he was named as leader. And Decius is his deputy, so he must be second. But, look, it's the middle star that's ringed.' She paused to let him study it. 'Who would that be?' she asked. 'Who is the middle star in your party?'

'A soldier named Pau,' he said slowly, his mind still working to catch up. He had been so sure of the harbour-master's code, and so certain that Decius was the threat he was being warned of, that he hadn't thought to study the coin too closely. 'The middle star is Pau, the officer in charge of the soldiers. But I cannot see what threat he is. And anyway, if he is not yet away at sea, he is safely in Zaiton where he can do no harm to the rest of us.'

He frowned for a moment longer, then to banish her anxiety he balanced the coin between his thumb and forefinger.

'Make a wish,' he said. 'Think of something you really desire.' And, before she could ask him why, he had spun the coin high into the air. For a moment it caught the sunlight as it twisted. Then it fell back and splashed into the deep green water below them.

'I can dive for it,' she cried anxiously, leaping to her feet, but he reached up and pulled her down beside him.

'No,' he said. 'Let it go. We've seen the message now, and the harbour-master of Genoa is many miles away. This place is far too beautiful to worry about that other world.'

And looking up towards the perfect stillness of the mountains, she felt their calm reach out to her and she smiled and gave thanks with all her heart for that sight, that place, that moment.

Three days later, for the first time she had ever known, he allowed his shirt to hang open after he had swum. It seemed to her a sign that the gentle rhythm of their days was working on him. More than once in the past, when he had been scouting ahead, she had seen him hasten to close his shirt when one of the party approached him. It was as if he believed that the mark on his chest must always be hidden. But now, lying beside her with the scent of the jacinta trees strong around them, he seemed to have forgotten.

Close up, she could see the lines of muscle beneath the scar. But also she could see the way the dark weal cut across them like a stain on the skin – puckered flesh that would never heal smooth.

He was lying with his head back, facing the sun. His eyes were closed but she knew he wasn't asleep.

He was simply absorbing the warmth of the sun after the raw cold of the water. Without thinking, she reached out and traced the outline of the scar with her fingertip, feeling its strange roughness running through her. He didn't move when he felt her touch, but she knew his eyes had opened and were watching her.

'So deep,' she said. 'You are lucky to be alive with such a wound.'

He said nothing, so she continued to let her finger move across his chest. 'Who did this?' she asked.

At first he said nothing and she waited, still not looking up at him.

'Strangers,' he said at last.

Again she waited, but he said nothing more. Yet he made no effort to move away from her touch. Finally she stopped moving her fingertips and laid her palm flat on his chest.

'Why?' As she asked the question she let her eyes move up to his face, but his eyes had moved away from her and were studying the distant mountains.

He could remember every second of it, right down to the sensation of the blade parting his flesh. At one time in his life it had seemed that the agony and anger of that night would never leave him. But lying there with her hand cool against his chest, it seemed that every slash of pain had had a reason. And this was it. The rest fell away.

'Why?' she asked again, more insistent this time, and so he tried to tell her how he had been travelling to a city on a distant island with a party of Jewish merchants. How he had been there to interpret, nothing more. How one night they had been set upon, ambushed out of hatred. There had been no fight. The mob was too many and the merchants were not fighting men. Their party had been instantly overwhelmed by their attackers' fury. Venn's resistance had been swept aside and he was held, pinioned, as the men who employed him were put to the sword, their butchered bodies flung aside. Good men with families, he knew. Learned, humane. He was made to watch their slaughter. His attackers knew he was not of the Jewish faith so instead of instant death, they had pulled open his shirt and carved a crucifix deep into his chest to remind him as he died of the true faith. It was their way of warning others against fraternising with heathens . . .

He had almost died where he lay. Not that night, among the still-warm remnants of the men who had employed him. Later, just after dawn, when the loss of blood began to tell. But women from the local village had come with the daylight, hiding their faces. They had staunched the bleeding and had left food and water within his reach. When the sun was higher, a passing miller found him and carried him to a convent. There the shape of his wound had roused a superstitious wonder among the nuns and novices, and he had been tended most diligently for many days. Later still, when the scar had formed, he found that pilgrims and peasants who saw him shirtless would take the mark for a symbol of his devotion, an heroic, God-fearing mortification of the flesh. Sometimes they would even fall to their knees before him in wonder.

He told her what he could, trying to explain to her the hatred and the poverty and the ignorance. She listened in wonder, imagining the scenes he described – the torches at night, the cries of mortal suffering, the lingering smell of blood.

'A brutal land,' she concluded softly. 'Is that where we must go?'

'No, not there,' he assured her, and placed his own hand over hers where it still lay against his chest. 'There is a place I know a long way west of here, a valley in the mountains with streams like this one feeding it from the snowline. It has a strange beauty all of its own.'

And while she lay there by the water, he told her of a valley edged with cedars, where orchards and vine-yards flourished and where villagers of different creeds worked side by side to make the valley fruitful, united by their shared need to prepare for winter.

'Can such a place exist?' she wondered, thinking of the stories he had told her of the western lands, and of all the suffocating strictures she had known in the land of her birth.

'It does. Many armies have passed near it. Many princes have claimed it. But each one leaves the place unchanged, for the people simply continue in their ways and in the winter the snow comes down and all is forgotten. It is a place that lives by its own calendar.'

'And is it very far from here?' Already she was seeing in her imagination the day of their arrival, her first glimpse of the orchards from the mountains above.

'A journey of many months, I fear, even on good horses.'

'I don't care,' she said, letting her eyes find his. 'The stars at my birth said I was destined to make a great journey.'

Without saying more she closed her eyes and lay still, and felt the warmth of his chest under her fingers. Somewhere higher up the valley a pheasant cried out. Beneath her palm she could feel the beating of his heart.

ζ

Sometimes, on the hottest days, a pink line appears across the horizon here and the sailors in the harbour grow nervous. That line of pink tells of a storm over Africa. From across the water, gulls appear, all flying in the same direction, and you know the storm will follow them.

It was on such a day that I returned from the hills to Málaga. Perhaps it was the strangeness of the light as the clouds gathered, but the town seemed different to me upon my return. Or perhaps the things I'd learned from the letter-writer of Granada had changed the way I saw things. I had always looked upon my son's disappearance as a case apart, as something that had happened to him alone, unconnected with his companions. But now I saw my boy was a part of other stories, stories more complex and confusing than his own.

In truth I had learned nothing. My son was still lost. There was no new information in Granada to change that fact or to tell me where to look. And yet I felt different. The discovery that the silent general who escorted him had troubles and passions of his own made the view less clear: as if, as I tried to peer into the past, I glimpsed another pink line, ominous above the horizon.

I decided to seek out Quintus Fabius, the Pope's officer, the man who had first told me something about Decius. I still believed that every story deserved an ending, and in questioning him further perhaps I still hoped to find some fragments of my son's existence in Decius's story. But on the evening of my return, the looming storm broke and kept me indoors, and the next day, before I could seek him out, there was a knock on my door and standing before me was the Catalan, Raymond of Nava, the first man to visit me with questions about my son. I remembered his restless, untrusting eyes. It seemed many, many days since he and I had talked.

'So you've come back,' he began, his quick glance taking in the room behind me. 'I wondered at your absence.'

'Yes, I'm back,' I replied, 'but I regret I have no time to talk to you.'

He raised an eyebrow at that but did not step away from my door.

'I see. And what has happened to make you decide that? You have not struck me these past months as a man for whom time is short.'

'For one thing, I have learned you are not a French count's agent. For another, that you came to me because you hope to earn a reward for information about Count Decius.'

'Ah, I see.' The thin man studied me closely. 'So you have received a visit from our friend Quintus Fabius, have you? And you have chosen to believe him?'

I made no response and waited for him to depart. But instead he stood his ground, his eyes now on my face, curious. 'He has probably told you that the Pope and his aides are quaking at the thought of Decius's return, and that they only wish to find him so they can secure the present peace.' He paused for a moment to see if I responded, then went on. 'What if I told you there is not a word of truth in any of that? What if I told you that this is all about something very different?'

Behind him the sky was still streaked with cloud from the storm.

'Tell me,' he said, 'just how much do you know about the Treasure of Montségur?'

After all, I had nothing to lose by letting him in.

'Fabius told you the truth when he said he works for the Pope,' the Catalan began.

I had seated him in the corner of my room and provided him with wine. By daylight his face seemed less furtive than I remembered it. There were lines around his eyes that suggested weariness and I saw he was older than he had first appeared. This time I could see in his face the strain of living by his wits.

'Fabius is genuinely a valued advisor to the Pope,' he went on. 'He doesn't bother himself with the unimportant or the trivial. Certainly not with the disappearance of an ageing general who probably died years ago. No. The matter he is involved in now is one that has bothered successive popes for many years. When I was here last, you told me you knew nothing of the Cathars. Is that true?'

'It was true then. I have learned more since.'

'Let me take you back to a darker time – to the year of the Siege of Montségur, to the last days, when the citadel was on the very brink of surrender. Have you ever asked yourself why the Archbishop of Narbonne and his henchmen were so eager to capture the fortress?'

'Their mission was to root out heresy.'

He rolled his eyes at that. 'Oh, come now. Wars are not fought over items of faith. Faith is just a flag to wave above the foot soldiers. No, they are fought over power and wealth and influence. And mostly over wealth, as that opens up the way to the other two. And this war in particular had its eye on the profits. You see, the Cathars were prosperous people. But to achieve a state of holiness, they had to renounce their worldly goods. This was common. So year by year the pool of discarded wealth grew and grew, and of course it was always closely guarded. For *two centuries*. Just think of that. Oh, there are wild rumours about it. Like the treasure, the rumours grew with time – foolish stories, wild tales about the relics of Christ's life. All of it untrue, I know. The treasure was a wordly one. Over time its guardians had converted the silver and gold into precious stones to keep it portable. It was not *relics* that the Church lusted after. It had plenty enough of those and no scruple about making more when required. It was diamonds and rubies the popes were after, a collection the like of which had never been seen before.'

The Catalan paused deliberately. 'That is no exaggeration, merchant. Year on year the Cathars had been shedding their wealth to achieve perfection. Wealthy men, rich farmers, prosperous tradesmen . . . No lord has ever enjoyed such a revenue as that. The Church's tithes are paltry in comparison, and the Church's expenses are high. But the Cathar treasure was rarely called upon. It simply grew. By the time of the siege, it was worth more than any Christian king could ever dream of commanding.'

His eyes glistened as he spoke of it.

'How do you know all this?' I asked. 'You speak as if you have certain knowledge.'

'Believe me, merchant, on this subject I am an expert. My family were close to its keepers. And I know for certain that the treasure was being held in Montségur when the fortress was besieged. That is why the besieging lords were so jubilant, for they knew they were closing in on wealth beyond their dreams. When the citadel fell, the treasure would be theirs.'

He paused and gave me that fleeting, sideways look of his. 'But, of course, they were wrong.'

'You mean they found no treasure?'

The Catalan smiled a crooked smile. 'Every soul who left Montségur under the terms of the surrender was stripped of everything but the shirts they stood in. You can imagine the thoroughness. And then the citadel was searched, room by room, inch by inch. The wells were dragged, the cellars excavated. And then the destruction began. Walls were demolished lest they should be hiding the treasure. Whole buildings were destroyed. Gradually, stone by stone, Montségur was razed to the ground.

'Of course, no treasure was found, though people still seek it there. But even before the final surrender there were rumours that the treasure had been smuggled away. Remember, there was much confusion in those final hours. At one point a trusted officer was told to take two men and two plain boxes and to try whatever he must do to get through the lines and find a place where they might be left in safety. There was no discussion as there were no alternatives.'

The Catalan paused to sip his wine, then raised his chin a little with a rare flash of pride. 'The man chosen was my uncle. His name was Peter of Girona. That is how I know.'

'And was he successful?'

'He was gone all night. The following day he and his men attempted to return to the fortress. All of them were cut down in the open space before the walls. My uncle alone made it to the gate alive; he was never able to speak. He died of his wounds soon after, on the last day of the siege.'

'But surely he must have left some word as to where the treasure had been taken?'

The Catalan looked at me and shook his head slowly. 'Not that anyone has ever found.'

'So that is it? The treasure is lost?'

Another sip of wine, and when he replied his eyes rested on his cup. 'There are rumours of other sorties similar to my uncle's, all of them designed to cover tracks and confuse the enemy. Which of them had the true treasure? We'll never know. Some say the treasure reached Italy or Aragon. Others still search the woods around Montségur. But it is not the peasants who peer down rabbit holes who are most eager to find the Cathar gold. Think of it. An expensive campaign had been fought, there were bills to pay and no spoils to pay them with. Worse than that, there was a pope with high expectations who had already begun to think of that treasure as his own. When the treasure of Montségur proved to have vanished from under his nose, the papal displeasure was extreme. There could be no excuses. The treasure must be found or those who had failed to secure it would end their lives in chains.'

I nodded, beginning to understand the determination, so many years on, of men like Quintus Fabius.

The Catalan sipped again, then went on.

'It wasn't long before the arrests began. In that period all those who had ever been close to the treasure began to disappear. I cannot tell you what became of them but it's assumed they died at the hands of their torturers. However, it seems none of them had the information that would have saved them, for the searches — and the disappearances — continued.

'It took six years for them to get around to Decius. After the campaign he had vanished. They found him living quietly in Sicily. If he had the treasure there, he certainly wasn't spending it, for he was living a quiet life in the hills. But by now the search for the Cathar gold had become a mania, a fixation for successive popes. Nothing must stand in its way. By chance, the Pope's agents arrived when Decius was away from home, but that did not deter them. His house and all his buildings were burned to the ground. That which wouldn't burn was demolished stone by stone. His servants were interrogated and then massacred. His child's throat was cut. When they had satisfied themselves his wife knew nothing, stones were tied to her feet and she was drowned in the well. And yet still they found nothing.'

I looked at him, horror on my face. 'That happened? You are sure of it?'

'I am. I tell you so you can see the stakes we play for.'

'His wife . . . I have heard of her. She sounded . . . like a good woman.'

'Indeed? Well, the same events were being repeated all over Europe.'

'And what happened to Decius?' I asked, still shaken by what I'd heard.

'When the Pope's men paid their visit, he was at the court of Manfred who was eager to recruit him to his cause. Up to then, Decius had always said no. Of course the destruction of his home and family changed everything. From then on Decius was always at Manfred's side.'

'But from what you say, he didn't have the treasure,' I interjected. 'So why so much interest in him now?'

The Catalan drained his glass.

'Ah, yes. You see, this is the crux of it. Twenty years after the Siege of Montségur, Manfred found himself in trouble.

The new Pope had ordered Charles of Anjou to take Sicily, and a massive Angevin force was being assembled. Manfred needed allies. You would expect the loyal Decius to be by his side at such a time. Yet around that time, Decius disappeared from sight. There were a number of rumours that he was dead. All we know — and there were papal spies aplenty to testify to it — is that around the same time a traveller with unusual eyes was seen in the vicinity of Carcassonne. The descriptions match Decius perfectly: he was an unusual looking man.'

'So he returned to Montségur?'

'So it would seem. Well, you can imagine, that news stirred things up considerably. At last it seemed the treasure might be within their grasp. His arrest was ordered and every soldier in the country was looking for him. But he slipped through their fingers and disappeared. The next sightings of him were in Genoa. And when he left there, it was to escort Antioch and your son on their journey.'

'So you believe the rumours are true? That he took the treasure with him?'

The Catalan shrugged. 'Why not? It was never found in Sicily. And that was the Pope's worst nightmare: that Decius had slipped away beyond his reach forever, taking the treasure with him. That way they would never get it back.'

'But Fabius says they are afraid he will return at the head of a Saracen army.'

Raymond of Nava laughed drily. 'That is their excuse for the reward they offer. They don't want to use the word 'treasure' too widely in case people like me start sniffing after it. But they would hardly be afraid of a general who must now be in his dotage. Besides, why would he come back? He had all he needed to purchase a kingdom for himself in the east, somewhere he'd be safe. Somewhere they would never find him.'

He drained his glass. 'And think about it, merchant. If Decius did find a kingdom of his own somewhere, that is where you will find your son.'

ζ

281

The Grasslands

Sometimes as they left the caravan during the hottest part of the day, Decius would watch them go, his eyes hooded against the sun. What did he think, Venn wondered? What lay behind that impassive gaze?

With each day that passed, the general's plots seemed increasingly fantastical to him. Popes, princes, power, the fall of empires ... Venn's world had shrunk to the sway of the horses, the sound of their hooves, the steady sweep of the sun overhead; and at night, the great disc of the moon, so bright that sometimes they had to cover their eyes to sleep. And this little world bounded by mountains had at its centre the daily excursions he made with Ming Yueh. They were the quiet heart that gave each day its pulse.

And with each day that passed, Venn wondered about Count Decius. Once, many years earlier, the interpreter had been trapped for part of an alpine winter in a shepherd's refuge. As the last days of severe weather passed, he had watched the gradual surrender of the ice to the warm earth that lay beneath it. Nothing in all that harsh winter had allowed for belief in a thaw. But when Venn was finally able to walk down from the high passes, the path behind him was already edged with flowers.

Was it fanciful to think that way of Decius? Perhaps it was. Nothing in the soldier's weathered face showed any sign of a thaw. But if Venn asked him when they were to slip away from Shuran's escort into the lands of the Khan, Decius would just shrug and look across at Ming Yueh and tell him that everything had its moment.

And if Venn's wariness of Decius was diminishing, so was his concern for Antioch and the boy. He had counted the new moons. By now the pair of them would be out at sea and many miles from Zaiton, looking out over the steaming Indies, watching the moonlight on untrodden jungle shores.

He couldn't know about the uncommon heat that had Lin'an in its grip, a heat so great that order in the city was beginning to fall apart. He couldn't know about the fever that was stalking the narrow alleys, the anger growing in the taverns. And he couldn't know that Antioch and the boy waited there and suffered, listening to the alarms which called the imperial guard into the streets in vain attempts to restore order.

The boy was anxious for many reasons. Antioch's fever had grown worse and his mind seemed to wander more and more. One of the court scholars had sent a great curiosity for his consideration, the solidified bones of an enormous beast, apparently turned to stone by magic. They were large objects and heavy. It had taken five men to lift them from the cart that brought them and lay them in Antioch's quarters. There the old man pondered them every day, pacing around them and muttering to himself. The great bestiary he had cherished so tenderly and for so long was discarded for this new interest; even at night the boy would hear him walking, talking to himself all the while.

'Such immense dimensions . . . We can calculate from the spine . . . Yet where were these beasts in the ark? Surely no craft could carry such giants. The Bible tells us the dimensions . . . Even one pair of these creatures would make the ship unsteady. And the man who sent them says there are more . . . Different creatures . . . All huge . . . No craft could carry them . . .'

And so it would go on, until he fell into an uneasy sleep. 'Buried in rock . . . Did the Lord bury them? Did he condemn them to drown in the flood? Where is his mercy *then* . . .?'

Each day the fever seemed to tighten its grip. The boy tried to get help for the old man but in truth they were largely shunned now. Yang the merchant was scarcely ever in the palace so there was no one to translate, and the unrest in the town meant that palace officials scarcely noticed them. He had the sense they were living in the hot breath of a looming tempest.

And yet when he lay at night listening to his master's ramblings, he could see that the storm need not destroy them. There was unrest in the city, yes, and the court officials were short tempered and anxious. The Emperor ignored everything and stayed on the lake, forbidding his ministers to mention anything that would spoil his pleasure. But he and Antioch were not the problem. If they could just stay quiet, beneath notice, then when the storm had passed they would once again be on their way . . . The boy would mop Antioch's brow and pray that the old man could survive the heat. If they did nothing to draw attention to themselves, they would be safe.

But his confidence would crumble into fragments whenever he saw Pau. Like Antioch, the officer appeared to be seized by some sort of malady, for his eyes were growing wild and his face was tense with twitching muscles. But he did not sweat. He simply watched and listened while rations were cut and he was ordered to stop his men from drilling outside until the situation in the town had calmed. And then, when he thought he was unobserved, the boy would watch his hands shaking as if a deep and uncontrollable anger was raging inside him.

'We are treated like beasts,' he would tell the boy. 'They treat us like beasts. They call us beasts. Are we to die in cages like beasts too?'

'Please,' the boy would say, 'I think we must wait until the heat passes. When things are back to normal we will be properly looked after.'

But Pau would look at him with uncomprehending eyes and the boy would return to Antioch with a sick fear in his stomach.

Then the fires started. Lin'an was always prey to fires but that summer surpassed all others. There were rumours of arson, of areas where the fever gripped being torched deliberately to burn out the sickness. From Antioch's room, the boy could see the night sky blossoming into flame. He could hear the cries of the soldiers as units were hastily rearranged and sent to fight the flames or keep the crowds in order. He could see Pau watching them go, could see him observing the weakness of the palace guards, calculating the strengths of his own waiting troops.

'I'm frightened,' the boy said. 'I'm frightened about Pau. I'm afraid he'll do something dangerous that will damage us all.'

And at first he thought Antioch was listening, for he too was staring out over the city. But when the old man spoke it was on a different subject.

'Could it be, Benedict, that the Holy Bible lies to us? These strange stone bones I'm shown are surely the remains of huge beasts. And these beasts are no longer living in the world. They cannot be, for they had no place in the ark and could not then have survived the flood. But we are meant to believe that all God's creatures were saved. Do you see what this means, Benedict? Do you see what I must conclude?'

And with eyes watering with passion he waved his hand at the bestiary.

'If we believe that God's mercy to his creatures is not infinite, then nothing is forever. If God made these great beasts and then allowed his own creations to be washed from the face of the earth, then it must be that he makes and destroys as he see fit. So these creatures in the bestiary that we have not seen for generations . . . Benedict, they may no longer live at all. God may have let them die. There may be no unicorn, no cockatrice, no dragon . . . And do you see, Benedict, if that is true, what are we? Are we not his creations?'

And with a great sob he reached his final questions: '*How can we be sure he will not one day abandon us?*'

There were tears in the boy's eyes, too, as he helped the old man into bed that night. It seemed that last outburst had overwhelmed the scholar, and he had gone quietly, obeying the boy's orders, suddenly meek and helpless. Sitting beside him, Benedict found himself remembering words he'd once spoken to Venn, that night in the desert when the interpreter had asked him what he prayed for. Well, he told himself, raising his chin defiantly, this was his chance. If the storm broke as he was sure it would, it would be his chance to prove his courage to the world. And he would make his father proud of him.

Venn came to think of them as the basilisk lands: the great stretch of the world from the water meadows of Zaiton to the towering mountains east of Karakorum. He had heard Antioch's tales. He had heard tell of the serpent that could blind a man with one flash of its eyes. And there, in those slow, sun-bleached days, when he could look up at any time and see Ming Yueh riding near him, Antioch's stories made sense to him. Here was a glimpse of something that dazzled him, a fiery joy so complete he could already feel himself lost in it; he was dazed, entangled; bewildered by the power of something far, far stronger than his own will. Love had struck him like a basilisk kiss, and left him reeling. He wasn't dead. It hadn't blinded him. Perhaps it was worse. It had deprived him of words.

Every day he longed to tell her what he was feeling, to explain how everything had changed because of the tenderness of her fingers and the squeeze of her hand; because of her courage and her grazed knees and the love he saw in her eyes; he longed to tell her that, in all his travels, it had never been like this; that he had never imagined it could be. He wanted to describe for her the shapes and colours and textures of his feelings.

But he could not. Paralysed by the basilisk's gaze, he did not know how. And so, while part of him gloried in every day he spent with her, another part of him suffered wretchedly, for how could she trust him if he said nothing? Without words, how could he make her understand?

She would watch him as he lay beside her and at first she would marvel that he did not speak, until, as the days passed, she became accustomed to his silence and learned to trust in other signs – the meaning in his eyes, his quick smile, the tenderness of his touch. Even when he rode ahead of her, she knew he was aware of her gaze. Often when she looked his way he would know it and would turn in his saddle to smile.

As for her, she did not ask how or why. She only knew that this unlikely companion had made the desert flowers bloom. She inhaled their scents as if each breath was her last.

Sometimes she tried to tell him this, but she too found speech had deserted her. Instead she would sit close to him in the sunlight, her fingers twined in his, and from time to time her grip on his hand would tighten as if to say, '*Please know that I am happy here, like this.*' And she would feel his hand reply to hers, and their eyes would meet, and she would be content.

In the end it was the mountains that broke Venn's silence. After many weeks of climbing through dusty valleys, the expedition came without warning to a high plateau, a flat, grassy meadowland that stretched away before them like a lake without shores. It was a change as unexpected as it was dramatic. The days of the narrow terraces cut out of the mountains seemed to belong to a different lifetime and they had seen no fertile soil since. To stumble after so long into rich grassland where wild horses grazed seemed hard to believe, a lost world hidden in the mountains.

Shuran halted the caravan on the very edge of the plateau and pointed. From where they stood, the blue mountains ahead of them were hidden by the haze rising from the grass.

'Rustum's land,' he said. 'Where the grass ends, the mountains go higher. His kingdom lies in the deserts below them.'

'And the other way?' Venn asked. 'Whose kingdom lies over the mountains?'

'The other way, the road leads up to the high passes. Beyond those the people are loyal to the Tartar chieftain.' He turned and spat into the dust. 'Now, let us rest here for a while. After today we will no longer have to stop in the afternoons, for it is cooler here than in the valleys below.'

'And the summer is ending,' thought Decius, looking up at the sky, calculating how much longer they could stay in the high pastures before the snows came. And he looked at Venn, wondering, still wondering, what Manfred's wishes truly were.

While the others rested, Venn and Ming Yueh returned a little way down the path, looking for a stream to bathe in. They both understood that the routines which had served them for so long were coming to an end, and there was a little melancholy in the air that day, as if both could sense the distant approach of winter.

But although the summer was drawing to a close, the afternoons were still hot. Even a few hundred yards below the plateau the dry heat prevailed, shimmering on the rocks, blurring the horizon. After fifteen minutes, the outline of the caravan was invisible to them and they had disappeared into one of the dry-sided gullies that trapped the heat like clay ovens.

It took them longer than usual to find a suitable pool. When they did it was a smooth hollow in the rocks, shallow-edged and clear, overhung with sprays of ferns. They undressed together on the warm rocks, each watching the other, unashamed and unembarrassed. When they were naked they drew closer and embraced. Very quietly, he took her face in his hands and kissed her.

'I have had so many chances,' he said. 'So many times to speak. Such closeness when I should have spoken. I've wanted to tell you what I feel. But all the words I know are other people's. And what I feel is so deep in me . . .' He paused, still struggling. 'It's as if there is a depth where the words run out.'

She nodded and kissed him. 'You do speak to me,' she said. 'Every day. You tell me all that and more. Even when we ride apart, with others in between us, you speak to me.' She moved her hand from his back and traced the line of his lips with her fingertips. 'I can learn new languages too. Every time you touch me, you speak. They way you move, the way you hold me. The way your eyes seem to open so wide.' She smiled then. 'You don't need to translate for me. I like your silent words that no one else has ever spoken.'

They swam together in the clear water, slowly, at ease; and when she lifted herself onto the bank, he swam to where she lay.

'I will never stop,' he said. 'Even if you cannot see me, even if I cannot be close to your side, I will always be saying these words that only you can hear.'

'And I will hear them,' she promised. 'Wherever you are, wherever I am, I will hear them. You will know it by my replies.'

That evening, when the caravan rolled out into the grasslands, she watched him ride ahead until distance blurred him, and she wondered at the force and the freedom of this love unshaped by words.

ζ

Raymond of Nava talked to me for two hours in my room above the town. When he was done, I asked him why he was telling me so much about Decius, things he had earlier tried to hide. He looked me in the eye and thought for a moment, then shrugged.

'When I came here first, I hoped you might point me towards a profit,' he said. 'I admit it freely. I take my fortune where I find it. I hoped you might let slip something of value about Decius's location.' He paused for what seemed a very long time, then went on in an altered tone. 'But they talk about you, you know. Down in the town. The sad English merchant. You make each of them recall their own loved ones. Sometimes a man forgets he loves until something reminds him. You remind them.'

'And that is why you came here today?'

In reply, he simply shrugged again and said no more.

I thought by then I had learned all he had to tell me. But because he had fallen silent I found myself speaking of his kinsman in Montségur, the man who had smuggled away the treasure. I told him I had heard the name before, from the old letter-writer, in connection with a child smuggled from the town.

293

Raymond of Nava nodded. 'Yes, the Infant of Montségur, they called him. The last child born there. But surely you know what became of him?'

'Only that he escaped to a monastery.'

He stared at me. 'But after that? You must know the child's history?'

I shook my head a little wearily and assured him I did not.

'That child was raised by monks, but he proved a troubled soul. They say from a young age he was unpredictable and vicious, as if the violence that accompanied his birth had stained his soul. When he reached the age of twelve, the monks would keep him no longer. Decius had sent him to them, so they sent to Decius for instructions. He arranged a military career for the child. I suppose he hoped that the boy's volatile character might be tempered by military discipline.

'But from what I've heard, the boy remained sullen and given to fits of anger. Later there were rumours about him. He was sent to serve in Acre for his first command, and something happened when he was there. A massacre of some sort. Whatever the truth of it all, the boy was sent home in disgrace. After that Decius made sure he only served under the toughest commanders. And when the young man had more experience, he called him to Sicily to serve as his captain on Antioch's expedition.'

This was something I hadn't anticipated. 'I see . . .'

The Catalan nodded, allowing it to sink in. 'Yes, the officer who went with Decius was that boy he had rescued from

Montségur twenty years before. In the end, both the Infant and the Treasure of Montségur were brought together. With Decius. And with your son.'

ζ

Tonight I stood for a few minutes on the walls above the town. From there, looking down, I watched a group of Arab sailors preparing to set sail. The tavern talk had been right after all, it seemed, with its tales of Antioch and an ill-fated treasure. And now I knew another part of the puzzle. Antioch, anxious and intent on finding animals to complete his bestiary; Decius, wounded and full of hate, carrying with him an ill-omened treasure; and Pau the orphan, sullen and irascible, given to fits of violence.

The Arab barque below me left harbour at sunset and I watched it leave on a smooth sea, the breeze fair behind it. Above it the evening star was unflickering in a deepening sky. On the horizon a sliver of new moon was stained orange by the sunset. It was a scene of great peace.

I would give much for such peace as that. But all I can hope now is that, amongst all the men who travelled with him, perhaps one of them was thinking of my boy.

ζ

The High Passes

When it came, Decius's signal did not surprise them. After their caravan had crossed the high plateau and reached the mountains beyond, the paths became rough and awkward. It was not unusual for Ming Yueh's wagon to fall behind the rest while Venn and Decius struggled to manoeuvre it.

It all happened very quickly, one such afternoon, when a dust storm blew up and for a short time hid the sky. Venn and the count came for the two women with spare horses tethered to their saddles. Words were impossible in the midst of the storm, so they were simply lifted across and dumped upon their mounts, hanging on to rein or mane or halter as best they could while hiding their eyes against the dust. And then they were away, holding on desperately, inching into the storm and away from Shuran's men, with the wind covering their tracks as surely as if they had vanished into the ground.

They rode into the night, praying the storm would not pass. When it did, they used the stars to confirm the directions that Decius seemed to sense by instinct.

By dawn they were already up among the high passes, but Decius did not allow them to stop. Rotating mounts so that each horse had a share of the lighter loads, they pushed on into the daylight, never resting for more than ten minutes, scarcely speaking. For Ming Yueh and her maid, unaccustomed to horseback, the pain was terrible. Inexperienced riders, they were simply strapped to their saddles like so much baggage so that even if they slept they could not fall. By noon their fingers bled and their skin was rubbed so raw the pain was almost insupportable. Ming Yueh felt herself pass in and out of consciousness, not sure if it was sleep or fainting. But neither woman asked to stop. All four riders knew that the present pain was better than the fate which would follow recapture.

Shuran's men must have pursued them but they saw no sign of it. After thirty hours Decius allowed a rest. Scanning the valley behind him, he watched and listened for a full ten minutes before he rejoined Venn.

'We are clear of them,' he said. 'We lost them in the storm and now they'll be trying each valley in turn to see which pass we're aiming at. It won't be long before they pick up our trail, but they won't push this high into the passes.'

'How can you be so sure?' Venn asked him. 'They will not be frightened of a brush with the Khan's men. And they trusted us. They will be angry at the betrayal.'

Decius shook his head. 'Not trust. Indifference. And right now they're at the stage of their journey when they simply want to get home. I've seen it many times. A good commander learns to watch for it. It's when any force is at its most vulnerable.' He shook his head. 'No, they've no appetite for a long search. And they know Lord Rustum has no desire to receive the cargo they are bringing. The girl is unwanted goods. Why risk a border skirmish when there are easier ways to save face? They'll probably spin a yarn about four weak foreigners succumbing to the fever. And Rustum will be glad to hear it.'

'And the Emperor?'

In reply the count turned and gestured to the path ahead. 'Can you smell anything, Venn?'

The interpreter shook his head.

'Wood smoke. It means there's a village beyond that ridge, an hour away, perhaps less. Which means we've crossed the highest pass. We've left his kingdom. The Emperor has no authority here.'

They rested in the village for three days, lying in huts that smelled of smoke and sweat. For the first time Ming Yueh would wake to find herself in Venn's arms. She would sleep with her back pressed against his chest, aware when she stirred of the rough scar against her, of the tenderness in the great arms that held her so close. Sometimes when the sun rose she would wake but lie still, pretending to sleep, postponing for every possible minute the moment when their embrace must end.

At such an altitude the mornings were cold until the sun crept above the valley sides. She learned to associate the smell of wood smoke and the pinch chill of an autumn morning with a sense of the most perfect happiness.

It wasn't much of a place. Shu-chen complained about the squalor and the filthy blankets, but when she looked at her charge's face even she could only shrug and fall silent. Such happiness, she knew, was rare to behold. In truth, Shu-chen was not displeased with her lot. She had been born in such a village and waking to the throaty chuckle of ducks and the whistles of the herdsmen brought back to her a childhood she had thought lost forever. She had been sold into service at the age of five. Now, as she rolled up her sleeves and bossed the goatherds, she knew herself an old woman, and she worried about her strength for the journey ahead of them. But to stand once again, free among the ducks . . . Well, she would do what she had to for as long as she could. And she smiled to herself as she went about her business.

On their second day in the village, Venn and Decius rode together down the valley, to a place where the valley floor widened and paths led off in several directions. There they paused and Decius pointed.

'That way there – the right-hand spur – that must lead east towards the Khan's court,' he said.

'And the other way, west,' Venn countered. 'It would not be hard from here to pick up the camel roads. From here to Kashgar, to Samarkand, and then Baghdad, Damascus. It would be a long journey, but they are safe routes.'

Decius looked at him. 'And you would choose to travel back to a land where tyranny reigns?'

Venn nodded, his eyes on the road ahead. 'I have seen tyranny everywhere, Count. I cannot judge one sort against another.'

Decius considered for a moment.

'And are you happy with that, Venn?'

'I am happier than I have ever been. I have found something I thought existed only in the imagination.'

Decius smiled. 'Like Antioch's beasts.' He turned back and considered the different paths for a moment. 'I'm happy for you, Venn. But what will you do? You have a plan?'

'There is a valley in the mountains north of Syria. It is a quiet place, just meadows and fruit trees. The rest of the world ignores it. Even if the Great Khan's armies come, they would leave us alone.'

For a long time Decius said nothing. 'I have dreamed that dream, Venn,' he said at last. 'But it isn't so simple. Nothing is so simple.'

The interpreter turned to him then. 'You could help us.'

'Only by breaking my promise to Manfred.'

Venn pursed his lips. 'You know, Count, you were right, that night on the road. All my life I've been too proud of this gift I have, proud that no new language ever defeated me. It was my excuse to hear everything and do nothing. I would prove myself by going to new places, fitting in, learning the customs, meeting women – showing that my skills were so special I could be accepted anywhere. But never belonging.'

'And now you belong somewhere?'

'I feel that way. And the hope terrifies me.'

Decius smiled to himself and began to turn his horse. 'Come, we will remain in the village another day or two. I see no reason to hurry, whichever direction we choose.'

But before nightfall, a messenger reached them – a tall Tartar, moustachioed and confident.

'Count Decius?' he asked as he rode into the village. 'I was told I'd find you here.'

Decius looked wary. 'Who told you? We've been a long time away from prying eyes.'

The horseman dismounted and grinned. 'We have been tracking your progress. Lord Tendiz says a great treasure depends on your safety.'

'And are you sent to lead us to him?' Venn asked, when Decius offered no reply.

'I have dispatches to deliver elsewhere. But you are safe now. If you take the road east you will come to a garrison town. They are expecting you. They will arrange for you to travel to the Khan's court in honour and comfort – once you have told the governor there exactly where we can find your precious stones, of course.'

With that the horseman prepared to remount. 'Also, I have news for you from Lin'an. The Lord Tendiz said you should know. It concerns events that took place a month ago.'

'A month?' Decius asked. 'How can news have travelled so far so swiftly?'

Again the horseman smiled. 'In the Khan's lands, news travels as fast as the birds fly. It appears there has been an insurrection in Lin'an, an armed revolt. The troops you brought with you have tried to seize the palace. There has been bloody fighting.'

'Our troops?' Decius and Venn exchanged puzzled glances. 'But they are miles away, in Zaiton. They were to be sent from there by sea . . .'

The messenger shrugged. 'Apparently not. They say it was a bitter, bloody business, a day of hand-to-hand struggle in the palace itself. Your men fought well and almost succeeded in seizing the Emperor. It took many hours to subdue them. They died fighting to a man.'

'What? All dead?'

'All dead. The scholar too. Afterwards, when they came to burn his books as punishment, he resisted. They killed him on the spot. Only the boy survives. He defended his master until he was overpowered. He was wounded but taken alive. From the reports he sounds like a brave lad.'

Venn's throat was dry when he asked his next question. 'And where is he now?'

'They say the Emperor has devised a special punishment. Every day the boy is hung from the palace walls in public view. At noon the crowds gather to see him beaten. Sometimes canes, sometimes the lash, but all very precise to be sure he doesn't die. If he does not cry out, they rub salt into his wounds until he does. The Emperor has decreed he must survive at least a year before they finish him. His surgeons are ordered to see to it. He wants all visitors to Lin'an to see for themselves the great victory he has achieved against the barbarians.'

It was a night she wished she could forget. Their conference in a low hut, the torch flaring with a ghastly yellow light. Decius unable to sit still, leaving sometimes to pace outside. And Venn next to her, his hand in hers, his face utterly changed, his eyes sunken, his skin sickly pale in the torchlight. She could feel his suffering. It seemed to flow through his fingers and into her, a hideous, choking poison of guilt and regret.

'I must go back,' he said, shutting his eyes as he spoke to spare himself the pain of meeting hers. In his

anguish he had fallen back on habit, repeating everything, even his own words, in Decius's language and
her own.

But it was clear from the outset that Decius
wouldn't agree, and the more Venn argued, the angrier
the general grew.

'It's pointless, Venn,' he raged. 'He may be dead by
now. How long can anyone survive such treatment?'

'A year, it seems. Can we take that risk?'

The count's hands clenched and unclenched. 'Even
if that's true, what good is our going back? The
Emperor will not release him at our request. Especially not when he knows we have betrayed him by
escaping.'

But Venn could only repeat the same thought, as if
every argument came back to it. 'I must go back,' he'd
say. 'I must go back.'

'I've no time for this!' Decius spat. 'You cannot help
him now. It cannot be done. You mustn't throw away
your happiness for this. You mustn't.' He nodded
towards Ming Yueh. 'She has trusted everything to
you. You have a duty to her now.'

She felt Venn's hand tighten in hers and she returned
the pressure.

'I cannot bear the waste, Venn,' Decius went on,
and now there was a note of pleading in his voice.
'Happiness is too rare. Grasp it. Cling to it. Do not
throw it away like this.'

But Venn was looking past him. 'What will he think each day as he hangs there? He will be waiting for us to come.'

'You cannot think like that! He may not be thinking at all. A body treated in that way is alive in name only. He will be scarcely conscious. Fever will dissolve the pain.'

'Perhaps.' Venn looked at him. 'But that is not what the surgeons are striving for.'

Decius slammed his fist into the ground.

'Well, what if you go? What if you rescue him? You think he will live? After so many months of torture? You think you can save his life?'

Venn simply shook his head. 'I must go back,' he said.

Then Decius turned to her and addressed her directly. Even before Venn repeated it she had understood the question.

'What about you?' he demanded. 'Will you allow this? Will you let him throw everything away, including his life? What you have is a blessing. A precious, precious thing. I beg you not to spurn it.'

Venn felt her fingers tighten then. She gripped his hand so long and so hard he couldn't believe her fingers had such strength in them. As she spoke, her grip did not slacken. Nor for a long time afterwards. And her words were for him, not Decius.

'With such a cloud above us,' she said simply, 'we would never find our way.'

Her tone must have said as much as her words because Decius reacted with a snarl.

'Very well,' he growled. '*I* shall go. I have nothing to lose and nothing to fear. I shall travel to Lin'an and try to buy his freedom. The treasure I left in Lin'an would buy his life a thousand times. It still lies in the woods outside the city. I will go back for it. But you must carry on. Go and find that valley you spoke of.'

Venn looked up. 'But, Count, what of Manfred's orders? What of your embassy to the Great Khan?'

Decius turned to him then and never had Venn seen such scorn in those dark eyes. 'I'm not so far gone as you think, interpreter. I still have some human blood left in my veins.'

Venn held his gaze, then smiled and shook his head.

'Thank you, Count. But it will not work. You cannot speak the language. How would you negotiate? And you have betrayed the Emperor once already. He will have you killed before you can even open your mouth.'

'Then write a letter and let me carry it. Offer him the jewels in return for the boy's life.'

Venn shook his head again. 'Why should he stick to such a bargain? Once he had the treasure, he could do what he liked. And he's too proud to go back on his decision. He will never let the boy live.'

Decius snorted. 'Then what can any of us do? Going back is futile.'

'Probably. But I know I can conceal myself better than you. And because I have the words, I can make something happen in a way you cannot. It's the price I must pay for having such a gift. For all your brilliance and for all your courage, it cannot be you.'

Venn felt Ming Yueh let go of his hand, then felt her fingers reach up and touch his face.

'Let me come with you,' she said. 'Please. I cannot bear to be away from your side. I was ready to die once. I will die again rather than be parted from you.'

Their eyes met for a long time then. Decius could only guess at all the meaning that passed between them before Venn shook his head.

'You know we would neither of us come back. It would be hopeless. But the other way we have a chance. Please, I beg you. Go on ahead and wait for me.'

'But how?' she whispered. 'How am I to make the journey without you?'

And Venn, as he had always known he would, turned to Decius.

Again no words passed. The torch flickered, but Decius's eyes threw back no reflection.

And then, very slowly, he nodded. 'So be it. It comes to this. I will keep her safe, interpreter. I will find your valley. Go quickly. Tread with care. We shall be waiting for you.'

He rose then and left them, stepping into the cold. Beyond the collection of huts, the mountains waited, still and silent. He could almost smell the gathering frost.

'My love,' he whispered softly, addressing the empty night, 'my dear, sweet Messalina. The decision is made. Manfred will forgive me. And if the greatest treasure on earth cannot buy us this one small thing, let it stay in the ground forever. It has caused too much hurt already. As for you . . .' He swallowed. 'You knew what I would choose. You've always known. Even when I did not.'

Then he smiled, and for the flickering of a moment thought he saw a small face framed by olive trees smiling back at him, behind it the fierce, unfathomable blue of the Sicilian sky.

The next day Venn left them.

Decius and Ming Yueh accompanied him to the head of the valley where the path led back to the high passes. Decius didn't linger.

'Go safely,' he said. 'And remember you must be across the grasslands before the snows come.' Then with a nod he turned and strode away.

Venn watched him go, half expecting him to turn again. But Decius did not turn, and Venn watched until the tall figure disappeared among the village huts.

'He's a good man,' Venn said quietly. 'Although I didn't know it. And a man of his word. You'll be safe with him.'

She nodded, but she was not looking at him. She was looking down, trying very hard to make the tears clear from her eyes. When she tried to meet his gaze she found she couldn't. Instead, desperate to divert him from her suffering, she pointed to something near her feet.

'Look,' she said. 'A plant with red leaves, like cassia. That's what the ancient poets used to say *come home*.' She still didn't dare look at him. 'Perhaps it's a good omen,' she went on. 'The opposite is applethorn, which means *lost love*. And there's nothing here that looks like applethorn.'

She tried to laugh, to make light of the moment, to make her words seem trivial. But when she looked him in the eye she could no longer contain herself and had to pull him close, burying her face in his shoulder.

'Be careful,' she whispered. 'Be so, so careful.'

He nodded and held her tighter than he had ever done, and wondered how his heart could survive such pain.

'Go now,' she told him. 'And whichever road it is I have to take from here, remember, I will still be with you.'

He tried to blink away his tears. 'Your road runs north from here,' he whispered, 'then west. The way is written in my heart. Every step of it. I'll follow you, I promise. Whatever it takes, I'll follow.'

She nodded and smiled but her eyes were full of tears again.

'There's an old poem,' she said. '*Your road angles north in expectation.*'

He watched her trying to control her face, trying to show him her courage. 'In expectation,' he murmured. 'In expectation of us being together.'

She didn't reply, she just moved back into his arms. The pressure of his embrace answered hers. She had never known such pain was possible.

Below them, in the village, Decius was waiting. When he looked up he could see the two small figures merged as one. They stayed that way for a long time, and when they finally stepped apart he had already looked away. It always hurt him to look at such bright sky.

She waited until he was no more than a dark dot against the rocks above her before she allowed herself to finish the poem she'd begun. *Your road angles north in expectation*, she whispered, *every valley, every rock, yellow with our regrets*.

It had become hard to tell if he was still there, or if the faint smudge of colour on which her eye rested was simply a rock darker than the rest. *Dearest, I will remember*.

The speck of colour seemed to move, but now her eyes were uncertain, watering from the strain. *If truth exists, it shall dress every day in cassia. Applethorn trailing ever downwards tells of you . . .*

Was that a face turning? A hand raised?

. . . Obscured, unseen.

She stood very still. Above her, nothing moved. He was gone.

ζ

Today I watch the sun set on this town for the last time. Tomorrow I take ship for Lisbon and from there to England. My time waiting here is done.

Nearly two years have passed since I first came here, hoping that some word of my son would reach me from the east. In that time I have come to understand the customs of the people and to speak their language. I know the signs in the sky when the hot weather ends and the patterns of clouds that presage a storm. But if I have learned anything here it is that perhaps, in the kindness I've found, there lies some future salve for the pain I brought with me. It is a small hope, but it is something. Now I must return to my family, to those who love me. In my affliction I have asked too much of their love.

Yesterday I paid my last visit to Leah Bathsheba. I couldn't leave without seeing her again. I have seen the Pope's officer, Quintus Fabius, in the streets but I have shied away from meeting him. But Leah is different. When she returned from Africa, I was waiting for her.

She entertained me in her apartments as she had done before, but this time it was I who talked. I told her the story of

Decius as I had heard it in every detail, from his love for his wife to his departure with Antioch. I told her of the Cathar treasure, of the murder done in its name, and of Pau, the Infant of Montségur.

She listened politely, although I knew her well enough by then to know that these tales of Christians killing Christians are things she feels do not concern her. When I had finished, she waited for me to speak again.

Hesitantly, still uncertain of exactly what I meant, I tried to form a question.

'I tell you all this because I have always seen a kindness in your face that told me you would listen. Now you have heard it all, there are things I must ask you. I know that your people are scattered all over the world. There is little of consequence that can occur without one of your race hearing its echo. I want to beg you now, dig deep into your memory. Have you ever heard of any Frankish kingdom in the east? Any stories of a Christian knight attempting to use his wealth to acquire such dominion? Could there be a land out there where my son might still be alive?'

Leah Bathsheba looked at me then. 'You still hope to find your son?' she asked.

'No. But I need to ask the question. You see, I have heard tales . . .'

She raised an eyebrow but said nothing, so I went on, a little embarrassed. 'The Christians tell tales of a man called Prester John, a great Christian king in the east. Once I dismissed them as legend. Now I cannot help but wonder . . .'

She shook her head sadly. 'I have heard the tales but I know of no such kingdom. But perhaps instead . . .' She trailed off, then sat for a minute or more in silence, until I began to think she would not speak. Finally she looked up again.

'There are two things I can think of that may be helpful to you. Neither are facts. Neither are even rumours. They are tales of rumours, stories about stories. The sorts of tales you hear in the bazaar and never think of more. And they reach back far into time, I don't know how long. They may precede your son and his companions by many years.'

'Tell me.'

'There is a tale told about the land of Sinim, about a pale lord who came from afar and offered his services to the emperor there. When these services were refused, the lord tried to seize the city for himself and only after a great battle were his armies defeated. They say the pale lord himself escaped, and disappeared into the lands from whence he'd come. Some say he was not a man at all but a ghost, sent by someone the emperor had wronged, to clamour for justice.'

I waited. 'And that is the end of it?' I asked at last.

'That is the end of it. As I told you, it is a tale, nothing more.'

'And the other tale?'

'The other tale is different. It is not easy to determine if its origins lie in one encounter or in many.'

'Please.'

'It concerns a Frankish beggar who walks the great road westward, from Khanbalik in the east. Some say he is a shipwrecked sailor travelling home. Others say he is Judas Iscariot, still bearing the mark of his betrayal, destined to walk forever without resting.'

As Leah spoke, she saw me move forward in my seat.

'You think this could be a survivor of Antioch's mission?'

'I think nothing,' she said softly. 'I told you the tale because you asked me to.'

'This beggar, what age was he?'

She shook her head. 'These are tales to entertain in the winter nights. The reports all vary. Some say he was seen in Kashgar or Samarkand, others say as close as Tarsus. That is all I can tell you.'

Leah gathered her skirts and rose.

'A beggar walking homewards,' I said. 'Back to those who love him.'

After a pause, I rose too.

'What will you do now?' she asked.

'I shall go home. Like that beggar. To the ones who love me. And if against all the odds my son should ever return, at least he will know where to seek me.'

Leah Bathsheba took my hand. I felt her strength. Our eyes met and we smiled.

Tomorrow I sail for home.

ζ

Requiescat

The Emperor was not best pleased when he heard that his carefully devised punishment had come to nothing. There was a storm in his face as he looked at his chief minister.

'Tell me again, Jao. How did this happen?'

'Something caused a disturbance in the crowd, my lord. The boy was hanging in chains in the usual place and the usual guard was posted. But a fight broke out in the marketplace, and while the guards were distracted someone slipped behind them. The guards have been dealt with, of course,' he added hastily.

'A rescue attempt, you think?'

'Rescue would be impossible. The irons were fast about his wrists. Perhaps that is why he chose to end the boy's suffering instead.'

'A knife in the heart . . . Yes, I suppose it must have come as a blessing. Still, we have the culprit?'

'Yes, my lord. The barbarian interpreter. The one we were told had died on the way to Lord Rustum's court. He was taken near the city gates.'

The Emperor shook his head. 'I scarcely remember him.'

'It is said he has a great gift for languages. They say his one and only joy is in the learning and speaking of new tongues.'

'Indeed?' The Emperor raised an eyebrow. People were constantly surprising him. 'Truly, Jao, there's no fathoming the barbarian heart.'

'No, my lord.' Jao was relieved. He had been expecting a trickier interview. 'Tomorrow we shall hang him in the boy's place.'

'Very well.' The Emperor nodded. 'Anything else, Jao?'

The council was over and the old minister had almost left the room before the Emperor called him back.

'I've changed my mind about that barbarian interpreter. I want you to let him go.' He watched with quiet amusement the look of surprise that spread across the minister's face, then allowed himself to click his tongue at the other's stupidity. 'Physical pain is not always the worst suffering, Jao. Let him go. Let him wander the roads in rags. But first cut out his tongue so he can speak no more languages. And his right hand too, so he cannot write them down. If he is the man you say, that will hurt him more than any early death.'

His cleverness put him in a good mood for the rest of the day. He even forgot to be angry about Rustum's inaccurate reporting of the barbarian's demise.

That was the last time the Emperor thought about the barbarian mission to Lin'an. A decade later, when the Great Khan's armies overran Lin'an and put the imperial army to the sword, any last record of Antioch's visit there was swept away. Once or twice after the city's fall, Lord Tendiz thought about the great hoard of gems he'd once been promised, but there was much else to do and so many other spoils to secure that he quickly forgot it. Perhaps, after all, treasures of such magnitude existed only in legends, he decided.

Some years after the English merchant left Málaga, Leah of Kairouan was taken by business into the mountains north of Syria. From there, she planned to continue with her small retinue through the passes and down to the Greek trading posts on the Black Sea where one of her sons had made his home.

One evening her path led her to a fertile valley high up in the mountains, where she and her party rested for the night. In the farmhouse where they lodged, Leah was served from a glazed platter and was struck by its decoration: a series of simple brushstrokes suggesting mountains and, around them, like letters, a pattern of slim, spidery designs.

The old woman who served them told her the pattern had been made by a woman who once lived a little out of the village. An unusual woman, she said, a heathen from the Steppes who had come to the valley many years before and had chosen to make it her home.

'She came with a man,' the serving-woman told them, 'not a husband but not a servant either. We weren't sure what he was. They were an ugly pair. She was tiny, like a bird, and her features were like none I'd ever seen. Eyes like almonds, my husband used to say. No one here had ever seen the like. The man had a cruel face, I recall. But he did no harm.'

She paused to wipe her hands on a cloth tied round her waist.

'They appeared out of the snow one spring with a string of horses to sell. With the money they built themselves a place high up the valley, looking out over the path they'd come by. They didn't speak our language then, though in time they learned it. And they settled down readily enough. They scraped an orchard out of the valley side and they kept a mare to breed from. He worked in the fields and planted apple trees and vines, he even tried to grow lemons. He had a passion for it, for making things grow. She had a way with the horses and sometimes she decorated plates for a man in the village. I didn't really know them but those who did said they were good people. They'd come down every year to help with the harvest.'

'And what happened to them?' Leah asked, a thought already stirring in her mind.

The woman shrugged. 'Same as everyone. Worked hard, grew old. They seemed content in their own way. When he died a few years back she buried him in the orchard he'd loved so much. We didn't see much of her after that. I'm told she wasn't well. They say she took up with some other man a few months later, some itinerant from the east who showed up and looked after her. I never saw him though. They just stayed up there together, winter and summer. Then, a couple of years on, one of my boys went up to see them and found the place deserted. They reckon she must have died. I don't know what became of the other one, though. I suppose he just moved on.'

Leah was unusually silent that evening, her companions thought. While the food was being cleared away and talk was turning to practical matters, she found herself thinking instead of an old story, and of a father waiting by the sea.

Before she left the following day, Leah rode up the valley to the pass that headed east. The early sun was warm on her face and a hot day was gathering: from the meadows around her, the skylarks were rising to meet it.

The house the woman had described was easy enough to find. It stood derelict, close to the road, with an unkempt orchard behind it. Inside she found the place stripped bare, as if the villagers, finding it deserted, had gradually claimed everything that could be of use. In the orchard she found two graves, each marked with a plain stone. On one had been scratched the single word '*Decius*'.

So this is where it ended, Leah reflected. The soldier who'd once startled the world, who'd been feared by popes and princes alike, here, planting vines and growing trees, scraping a living from the soil. With a good horse he could have been in Jerusalem in days. He had credit there. Reputation. As an advisor to any prince or lord he could have lived a rich old age.

Leah looked around, at the narrow valley and the distant mountains, and wondered why he'd stayed.

The second grave was marked in a different hand, in characters she didn't recognise.

That was all. Or nearly all. Before returning to her companions, Leah led her horse down to the stream she could hear a little beyond the house. She found it running through a low gully that trapped the sun and which led down to a pool that reflected the sky. There, while her horse drank, she sat in the sun on a rocky platform above the water and noticed something scratched in the rock.

Then she smiled. It was the sort of mark lovers make when they are happy together, linking their names in stone for all time. But the names themselves meant nothing to her, for they were written in that same unknown script. She could make out nothing in it – nothing but a strange, elusive beauty.

ζ

Today, when I was out riding with my eldest son, a beggar came to the gates of my house.

I am seldom away from home nowadays. My eldest son has run my business for many years. His sons, my grand-children, work with him. They are five boys, dark and thick-set like their father, quiet and confident in their surroundings. With them to help, there is little need for me to travel from my door. But sometimes my son takes me out, pretending that he needs my opinion over some piece of business. And I go with him happily. I have been with him too little these last few years.

Today, while I was out, the beggar called at my door. My steward, who dealt with him, says he was a decrepit fellow. His clothes were not rags but were soiled and very worn. He could not speak. My steward gave him a copper coin. When the beggar was gone he noticed a letter affixed to my gatepost. He took the letter in. He did not mark which way the beggar went.

On my return, I roused my entire household to seek him. But it was too late. There are many beggars on these roads. To find one among so many is a difficult thing.

The letter, when I opened it, contained a golden chain and, attached to it, a golden tablet. It had been my father's. And my son's.

The letter was scrawled in unsteady characters as if by a wavering hand, but the language was that of someone who spoke well.

'Sir,' it began. *'Much of my life has been spent in travel in lands beyond our maps. Sir, I knew your son. He was a fine boy who grew into a fine man. It was his greatest desire to make you proud of him.*

'The journey home has taken me many years. It is my regret that this news and this token have taken so long to reach you.

'He died in the land of Cathay, from wounds sustained in action, defending his friends. He showed great courage and many owed their lives to him that day. He felt no pain. He died serenely in my arms and in the company of many who loved him, having made his peace with God. His last words were of you, sir. He charged me to deliver this to you and to tell you of his love.

'I know this news will bring you grief. I hope you may also find peace in it.

'I am your servant,

'V'

If I could find the beggar who delivered that letter, I would bind his wounds and dress him in velvet. And I would beg him on my knees to take me to this traveller who knew my son, the man who held him as he died. I would give my life to have but ten words with him.

323

And yet, the locket sits now in my palm. Today, for a time, I shall grieve. Tomorrow I will give thanks to God for the memory of my son. The locket, I think, should go to my other son, who through so many years has been kind and patient with me. I will be proud for him to wear it.

ζ

Today I was brought news of a curious incident in one of the taverns of the city. Yesterday a beggar called there and showed by signals that he wished for water. The tavern keeper, being a charitable man, rather than show him the well, gave him water in a wooden cup and bade him sit at the bench outside his door.

The keeper's wife, who observed from her window, says the beggar took from his shirt a green silk pouch and from it poured a powder into his cup. Having swilled the cup around, the beggar closed his eyes and drank. When he had drained the cup, he leaned back and rested himself against the warm stone wall.

Later that day a fellow of similar type was found dead beside a stream, a mile or so from the city. It seems he must have lain down in the sunny corner of a meadow to rest by the water. Death must have come to him in his sleep.

ζ

Historical Note

The Unicorn Road is a work of fiction, but it is based on a number of real events that took place in the same period . . .

Manfred and the Papacy

When Manfred was elected King of Sicily in 1258, he had established himself as ruler of a prosperous and attractive land. But Europe was in the grip of a bitter struggle for power and the vindictive policies of successive popes towards Manfred meant that peace proved impossible and in the end Manfred had no option but to fight his corner. It is known he actively sought support from non-Christian forces in his struggles against the papacy, but to no avail. He died fighting Charles of Aragon, the Pope's ally, near Benevento in 1266.

Expeditions Eastwards

Even before that date, Christian kings had increasingly begun to look to the distant east for salvation from their enemies. Rumours of a lost Christian kingdom (popularly thought to be ruled by a great king called Prester John) led to increasing numbers of expeditions being sent eastwards beyond the maps of Christian Europe. Well before Marco Polo arrived at the court of the Great Khan, other missions and missionaries had already travelled the routes east. Many never returned.

The Fall of the Song Dynasty in China

The Emperor who reigned in Lin'an at the time was Emperor Duzong, a man famous for his decadence and his sexual appetites. His end came only a few years after Manfred's, when his armies were swept aside and his entire empire fell into the hands of Kubla Khan and his generals.

The Women's Script

The origins of the women's language of Yunnan province are lost in time. For many years, very little was known about it. It was simply ignored. When Yang Huanyi died in 2004, she was widely considered the last woman to have learned the women's script (*nushu*) in the traditional way. It had always been a language handed down from one generation of women to the next, expressing the sorrows and the heartache that was common to each.

The Cathar Treasure

There is no shortage of theories about the contents and the fate of the Cathar treasure reputed to have been smuggled from Montségur in the last days of the siege. All we can be certain of is that, despite centuries of hunting across Europe, it has never been found . . .

And a final footnote to *The Unicorn Road* . . .

After Manfred's death, his three young sons were imprisoned for the rest of their lives in the Castel del Monte in remote Apulia. There they were effectively forgotten by all but their jailers. It is said that each was held in solitary confinement, seeing no other humans for the remainder of their lives, and so grew up with no language of their own, and able only to grunt like beasts.

Acknowledgements

My heartfelt thanks to all the friends and family – too many to mention – who put up with me during the writing of this book. In particular to Lorna and to Nick and to Teresa who must all have thought there'd be no end to it and who were, in different ways, miracles of patience. Thank you!